HER
LAST
WORDS

BOOKS BY CAROLYN ARNOLD

Sacrifice

Found Innocent

Just Cause

Deadly Impulse

In the Line of Duty

Power Struggle

Shades of Justice

What We Bury

Girl on the Run

Her Dark Grave

Murder at the Lake

Life Sentence

SARA AND SEAN COZY MYSTERY SERIES

Bowled Over Americano

Wedding Bells Brew Murder

MATTHEW CONNOR ADVENTURE SERIES

City of Gold

The Secret of the Lost Pharaoh

The Legend of Gasparilla and His Treasure

STANDALONE

Assassination of a Dignitary

Pearls of Deception

Midlife Psychic

HER
LAST
WORDS

CAROLYN ARNOLD

bookouture

Published by Bookouture in 2023

An imprint of Storyfire Ltd.
Carmelite House
50 Victoria Embankment
London EC4Y 0DZ

www.bookouture.com

ISBN: 978-1-80314-790-1
eBook ISBN: 978-1-80314-789-5

PROLOGUE

Her heart was beating like crazy as she paced back and forth across the living room, the phone pressed to her ear. The line just continued to ring and ring.

If only she'd left well enough alone. But no, she had to push and push until she knew too much, and now she may have very well put herself in danger.

With every ring that traveled the line, breathing became more difficult.

Please, please, pick up!

As if to mock her, the ringing stopped—

"You've reached the voicemail of Detective Steele. Leave a message and your number, and I'll get back to you. If this is an emergency, call nine-one-one."

Should I?

Her entire body was shaking as she contemplated the enormity of her situation. She was quite sure this person was onto her, but how far would they go to keep their dark past a secret? Would they come after her and try to silence her? Or was she making too much out of this?

No, I'm not!

Her mind shot back the answer, the internal voice having power and standing on logic. This person had already proven themselves dangerous.

All these thoughts swirled in her head for several seconds until she realized the line was blank. Silence struck her ears with the impact of thunder.

She cleared her throat. "Detective Steele? It's Felicity Kelley. I need to talk to you. In person would probably be best. Please call me when you get this." As the words left her lips, she heard the voice of a calm and rational person. Where had she gathered such self-control when her entire body was quaking with a mix of adrenaline and fear?

After leaving her number, she ended the call and stared blankly across the room. She was at home, a place she should feel safe. A haven. But even sitting on her couch, she wasn't comfortable. Nothing in her world was making sense. It was as if someone had tilted it upside down, and there would be no setting it right. At least not until she spoke to the detective.

For a moment, she considered calling 911, but her mind chastised her. *Keep the lines open for an actual emergency.*

It wasn't like she was in immediate danger.

She took a few deep breaths, trying to convince herself that she was being paranoid. She could have exaggerated the way they had glowered at her, their eyes constricting, their look hardening.

Maybe if she occupied her mind with something else...

Surely Detective Steele would return her call soon. Hopefully. But she'd been so calm in her message, speaking as if there were no rush, as if nothing was at stake. Who knew when the detective would call back.

Taking a few deep breaths, she let her wild thoughts drift away. What she needed was a moment of normalcy to reestablish rationality. She ordered a pizza—thirty-minute delivery guarantee—and wrote while she passed the time. Playing in a world of her making was always therapeutic, and she was already past due turning in her manuscript.

Just as she was sinking into the story, letting the muse take the wheel, her doorbell rang.

She flinched, her heart rate spiking. A look at the bottom corner of her screen told her thirty minutes had almost passed. She shook her head. *It's just the pizza...*

She answered the door armed with a twenty-dollar bill and a smile on her face. But it disappeared at the sight of her visitor. It wasn't the delivery guy. Her entire body trembled and turned to liquid, but she nudged out her chin, trying to project strength. "You need to leave."

"I'm not going anywhere. You and I need to talk. Just a few minutes?" Her visitor smiled at her.

The expression had her going cold despite the summer heat seeping into the house. But if she played along, swallowed down the fear that threatened to devour her alive, she might take control of the situation.

"Okay, come in." She stepped back and listened to the sounds of the neighborhood—young children laughing and lawnmowers buzzing. Somewhere close by, meat was grilling on a barbecue, its smell heavenly. She squeezed her eyes shut and hoped she'd be able to savor all those things again.

Because she was quite sure the person she'd just let into her home was a killer.

ONE

The Next Day, Wednesday

How had she gotten herself into this predicament again? All alone, the house to herself, time to pass...

Amanda dropped onto the lounger in her backyard. Freshly cut grass and fragrant summer blooms traveled over the fence from her neighbors' gardens and were intoxicating. The sky was a rich blue, and the sun was a blazing yellow orb. Dumfries, Virginia, was the picture of perfection on this summer day, and even the birds were singing their approval. She lowered her sunglasses over her eyes.

Given all the sunshine and heat she'd had in Orlando, Florida, last week one might think she'd have had enough. Not even close. And despite the incredible weather, there wasn't much downtime between Disney World, Universal Studios, water parks, miniature golf, and on it went. But it was awesome being able to treat her adopted daughter to such a vacation to mark her eighth birthday. Seeing Zoe's eyes light up and hear her laughter was more than enough reward.

Zoe delighted in the costumed characters in the theme

parks, never passing up a chance to hug one. Amanda had been on guard, wary of strangers touching her child, even in that context. The negativity was an occupational hazard of her job in homicide with the Prince William County Police Department. With all she'd seen, darkness lurked everywhere, even when all seemed light and innocent—especially then.

But that wasn't her issue right now. She had five more days of vacation to enjoy before work on Monday, and currently had the house all to herself. Zoe was with Amanda's sister Kristen and her daughter, Ava. They had a pool and, as Amanda had discovered this summer, Zoe was part dolphin, though she preferred to be called a mermaid.

Logan Hunter, who had moved in with Amanda and Zoe at the start of summer, had also been on the Florida trip. The way their relationship had bloomed couldn't have been planned any better. They just fit. Today, he was off golfing with friends.

That left her with all the time in the world to relax. *Thinking, thinking, thinking.* And B-O-R-E-D.

Between her job and personal life, she didn't have the luxury of much downtime. Because of this, she had zero hobbies and hadn't read a book for fun in... She couldn't remember how many years. It might be time to crack the spine on one of the two novels on the table next to her. They'd already endured the trip south without a single word being read.

Why not give it a go...?

She grabbed one, and taking her lemonade with her, she moved to the patio table and cranked up the umbrella. With her light, freckled skin, inherited from the Irish in her blood, she burned easily. She leaned back in a chair, lifted her legs, and rested her feet on the table.

She opened the cover of the paperback. Then looked up. Her mind wandering at just the thought of dipping into a fictional world. Why did the concept of having time to herself sound wonderful, while the execution, not so much? In place of endless possibilities was an endless void of nothingness. But, no, she had to learn to just *be*. Even Logan had told her that.

She took in her modest-size yard. At the back fence line was a children's play set with a climbing frame, swings, and a slide. Kevin, her late husband, had built it for their daughter, Lindsey. It was hard to believe last month had marked eight years since she'd lost them in a car accident. The sorrow and sense of loss still lingered, but mostly, it lay dormant in her heart. She came to think of her grief as a symbiote, like from the sci-fi enterprise *Stargate*, of which Kevin had been a fan. Just like how the alien lived within a host's body, bringing it benefits, so did her grief. It made her ever aware of how precious and fragile life was, how things could change in the blink of an eye. This made her more conscious of how and with whom she spent her minutes and hours.

And she certainly didn't want to sit here caught up in memories. She had Logan and Zoe in her life now—not that they could ever replace the family she'd lost—but they had made her life whole again.

Amanda took a deep breath. *Be*, she coached herself. Logan had told her that meant existing within the present moment. She was trying, but clearly failing.

She tossed the novel onto the table and pulled out her cell phone, checking for new messages. None. And she'd been in touch with everyone since they got home yesterday. There was no one else to call. Except...

She had received a voicemail yesterday during the flight home. After landing, she'd listened to it with the intention of calling the person back. That just hadn't happened yet. But she suspected how the conversation would go.

The caller had been Felicity Kelley, a local mystery writer, who Amanda had met during a previous murder investigation. Amanda had told Felicity that if she had police procedural questions, she'd be willing to help. It would seem the time had come to make good on her offer.

Amanda would call her now, answer what questions she might have, and then call her best friend, Becky Tulson, and see if she could meet up for lunch. She'd be working but might find time to take a break. Becky was also in law enforcement as a uniformed police officer with the Dumfries Police Department, a smaller PD than where Amanda worked.

She hit Felicity's number and listened as it rang and rang and—

"Detective Steele?" A man's voice. "Why are you calling this number?"

She removed her feet from the table, her brows pressed down in confusion. "Who is this? How do you know who I am?"

"This is Detective Hudson." Spoken off-the-cuff, as if he were insulted that she hadn't recognized his voice. But it was also about context. Why would she expect him to be answering Felicity's phone?

Why is *he answering it?*

Fred Hudson was another detective in the Homicide Unit with the PWCPD. His being on the other end of the line couldn't be a good sign. Goosebumps rose on her arms, the hot, light breeze doing nothing to warm her now.

"In answer to your other question," Fred said, "your name came up on caller ID. How do you know Felicity Kelley?"

She'd choose to ignore the judgment in his tone and focus on the more urgent matter. "Why are you answering Felicity's phone? Is she okay?" The question dangled, vulnerable, as she wished for an innocent explanation. *Felicity is just in the other room. He is a friend or a relative or...*

"Felicity Kelley has been murdered."

That couldn't be right. She'd just called Amanda yesterday. She was alive... *yesterday*. And there it was again, things changing in the blink of an eye.

"Are you still there?"

"Yeah, I'm—" Her job was dealing with murder, but that was the last thing she'd expected to come at her today. Her mind must still be in vacation mode. Normally she was far sharper, ready to go, not stuttering and floundering in shock. "Murdered? Are you sure?"

Fred let out an exasperated sigh.

There hadn't been any urgency in Felicity's voice or in the message itself—or had she missed it? She'd need to listen to it again. All Amanda remembered was she had said, "in person might be best." But people said that even when a phone call would suffice. "Of course, you wouldn't say it was murder if... I'm just shocked is all," she eventually said, filling the elongated silence. "Where are you? Where is she?"

"No need to concern yourself with that. Ryan and I have this handled, but we will need to question you."

Natalie Ryan was another detective with the unit and Fred's partner.

"Question me?" *Like I'm a suspect?* She and Fred had never exactly been buddies and his attitude shouldn't surprise her, given their past encounters. "Tell me where you are. I'm heading over."

Another loud, exaggerated sigh. Then Fred told her he was at Felicity Kelley's house. He didn't need to provide the address. It was one Amanda remembered from her first meeting with Felicity. She and her partner, Trent Stenson, had gone there to notify Felicity her only sister had been murdered. And now, flash forward a year and a half, someone had taken Felicity's life. Was the family cursed?

"When you get here, Steele, I hope you have a good explanation for why you were one of the last people she called." He hung up, and she was left holding the empty line.

She wanted that explanation more than anyone.

TWO

Amanda stood on the sidewalk, looking up at the two-story, white-sided house. A rather ordinary home, in an ordinary neighborhood in Triangle. It was a small community, which was part of Prince William County, and located five minutes from Dumfries—where Amanda lived—and fifteen from Woodbridge, where the PWCPD Homicide Unit was stationed.

Uniformed officers had the area cordoned off, and an unmarked department car, likely the one that Fred had signed out, sat at the curb. There was no sign of Crime Scene or the medical examiner's vehicle yet, though they came from Manassas, thirty minutes northwest of Triangle. The scene felt fresh, and it was likely Felicity was discovered rather recently.

Detective Natalie Ryan was with a man and woman, both in their late twenties, early thirties. He had his arm around her, and she was pawing at her cheeks, visibly distressed from this distance. Probably wiping away tears. Amanda suspected she had found Felicity.

An officer stood by the front door of the house, watching her closely.

Amanda was finding it hard to move, her legs frozen in

place while her conscience ate away at her. Ever since Fred had answered Felicity's phone, guilt had stepped in, plaguing her with *if onlys* on a never-ending loop. *If only I had called her back sooner, would she still be alive? If only I had answered* when *she called? If only...* Two words, their implication brutally painful.

After hanging up from Fred, Amanda made two calls—one to Trent Stenson, the other to their sergeant, Scott Malone. He was also a family friend and had known Amanda from the time she'd entered the world. She'd told him she was back from Florida, and he'd asked about her trip and told her to enjoy the next few days off. Her counter was to request an early return to the job. Her conscience told her she owed Felicity Kelley this much. And just as she had found justice for her sister, Amanda was determined to do the same for Felicity.

Malone agreed to her going to the scene and roping Trent in "for the time being." His words. They didn't bring much hope that he'd reassign this case, but once face to face with him, she was certain she could make him see how important it was that she be the one to investigate Felicity's murder.

"You don't need to do this, you know." Trent walked around the nose of the department car he'd driven them here in, having met Amanda at Central. "You still have a few vacation days left. I say let Hudson and Ryan continue to run with this."

She shook her head. "We covered this already. I just can't do that. And how could you? We knew her, Trent."

"Yeah, I know."

"You also know how Hudson and Ryan can steamroll their investigations." She didn't need to spell it out in detail. A year ago, they'd witnessed the duo's shoddy detective work when they investigated the murder of Logan's estranged wife. One could blame the management at the time, an interim sergeant named Katherine Graves, who had exerted her authority and pressured for a quick resolution to look good to the police chief.

But Amanda couldn't forgive Hudson and Ryan for playing along and jeopardizing justice.

"Well, no time like the present, I suppose." Trent gestured toward the house, but she picked up on his reluctance. He wasn't looking forward to the inevitable confrontation with Fred any more than she was.

They didn't need to wait long. Fred stepped onto the porch —hands on hips, lips pressed in an unquestionable scowl, eyes squinting in the afternoon sun. "Stenson? I didn't expect you. Don't you have other work to do?"

Amanda squared her shoulders and took a step toward Fred. "I called Detective Stenson." She'd hold back that she'd cleared their presence with Malone.

"I can't have everyone tramping around my crime scene."

"Don't consider us *everyone*." She bit back saying, *Consider us the new leads on the case.* She was confident it was only a matter of time. She put booties over her shoes, and Trent did the same.

"Fine. Just don't touch anything." Fred retreated into the house without bothering to pass the door off to Amanda. The spring on the frame was tight, and it closed in her face.

She took a deep, centering breath and got the door for herself and Trent.

The place was muggy with a touch of cool—the central air conditioning likely working overtime to offset the front door's frequent use. The layout was open concept from the entry. Straight ahead was a hallway that Amanda assumed led to the kitchen. Beyond that, she didn't know.

A walnut staircase was on the right. Its newel post, caps, and balusters were original to the home, but the steps had been carpeted at some point over the years.

The living room was on the left, and most of it was visible from the front door.

Modestly decorated. Tidy. No artwork adorned the walls.

Chairs bookended the main window through which sunlight was pouring in and drenching the wood floor. Felicity had sat in the chair on the left when they'd informed her of her sister's death.

Amanda pushed the memory aside and continued dancing her gaze over the space.

A couch and two end tables faced a fireplace on the far wall. Fred headed there, and Amanda and Trent followed.

Rounding the couch, she caught her first glimpse of Felicity. She was on the floor. Amanda's breath caught in her throat.

Remember, you're a professional.

A reminder she didn't normally need but being off had made her rusty, wiping out years of auto-response. Or was it because she had known the woman and liked her? In the least that aspect explained the guilt trying to suck her down in its powerful undertow. But it wasn't the time to surrender. It was time to focus and be present.

Felicity was on her back, arms at her sides, head angled to the right. Her face appeared haunted—eyes widened, lips parted. Her long, light-brown hair fanned out beneath her head and was haloed by a pool of deep crimson that reached her upper torso. The color and tacky-looking texture indicated the blood had coagulated, meaning Felicity had been dead for several hours.

A knife was sticking out of her chest, a bloom of red around the entry point.

Their first meeting rushed back to Amanda. Felicity was quiet, slightly awkward, giving the impression she was far more comfortable with her characters than interacting socially in real life. She was caught up in the worlds of her creation, living peacefully, and getting paid to do what she loved. That someone did this to her had a redhead rage blinding Amanda.

Deep breaths... She'd be no good to Felicity if she let herself become sideswiped by emotion.

Amanda moved closer, mindful of her steps.

Felicity was barefoot but wearing jean shorts and a gray tee. Gold studs and dangling dragonflies adorned her ears. Three gold chains of different lengths and thicknesses dipped above the rounded collar of her shirt. Her fingernails were deep purple. It was impressive with her busy schedule she had time to paint them or get a manicure.

She'd been hitting against a writing deadline when they were here last, stacks of paper everywhere. Today, there wasn't a stray piece in sight. In fact, the entire room was tidy and more sparsely furnished than before.

Or does it just seem that way without the clutter?

She lifted her gaze to the mantel. Several framed photographs of Felicity and her late sister, Eve, were displayed there. They served as a time capsule, capturing the siblings at different ages.

Yet again, murder served up an irony—chaos and death in a homey setting.

Amanda was about to turn around when her eyes landed on the hearth. She headed toward it for a closer look.

"Steele, what are you doing?" Fred asked.

She stopped walking and pivoted.

"I've given you the courtesy of letting you into my crime scene, but you need to leave now."

"I'm not—"

"*We're* not," Trent interjected.

"Going anywhere," Amanda finished.

Fred's cheeks shot crimson. "Oh, yes, you are. You're getting out of this house. Now."

"Nope." Malone stepped through the threshold, and the officer at the front door scurried behind him, urging him to put booties on over his shoes. Malone snatched them and conceded. "She's staying, so is Stenson."

"Excuse me, Sarge," Fred said, "but Natalie and I were the first from Homicide to respond."

Malone would have sent them here, but Fred wisely kept his mouth shut on that point.

"Yep, and now this is their case." Malone flailed a hand toward Amanda and Trent. "They have history with the victim."

Amanda resisted the urge to smile at the win. She knew that Malone would come through for her.

Fred's cheeks blazed even hotter, and his lips quirked. "Shouldn't that be a reason for them *not* to take the lead on this?"

"Usually," Malone said, "but they are familiar with the vic, and it might move the investigation to a speedier resolution. I assume justice is something we're all after?"

Silence, except for the faint buzzing of a lawnmower.

Both men locked in a stare down, but Malone always won. He was a tough old bird that Amanda was happy to have on her side—at least he was most of the time.

"It is, Sarge," Fred eventually said. "But you might want to ask yourself why Amanda was the last person the victim called... well, besides Lorenzo's for pizza."

Malone's turn to ride the silence, and he touched his groomed beard and leveled his gaze at Amanda. "Do you care to chime in here?"

She opened her mouth, but no words came out. *The last person...* Fred had prepared her for that, but it wasn't any easier to hear a second time.

THREE

Time suspended as Malone, Fred, even Trent, looked at Amanda for an answer. She was still processing being one of the last people Felicity Kelley had called.

"Steele?" Malone prompted.

"Honestly, I don't know why exactly. She called when I was on the flight home, and we never connected. I was returning her call this afternoon. That's when Detective Hudson answered."

Fred's shoulders relaxed, and he had this smug look on his face that Amanda would be happy to wipe off—if she wasn't so busy mentally beating herself up and entertaining the flood of *if onlys* again.

"Apparently, the two were close enough, boss. Amanda was also in the vic's contacts. I'd say this all points to a conflict of interest." The latter, a remark he obviously had to get out.

Malone narrowed in on her again, his brow pinched. "How close were you?"

Damn you, Fred! Malone knew she'd had dealings with Felicity, but Fred's comments opened her up for an inquisition. "Felicity was a mystery writer," she started calmly, "and I told her she could call me if she had questions about police procedure. Yesterday was the first time she reached out to me."

"And that's why she put your number in her phone?" This was from Fred, no attempt at masking his skepticism. He was desperately trying to make their connection appear stronger than it truly was—whatever would get Amanda off the case and him back on.

She wasn't the rollover type. "I can't control how a person organizes their life. She probably just wanted to make sure that she didn't lose my number."

"Huh, well, that makes sense to me." Malone looked at Fred. "Satisfied?"

Fred mumbled something incoherent.

"I asked you a question, Detective," Malone said firmly.

"I have to be, apparently."

"Detective Steele isn't hiding her relationship with the victim, though I think *relationship* is stretching things," Malone said.

"It is," Amanda agreed.

Fred fired daggers at her and went to leave the room.

"Wait, where do you think you're going?" Malone called out.

Fred stopped walking and turned around. "You've given the case to Detectives Steele and Stenson, unless I misunderstood?"

"Oh, no, you got the message loud and clear, but have you already brought them up to speed? Or were you just going to leave them to scuttle through and waste not only man hours but squander precious time that could be better used in catching up with the killer? Start talking." Malone pointed from Fred to Amanda and Trent. "And if you two have questions, ask them now."

Fred walked back to them as he pulled a notebook and pen out of a pocket. He flipped it open. "Victim is Felicity Kelley, twenty-eight years old, single—"

"That much they'd know," Malone huffed and shook his head.

"Very well. Felicity was found by her friend Celeste Sweeney at eleven thirty AM, that being this morning, Wednesday, August—"

Malone held up a hand. "We know what day it is."

"Sweeney was here because she was checking on Felicity. Said she's been worried about her."

"Did she say why?" Trent asked, beating Amanda to the same question.

"Didn't get that far. Detective Ryan might have by now, but Sweeney's a mess."

That was easy to imagine since she'd found her friend with a knife in her chest. Though they didn't know if she had entered the house. "Did Sweeney come inside? Touch anything?"

"Nope." Fred pointed the tip of his pen toward the front window. "She caught a glimpse through there. She resorted to that when Felicity wasn't answering the door or her phone."

"Speaking of Felicity's phone," Amanda said, "we'll need that before you go."

"It's currently in an evidence bag with the officer at the front door."

"Where did you find it?" She wasn't even sure how his response might affect the investigation, but it had taken several rings before Fred had answered when she'd called.

"It was tucked under the couch cushion, like it was put there on purpose."

"Strange place to keep a phone." She turned to Trent, who nodded. Fred shrugged. "How did you unlock it?" she asked.

"I used her fingerprint."

The room fell silent for a few seconds.

"Anything else?" Malone prompted Fred.

"Actually, I have a question," Amanda said. "You told us

that Felicity called Lorenzo's after me. I assume you confirmed she ordered a pizza?"

"I did, and before you ask, the delivery kid checks out."

Something only an iron-clad alibi could guarantee. "How is that possible? Do we know the time of death?"

"No ME here yet, so no. But Felicity didn't get her pizza."

"What time was the attempted delivery?" Trent asked.

"Six-oh-five. But this delivery guy isn't suspicious in the least. He was at his next stop ten minutes later and delivering pizza until midnight. Confirmed with Lorenzo's. After that he was with his girlfriend until this morning, which she confirmed."

Likely safe to take him off the suspect list then. "And Felicity called Lorenzo's at what time?"

Fred consulted his notes. "Five forty."

After she called me... That should ease her guilt. After all, such a routine thing didn't indicate that Felicity was fearful for her immediate safety. It also allowed Amanda to build a time-line. "Then in all likelihood, Kelley's killer gained access to her house between five forty and six-oh-five."

"We could be looking at the same for time of death," Trent said.

"Possible, though not necessarily," Amanda replied. "Her killer simply would have had to prevent her from answering the door."

Trent nodded and turned his attention to Fred. "What size was the pizza?"

"A small."

"Then she wasn't expecting company to share it with," Trent reasoned. "Whoever turned up, it wasn't for a planned visit."

"Exactly what Ryan and I figured."

"Anything else they should know before you leave?" Malone asked Fred.

"Think that's about it."

"All right, then." Malone clapped his hands together, an obvious dismissal.

Fred picked up on it and left.

"First thoughts?" Malone asked her and Trent.

"Far too soon to leap in any direction," Amanda said.

Malone smiled, bobbed his head, and left the house with, "Keep me posted."

Trent turned to Amanda. "I'm going to assume you haven't seen the news recently, about how well Felicity's latest book has been doing?"

"I do my best to avoid the news." She had precious little free time, and she wasn't spending what she did have filling her head with more bad news.

"As I figured. Well, it's apparently blowing up the bestseller charts. I'm not a reader, so don't ask me what it's called, but its success resulted in a movie deal. And I'm talking box office, blockbuster huge. Apparently, Chris Hemsworth is set to play her lead detective."

That made her momentarily speechless. "Wow. That's incredible." And it was, but it might also complicate finding Felicity's killer. Was it someone envious of Felicity's success? An avid fan? A rejected lover? The list was truly endless.

"Just wanted to give you a heads-up. Obviously, I don't know if it will factor into the case."

"Again, too early to say. But if I were to ask your early thoughts, what are they?"

"Assume you're asking?" A brief smirk, then, "I'd say an isolated incident. You know how I feel when it comes to people getting struck in the heart."

She nodded, recalling he saw it as testifying to a love affair gone wrong. "We'll talk to her friend, Celeste Sweeney, see if she knows of any boyfriends or exes Felicity had."

"On board with that. We also need to find out if there is any sign of forced entry. If not, Felicity may have let her killer in."

With this statement, Amanda conjured a sad possibility. Had Felicity answered her front door expecting the pizza she'd ordered to find her would-be killer standing there instead? "Yeah, we'll need that answer."

"You must have missed this." Trent gestured back and forth between them.

Her cheeks heated, not exactly sure what he was implying.

"I just meant all the questions," he rushed out. "After all, you did come back early."

Mostly wracked with guilt and spurred on by compulsion... "I wouldn't go that far, but sitting around does get kind of tedious."

"You? Sitting around? I'd have to see it for myself."

"Very funny." She bristled some, probably because his jest was so accurate.

"It's true, though, isn't it? What you are basically telling me is you were bored once you got back from Florida."

"Fine, yes, I was. Today, anyway. Not that I wanted this"— she glanced over at Felicity's dead body—"*excitement* to liven things up." If it meant Felicity Kelley were still alive, Amanda would have happily stared into space for days on end.

FOUR

Amanda and Trent stepped outside and found that detectives Hudson and Ryan were gone. Malone wasn't in sight either. Officer Wyatt was with the man and that upset woman. Appearance-wise, they were a mismatched couple. Him around six foot two, her about five foot five. Both were dressed casually. Her fair-haired, him dark. Her with a round face, him oval.

Amanda wasn't privy to their relationship, but they appeared comfortable and familiar with each other. His arm was around her, and while she currently wasn't crying, she was tucked tightly against his side.

As Amanda got closer, she noticed they wore wedding rings and the woman had the beginnings of a baby bump. Amanda dipped her head to Wyatt in greeting and dismissal, which he picked up and excused himself. "Celeste Sweeney?"

"That's me." Celeste's lips quivered, and Amanda felt for her. If merely confirming her identity was hard, the rest of this conversation would be hell.

"I'm Detective Steele, and this is Detective Stenson." No need to announce themselves as being with the Prince William County Police Department as they'd assume as much. "We understand you spoke with Detective Ryan," Amanda started, wishing that Natalie had stuck around long enough to bring them up to speed before she jettisoned. "We're going to be the detectives in charge of investigating your friend's murder."

Celeste's eyes filled with tears, turning the steely blue to cobalt, and a few fell. She let them, unabashed, unlike earlier when Amanda had noted her wiping them away.

"And you are, sir?" Amanda turned her attention to the man.

"Barry, Celeste's husband."

"I wish we were all meeting under better circumstances," Amanda said softly.

Celeste hiccupped a sob and rubbed her baby bump.

"How far along are you?" Asked out of genuine interest, but the brief detour might relax the woman some.

"Four months. It's our first."

Amanda squeezed out her own memories of being pregnant with Lindsey. How it was all so strange and exciting at the same time. The thought of a life growing inside her had been surreal, but due to the accident, she'd never experience that again. While it had claimed both Kevin and Lindsey, it had also taken her unborn child and her ability to have more children. She'd spent so much time processing the loss of her husband and daughter, she hadn't fully addressed the emotions surrounding that yet. Whenever she started to broach that territory, she turned back. "That's exciting. Congratulations to both of you."

"Thank you," Celeste said.

It would be easy to get caught up in asking about names and gender, but Amanda wanted to stay on track. "I appreciate this must be difficult for you, but we have some questions we need to ask."

Barry rubbed the top of Celeste's shoulder and said, "We talked with Detective Ryan and Officer Wyatt. Now you? I'm not sure there's anything left to say."

"My partner and I will catch up with both Officer Wyatt and Detective Ryan, but until then, we apologize if some of our questions seem repetitive." She provided a version of this caveat with most cases. Typically, a uniformed officer took an initial, brief statement from the person who found the body. "When did you arrive?"

Trent pulled out his notebook and a pen. He was better at detailing everything in writing than she was. If she had notes to make, she used an app on her phone.

"I got here around eleven thirty." Celeste sniffled. "I'd tried reaching her so many times, but she never answered."

Amanda noted how Celeste had slipped into autopilot, prattling off details devoid of emotion. "And that's why you came over? Or did you have plans?" She recalled what Fred had told them but wanted to hear directly from Celeste.

Celeste shook her head. "No plans. It's been hard to pin her down for months. She's been like the wind."

"So, you thought you'd stop by and check on her?" Amanda asked.

"Yeah."

"She's come into a lot of success," Trent said, "what with her book hitting the charts and the movie in the works. That must have made her life more chaotic."

"It felt like there was more to it than that. She was obsessed, guess that's the most fitting word, with her work lately."

"A new book she was writing?" Amanda asked.

"Uh-huh. She was tight-lipped about it."

"That wasn't usual for her?" Call it a feeling based on Celeste's tone of voice.

"Not really. She doesn't normally spill all the details about her WIP, but she seemed to hold this one even closer to the vest than normal."

Trent looked up from his notepad. "Her what? You said WIP?"

"Work in progress." Celeste shook her head. "Now she has me talking like her. Writers have their own lingo, and I've picked it up."

"How long have you been friends?" Amanda asked.

"Since public school when my family moved into town. And I can't believe that... *that...*" Celeste clamped a hand over her mouth as a fresh batch of tears fell.

"Losing her sister was hard on Felicity," Barry interjected, speaking on Celeste's behalf as if he were picking up on some unspoken message from her. "Is that where you were going?" He softly nudged Celeste, who nodded. The two were obviously close for him to read her mind—not all married couples were that in tune.

"I imagine that time would have been very hard on Felicity." Though Amanda didn't need to imagine; she could draw from personal experience.

Celeste's crying subsided, and she dug into her purse. She came out with a ratted tissue and dabbed it to her nose. "The movie deal was bittersweet for her. She really wished her sister was around to celebrate with. Eve would have held a huge party for her. She was an incredible woman. They both were."

It made sense that Celeste would have known Eve Kelley given the length of her friendship with Felicity. Now that her name had come up, Amanda was curious what happened to Eve's cosmetic company, Pixie Winks, after her death. Most likely Eve had left it to her sister, who was her sole surviving relative. It was a mystery what would happen to it now. Had someone killed Felicity to get their hands on it? Due diligence made it necessary to ask. "Celeste, do you know who will inherit Felicity's estate? Her house, her assets, Pixie Winks...?"

"Wait. You said Detectives Steele and Stenson?" Celeste blinked and palmed her cheeks. "I thought those names sounded familiar but couldn't place them until now. You investigated Eve's murder."

Not a question, but Amanda answered, "We did."

"Then I'm so happy you're on this. I know you'll find out who did this to Flick." Celeste took a staggered breath as if saying her friend's nickname hurt too much, but her shoulders raised with her statement of confidence.

Amanda hoped she and Trent could live up to the woman's expectations. "We will do all we can. Do you know who will get—"

"Sorry, yes. She made her own will after Eve died—said it was the responsible thing to do. I know because she told me she'd left *me* everything. I never thought... I figured she'd meet someone and change it, you know? But I don't... I don't want it. I just want her." She set off in a fresh crying jag.

Amanda waited for a few seconds, then spoke. "You said that she had been very busy in the past few months."

"Yeah. She rarely canceled our dates together. We'd often bike on the weekends and catch a yoga class or two here and there." She smoothed a hand over the hair tucked behind her ear. "We'd have lunch, drinks out. Virgin ones for me now, of course." She rubbed her baby bump again.

"I get the picture," Amanda said softly. "But more recently, she was canceling on you?"

"Yes, and sometimes last minute. She'd say something came up but never give me details."

Given what Celeste was telling them about the relationship, that was certainly unusual behavior, but did it factor into Felicity's murder? "When did you see her last?"

"Two weeks ago. I begged her to have a quick coffee, and she agreed."

The distinct sound of car doors closing had Amanda turning to see who had arrived. Crime scene investigators Emma Blair and Isabelle Donnelly were trudging toward the house. Amanda made eye contact with Blair and dipped her head in acknowledgment but focused back on Celeste. "What was she like?"

"Frazzled. She wasn't wearing any makeup, and her hair looked like she'd stuck her finger in a socket." Celeste paused there, a slight smile at the mental imagery she must have conjured with the memory. "I don't think she was sleeping properly either."

"And didn't you tell me she hung around for all of twenty minutes?" Barry said to Celeste, who nodded.

"She said she had to go," Celeste added.

"Any reason as to why?" Trent asked.

"No, but I wish I'd pushed her on it." Celeste bit her bottom lip, and her eyes glazed over.

Death piled up regrets, but there would be no going back in time. If she and Trent were going to find Felicity's killer, they had to move forward. Just where was that lead to follow?

FIVE

Amanda continued with the questioning, drawing from her earlier conversation with Trent. "Did Felicity have a boyfriend?"

"She used to. Oh my god, you don't think that—" Her body shook, and Barry enveloped her in a hug.

Celeste's powerful reaction to her question gave Amanda a sinking feeling there was a story about this ex that she and Trent needed to hear.

"Just breathe," Barry told Celeste, drawing back from her. "Inhale slowly. Hold a few seconds. Exhale. Repeat."

Celeste did as her husband suggested and was better for it a moment later.

"She is prone to having panic attacks," Barry explained and took Celeste's hand.

"What was the boyfriend's name?" Amanda tamped down the urge to jump right on why Celeste's suspicion went to him. Tentative steps in that direction would keep Celeste settled and the story unraveling.

"Luis Navarro." Celeste pinched her earlobe and the gold

bar earring there and added, "He's a piece of work. I was happy when she told me she finally broke things off."

Piece of work, and she *had broken things off...* Luis might not have been on board with the split.

"How was he a 'piece of work'?" Trent's sensitivity to domestic violence was high.

"He was a player. I saw it clearly from the start, but Felicity turned a blind eye. Thankfully, she eventually saw sense and when she told me she suspected he was cheating, I told her if she was feeling that way, she was probably right."

From the sound of it, the termination of the relationship hadn't been mutual, rather one-sided. Trent might be onto something with the positioning of the stab wound. To the heart from a jilted lover? "How did Luis take the breakup?"

"Not well. At all." A swoosh of her hand emphasized the point.

Her response didn't help alleviate Amanda's suspicion. They needed to speak with this guy.

"It was just days after the movie deal was finalized too, wasn't it?" Barry asked his wife.

Celeste shook her head. "Not right away. That deal was signed a few months ago, but she ended things, say, three weeks ago."

Was Luis bitter Felicity had ended things not long after she came into money? They weren't married, but he could have deceived himself into thinking he'd financially benefit anyhow. He might even have thought he contributed in some way toward her success. "How long were they together?"

"Seven months, somewhere in there," Celeste told them.

"Safe to say it was a serious relationship then, exclusive?" Trent asked.

"As serious as Luis could be, I suppose. He was a cheat, as I said. I can't believe he proposed to her."

"He proposed?" Amanda nearly choked on that revelation.

The stakes in this breakup just got larger for Luis Navarro—cut off financially and left with a broken heart.

"Yep, right after she signed the movie contract. What a slime bucket!" Celeste was shaking her head and looking at Barry. "Thankfully she had the sense to turn him down. I still can't believe she stayed with him a while longer though."

Sadly, Amanda could believe that Luis would want to cement his union with Felicity. He probably imagined her payday benefiting him, and she'd burst that bubble. Thinking back to the murder scene, there hadn't been signs of forced entry as of yet, which meant Felicity may have let her killer inside. Had that been her ex? Though there was another option. "Do you know if Felicity gave Luis a key to her house?"

"She did, a while back now."

Luis could have let himself inside and pleaded for Felicity to reconsider their relationship. When that didn't work, he snapped and killed her. "Did Felicity get the key back?"

"I don't know that for sure."

Luis Navarro had potential motive, but she couldn't afford to pigeonhole the investigation this early. "Going back to Felicity's recent success, those in the spotlight often attract certain types—stalkers, obsessed fans, even haters. Did Felicity ever mention anyone like this bothering her?"

"Sometimes she'd gripe about fans bombarding her with messages of a rather personal nature, but she didn't say it was anything that had her concerned."

"A personal nature?" That alone had the skin tightening on the back of Amanda's neck.

"They'd overshare and ask probing questions, trying to get Felicity to reciprocate."

"Then nothing lewd or sexually inappropriate?" Trent asked.

"Not that she said."

Celeste had used that caveat twice now, and it wasn't reassuring. All it meant was if Felicity was contacted by dangerous types, she never shared her concerns with her friend. "Can you give us any examples of what the messages were about?" Having a better understanding in this area could help immensely. It would tell them how much effort to concentrate on this angle. Though, they'd pick up the topic again with Felicity's publishing contacts regardless of what Celeste had to tell them. But one step at a time.

"Some wanted her to talk about her next books, connect online, follow them back. But if they wanted updates, all they had to do was follow her social accounts. Do they want her to write books or chitchat her days away?"

Celeste made fans sound like irritating flies buzzing around, but without them, Felicity wouldn't have had the success she had.

"Actually, that didn't come out right," Celeste backpedaled. "And Flick adored her fans."

Amanda nodded, placated. "Did she ever mention any one person in particular?"

"Not to me, but her editor or agent might know of someone."

An agent didn't surprise her, but... "Her editor...?" Amanda wasn't familiar with the world of publishing aside from the fact publishers acquired works from authors and put them into the marketplace. As for an editor, she imagined their role was limited to proofing manuscripts for grammatical errors.

"Her point of contact at her publisher," Celeste said.

Apparently, the position was more involved than punctuation. "And who was that?"

"Melody? Sorry, I don't remember her last name. But Flick's publisher was Garrison & Marrow. They're the second largest publisher in the world." As Celeste added that tidbit, her shoulders lifted, as did her chin, showcasing obvious pride in her friend's accomplishments.

A publisher with serious clout wouldn't have hurt Felicity's chances of success, though it probably had a lot to do with talent and luck as well. "We'll find Melody. Do you know the name of Felicity's agent?"

"Justine Livingston, apparently one of the best there is. Not that I've met her, but that's what Flick told me about her."

"All right, thank you for taking the time to answer our questions," Amanda said as she withdrew a business card and handed it to Celeste. "You can go now, but if you think of anything, call me anytime. I mean that."

"Thank you." Celeste stepped forward to hug Amanda.

Amanda's instinct was to move out of reach. Touch made things personal, and she needed to remain detached for the benefit of the investigation. But to turn her back on this woman's suffering would make her feel like an anatomic robot. She let the embrace happen but kept it brief.

Celeste palmed her cheeks as she drew back. "If anyone is going to find out who did this to her, it's you."

She appreciated the faith, not the pressure. "We'll do our best."

Barry and Celeste walked off while Amanda and Trent stayed put.

Officer Wyatt came over. "She's so distraught. Poor woman."

"Any highlights from your conversation with her we should know about?" Not that she suspected that Celeste had lied or was Felicity's killer—her grief and angst struck Amanda as genuine—but due diligence required they compare what they'd been told.

"Just the ex, and that guy sounds fishy. Did she mention him to you?"

"She did." Amanda shared the overview of the story they heard, and Wyatt confirmed he'd been told the same, short of the proposal.

"Just a heads-up that canvassing will start once we know time of death."

She nodded, expecting that would be the case. Hopefully, a neighbor saw or heard something that would give them a lead.

Wyatt walked off toward a cruiser, and Trent turned to her. "Luis Navarro sounds like someone we're going to want to speak with soon."

"Agreed. Turned down and set loose after seven months— just after Felicity struck gold. That would hurt anyone's ego. Did it wound Navarro's pride enough to make him kill Felicity Kelley?"

"Guess we'll have to wait and see."

Amanda and Trent walked up to Felicity's front door. Again, she was thinking what an ordinary neighborhood it was for such a violent act. But the thing was, murder didn't discriminate between class, color, or age.

SIX

As Amanda walked inside the house, booties back over her shoes, she was somewhat conflicted about whether they should hang around longer, or go have that talk with Luis Navarro. But it would be beneficial to glean whatever information they could first. One thing that niggled was why Felicity's phone had been under a couch cushion. The spot suggested she'd been trying to hide it and keep it from someone. If so, was something on there she had wanted to protect?

Amanda and Trent found CSIs Blair and Donnelly hard at work processing the scene. Donnelly was snapping photographs, and Blair walked into the living room area taking video of the scene in situ with a tablet. A couple of yellow evidence markers were in the middle of the room, but Amanda couldn't tell what they were indicating. "What are these for?" Amanda asked Donnelly.

"Shoe impressions."

Amanda nodded. CSIs could lift shoeprints even when they were invisible to the naked eye. They'd use an apparatus that magnetically charged Mylar and lifted dust particles, retaining the tread pattern. Shoeprints, often as unique as fingerprints, could go a long way in building a case against someone. Just one more reason it was so important not to traipse all over a crime scene. "Well, everyone with the PWCPD is wearing booties. Felicity isn't wearing shoes. I know it's possible these could belong to a pair from her closet—"

Donnelly shook her head. "They are too large. A man's size-ten running shoe."

"A running shoe," Trent said slowly, as if chewing on the words. "So, whoever this guy was, he was dressed casually." He looked at Amanda, and she thought she read his mind. If so, he was also thinking about Luis Navarro.

"If only we could determine *when* they were left." Not to be negative, just trying to keep this potential lead in perspective.

"I'm not that good." Donnelly smiled. "But I can tell you one print was headed toward the front door, another coming into the living room."

"The same person came and went. For however much that helps us," Trent said.

"Unfortunately, not much," Amanda conceded. She turned and looked around the room, her gaze landing on Felicity. She wanted so badly to find her killer. Was it the man behind those shoeprints? And just because they belonged to a casual shoe, it didn't indicate that Felicity had a relaxed relationship with the man wearing them, or that they were welcomed in her home. It could have as easily belonged to an intruder. Speaking of... "Felicity had planned to eat alone. The small pizza tells us that much." She stalled there, thinking again how Felicity's time of death may have factored in timewise with the failed delivery attempt. She was about to carry on when Blair spoke.

She set down her tablet, video supposedly finished, and weighed in with, "There's only one used water glass on the kitchen counter. Nothing to show she had company, period. Well, except for..." Her lips set in a thin line as she glanced at the body.

Amanda asked what she'd been about to a moment ago. "Is there any sign of forced entry?"

"We haven't gotten that far yet, but we'll get there," Blair said.

"Fair enough." Amanda stepped to the side of the room with Trent and gave voice to what was gnawing on her. "Whoever this person was, Felicity didn't want them to get her phone, considering that she hid it under a couch cushion."

Trent nodded. "Right. As Hudson said, it was like the phone was deliberately placed under the cushion. It wasn't like it just slipped down between it and the couch. But why hide it?"

"Add it to the list of questions. Is there something on it she didn't want her visitor to see? All I can conclude."

"Either way, it suggests she had been aware of their presence and had time to tuck it away."

"Huh. Good point. So, she let this person in, thinking she had things under control?" Amanda gnawed on that.

"If that's the case, we could assume her killer was someone she knew. This Navarro guy or someone else."

Amanda's heart ached at how Felicity may have been betrayed in the worst possible way. She could only imagine how horrible it would have been for Felicity if she'd misplaced her faith in the person who ended up taking her life. "We'll need to take a good look at her phone, see her recent contacts—beyond myself and Lorenzo's. It might help us figure out why she hid it." She didn't much relish pressing Felicity's dead finger to her phone as Fred had done. And if it housed glaring evidence, Fred hadn't mentioned it. She'd wait to access the device for now. Besides, learning more about Felicity—outside of the device— might be crucial for putting what was there into perspective. "Let's walk around the house and see what we might find out," she suggested.

"Sounds like a plan. If we're lucky, a laptop or computer could shed light on why she was killed."

Amanda appreciated that he was keeping objective and not obsessing about where Felicity had been stabbed. With the investigation so young, there were many possibilities for suspects. Too many. They had to keep open minds.

SEVEN

Amanda and Trent made their way through the house. There was a dining room at the end of the living area, off the kitchen. From the looks of it, Felicity had used the space for storage. Clear totes were stacked along a wall and from a quick glance, each one was empty.

"Huh. That's not strange at all." Her words dripped with sarcasm, and her observation brought her back to the one she'd made not long after entering the house. "Do you remember our first time here?"

"Hard to forget. I think every notification we've ever done is stored in my head."

"Sad truth." Much like storage totes, her mind housed those memories. "I'm thinking more along the lines of how the place looked. There was so much paper in her living room, there wasn't a place for us to sit."

"That's right. I kept thinking, how many books has she written?"

"And did she ever sleep? I thought she must have kept every manuscript she ever printed, every revision."

"Could have included printed research too."

"Sure, but today, not one scrap of paper and empty totes."

"She could have cleaned house. Purging is the thing to do these days, or so my sisters tell me." Trent had two—one younger and one older.

"Suppose so." She'd leave it there for now, but the lack of printouts in an author's house was unusual. But did it tie into her murder?

They moved on and toured the L-shaped kitchen that hugged the rear east and south sides of the house. They passed a modest table and matching chairs and ducked down to the basement using the stairs just beyond the eating area. It was unfinished with exposed cinder block walls and a concrete floor. A rackety furnace, sounding much like a rattling tin can, kicked out cooled air from the air conditioning unit.

Next, they headed upstairs. Two bedrooms—one used as a home office—and the home's only bathroom.

The office didn't give up any secrets or a laptop. The only documents were bills—utilities and property tax—all paid up to date.

"Where the heck is all the paper?" Trent gently tossed one of the invoices back to the desk. "It doesn't make any sense."

"Nope."

"She could have purchased or leased a place to do her writing. I've read that authors can be particular about where they commune with their muse."

She shook her head. "Commune, muse... Though I suppose it's possible. We can make a note to ask Celeste. But there aren't any rental statements lying around. Besides, she had a lot of space here with living on her own."

"The muse can be a demanding son of a—" He closed his mouth; she was smiling.

Pockets of light reprieve aided in keeping one's sanity at a murder scene, but she said, "All right, let's be serious here."

"Sorry. You're right."

Silence fell between them, and they headed back downstairs to find that the medical examiner, Hans Rideout, and his assistant, Liam Baker, had arrived. Both were near Felicity's body. Rideout was hunched just outside the blood pool.

Amanda approached from the dining room side. "Afternoon," she said to them.

Both returned the greeting, but Rideout didn't take his eyes from the body. Amanda let her gaze dip over Felicity to the surrounding floor where the sun came through the front window and kissed the wood. It accentuated an area that was lighter than the surrounding planks.

She indicated what she'd noticed to Trent—a spot about five feet by seven feet.

He stepped up next to her. "There might have been an area rug here at one point."

At one point... Amanda suspected her mind was reading too much into that. "Don't remember the rug, but I recall a coffee table in front of the couch."

"Now that you say that, me too. It was a long one."

But where did this trip down memory lane take them? Did the missing items factor into what had taken place here? And really what was she suspecting—that the killer packed up Felicity's paperwork, table, and rug? For what purpose? Either way, they'd talk to Celeste about all of this, see if she had any answers.

"Time of death was approximately between ten and midnight last night," Rideout said, cutting into her concentration.

"Then she was alive when the pizza guy knocked on the door at six-oh-five." It might be best not to give too much thought to what had transpired between then and ten o'clock. "Cause of death?" It felt counterintuitive to ask given the knife in her chest, but it might not be what had killed her.

"One would assume it was due to this"—Rideout gestured toward the knife—"but if so, I'd have expected far more blood."

"What are you saying? It was added after the fact?" It wouldn't be the first time a killer had staged things to look the way they wanted. Could that be the case here?

"I'm not concluding anything at this point. I'll only know definitively once I have her back at the morgue. But, preliminarily, the lack of blood tells me her heart may have already stopped beating when the knife was put in her chest."

"Nothing disturbing about that," Trent muttered.

"When do you expect to perform the autopsy?" she asked.

Rideout gestured toward Liam.

"The morgue is quite busy these days," Liam said as he took out a tablet, presumably consulting Rideout's schedule. "It won't be until tomorrow afternoon at three."

"Twenty-four hours from now?" Things took time, but this delay seemed excessive.

Liam pressed his lips. "Sorry, but that's the soonest." He tapped on the screen, likely adding Felicity's autopsy to the calendar.

"Let's load 'er up, Liam. We've seen all there is to see here." Rideout rose to full height, groaning as if he were going on eighty and wasn't just forty-something.

Amanda moved back to make more room and looked around. Her eyes landed on the mantel of the fireplace, and it prompted her memory. Before she was distracted by Malone's arrival, etcetera, she had noticed something on the hearth.

She walked over there now, watchful of the placement of her steps. As she drew up next to the fireplace, she pulled out her phone, turned on the flashlight, and set the beam on the grate. And sure enough... Ash. She hunched down and rolled some between her gloved fingers. Cool to the touch, but she'd still wager the fire had been rather recent. "Trent, come here."

He lowered next to her.

"She had a fire recently..." She met his gaze and was curious if his mind was headed where hers had gone.

"Could it explain the missing paperwork? But why would she burn all her manuscripts and research?" Trent's brow furrowed with confusion.

"She might not have set the fire. I'm thinking maybe her killer did."

"To destroy her work? But why? And who burns a fire when it's a hundred degrees outside?"

"Ah, guys..." Liam was waving for them to come over. "You'll want to see this."

Amanda and Trent hurried over. Felicity had already been set inside a black body bag—zipper undone—and loaded onto a wheeled gurney. They'd use it to transport her out of the house and into the van.

Rideout was dipping long-pronged tweezers into Felicity's mouth.

"There is something wedged in her throat. I caught a glimpse of it when we lifted her," Liam said, providing explanation.

The entire room fell silent as the investigators, Amanda, Trent, and Liam watched Rideout slowly withdraw his hand. And there, gripped in the tweezers was a piece of cardstock folded into a small square.

CSI Blair rushed over with a plastic evidence bag and set it on Felicity's torso.

"Thank you." Rideout set the find on the plastic and unfolded it with gloved hands. "A playing card, folded into eight even squares."

Creased in half, half again, and half again...

"Things are getting strange now," Liam said.

Even stranger than the suggestion the killer stabbed Felicity after she was already dead?

"Yep, weirder by the second." Rideout held up the card.

The Queen of Hearts.

First, a knife to the heart. Now this. It was time to talk with the ex-boyfriend.

EIGHT

Amanda couldn't completely set aside Trent's strong feelings about murders involving a wound to the heart. In this case, it might not be cause of death but it had to serve some purpose. To manipulate the investigation? To throw suspicion on Luis Navarro? If so, the killer needed to know about him in the first place. Or was she complicating things? Had Felicity's ex exacted revenge and decided to make a statement with the knife and playing card?

Whatever the case, it was too early to leap to judgment, though it also couldn't be ignored that Navarro deserved a hard look. The fact remained that Luis was given good reason to feel slighted and pissed off. After all, he'd spent seven months with her only to be dumped shortly after Felicity met with huge success. Typically, a man's pride only had so much tolerance for a bruised ego. Had this slight triggered Luis to murder?

"Right there, Trent. You"—Amanda pointed emphatically from the passenger seat, then lowered her arm and looked back —"passed it."

"Oops." He'd driven right by Navarro's address. "Sorry, I'll just..." He pulled a tight U-turn and parked in the lot for Luis Navarro's apartment building.

"You seem deep in thought." Obviously, whatever was on his mind had him distracted.

"I am."

Two words, and it would seem the conversation would end right there. While she sensed his thoughts were complex, possibly personal, she tried to lighten the air. "Don't tell me the playing card has you thinking this is a serial killer?"

He hesitated just long enough to disclose that wasn't what had his focus, though he said, "You got me," and flashed her a smile.

She continued playing along. "It's too soon for that. Come on." She reached for her door handle and got out.

He shut off the car and followed her lead.

"The Queen of Hearts doesn't need to be a serial killer's calling card. It could have been left for any number of reasons," she added, more because she wanted to talk this out than being under the impression her partner was actually thinking this was a serial killer.

"Not going to argue. Honestly, based on what Celeste told us about this Navarro guy, we might have this investigation all wrapped up in the next few minutes. Well, plus paperwork." He winked at her. "That will tack on several more hours."

"Since I'm not really back until Monday..." The implication being she'd cut and run.

"Very funny." He held the door to the building open for Amanda. Navarro was apartment 310, and they could walk right up.

She knocked while Trent stood next to her, but there was this undercurrent of tension between them. Sometimes their past came back and manifested itself this way. All because they'd kissed—crossed a line they never should have. Despite vowing to forget it ever happened, it had a way of slithering up for light on occasion. Blame it on the indisputable attraction and the fact they cared for one another, but she had Logan now, and Trent was dating. It might be the thought of facing Luis Navarro, a man rejected in love, that had Trent feeling the same way. But she shook the thought aside—discounting this as her ego—and knocked again.

"He could be at work," Trent said.

But Trent had spoken too soon. Shuffling feet were coming toward the door.

Something inside the apartment hit the floor and made a loud bang. Following that was a string of expletives.

The security chain slid aside, scraping against the door, and then it swung open. "Yeah?" A man in his late twenties, early thirties, stood in front of them, shirtless and wearing cotton shorts. His hair was sticking up, and he rubbed a hand over it, an obvious self-conscious move.

Amanda caught a blur of movement in the apartment behind him. A woman by the look of it.

Trent took the lead, holding up his badge. "Detectives Stenson and Steele." He gestured toward Amanda. To the man, he said, "Are you Luis Navarro?"

"That's me."

"We need to talk to you about Felicity Kelley."

He scratched his chest and drew back. "Ah, sure. Come in." Luis showed them to the living area, which was a couch and a media stand with TV and a gaming console. Sparse furnishings, but a tornado had passed through, leaving articles of clothing draped on the cushions and floor. Shirts, shorts... a bra.

Luis snatched it up as if he just realized its presence and tucked it into a pocket of his shorts. He cleared his throat and crossed his arms. "What's this about Flick? Felicity?"

"Why don't you sit?" Trent gestured toward the couch, and Luis did as he'd suggested. Then, Trent laid out the notification matter of fact, "Felicity Kelley was murdered last night."

"She was... *was* what *now*?" Luis rubbed his face as if he were just waking up and trying to shake the cobwebs.

Trent added, "She was found in her home this morning. Stabbed."

Though Rideout hadn't concluded it as the cause of death, Trent's statement was accurate in a vague sense. A knife was plunged into her chest.

"I... Wow." He flexed his hands on his forehead, massaging it as if an instant headache had moved in.

"That's all? I tell you that your girlfriend is dead, and all you say is 'wow'?" Trent's voice was full of disgust.

"*Ex*-girlfriend."

Navarro's correction would have played right into Trent's hands. He opened his mouth to speak just as a woman with blond hair, dressed in a man's T-shirt and shorts, the drawstring pulled tight, slinked into the room. She dropped on the couch beside Luis and put a hand on his shoulder.

"Everything okay?" She never acknowledged Amanda or Trent with any eye contact.

"These are detectives," Luis said. "They just told me that Flick has been murdered." His voice broke on the last word—for show, shock, regret? Amanda wasn't sure.

"Oh my god." The woman's eyes widened, and she clamped a hand over her mouth.

"Did you know Felicity Kelley?" Trent asked.

The woman shifted her blue eyes to Trent. "I knew *of* her. Didn't really know her."

The energy in the room changed, and Amanda had a hunch. "Were you together"—Amanda drew a finger from Luis to the woman and back—"when you and Felicity were?"

"Not that I'm proud of that fact," Luis said.

"Hey!" The woman slapped his arm.

"Not that I'm not proud of you, just that I was cheating on Flick."

That seemed to satisfy the woman as her body language softened—at least some.

"What's your name?" Trent asked her for the record.

"Kaitlyn Avery."

Trent took out his notepad and made a note of her name. "How long have you been seeing each other?"

Kaitlyn answered, "A couple of months?" She looked at Luis as if to verify.

"Sounds about right."

"We understand that Felicity broke things off with you only a few weeks ago." Amanda phrased it that way, putting the split relationship as being outside Luis's control.

"It was mutual," Luis said. "We'd been growing apart."

"That's not how we heard it." The fact he was bald-faced lying to them had Amanda's hackles going up.

"Let me guess... Celeste blabbed to you. That's why you're here in the first place." Luis leveled a glare at them.

"Blabbed to us?" Trent prompted.

"Yeah, well, Celeste never liked me."

Amanda could see why. Luis Navarro struck her as arrogant and a player. It wouldn't surprise her if he had another girlfriend in addition to Kaitlyn. "You were cheating on Felicity, and she found out. You also proposed, and she turned you down. If I were you, that would have had my blood boiling." She had added that latter part to hook a reaction, but Luis remained calm.

"It just wasn't meant to be, I guess."

"Huh." Trent looked at Amanda and spoke to her. "He's taking it much better than I would."

"Sounds like he was cool-headed about it," she replied.

"Hello? I'm right here. You can talk to me." Luis was wildly waving his hand.

"Let's just say, I don't think either of us are buying this cool act of yours. Felicity was with you for months and decided to break up with you just after coming into serious money. How could you have been okay with that? The timing alone had to sting." Trent was pouring acid on the open wound in Luis's ego, but Amanda was letting it happen.

"It was what it was. I've got Katie." Luis put his arm around the woman.

"Where were you last night between ten and midnight?" Amanda asked.

"Here with Katie." Stated calmly, Luis had shed all guilt about his affair.

"That's right." Kaitlyn bobbed her head like one of those bobble dolls.

"What about between five forty and ten o'clock?" That time window accounted for approximately when they figured Felicity's killer had arrived until the early end of time of death.

"I would have just been getting home from—" Luis clamped his mouth shut.

"From?" Amanda pressed.

Luis licked his lips and passed a nervous side-glance at Kaitlyn. "I picked up a burger, came home. That's all."

"You have a receipt?" Amanda countered.

"No. I paid cash and told them to throw it out."

"Otherwise, you were here all day?" Trent asked.

"Between jobs at the moment."

Huh. No income and *dumped by his wealthy girlfriend...* "Can anyone else confirm you were here last evening? Neighbors? Other friends who might have popped by?"

Kaitlyn bounced up and pivoted to face Luis. "Cat Lady saw me in the hallway."

Trent looked up from his notebook. "What time was this?"

"Nine."

That was outside the TOD window, and even if "Cat Lady" confirmed seeing Kaitlyn, it didn't mean that she and Navarro hadn't left. Or even that Navarro was home in the first place. "And who is Cat Lady?" Amanda asked on a sigh, hating the moniker.

"The bat who lives across the hall." Luis scrunched up his face. "Never bothered to remember her actual name."

"I see." Trent tapped the tip of his pen against the page, leaving little blue dots in its wake. "Did you let yourself in, Kaitlyn, or did Luis?"

"I did," Luis said.

"Can anyone confirm you were home, besides Kaitlyn?" Amanda stiffened her posture, her attention fixed on Luis.

Luis let out a puff of air. "Not that I know of."

"You must realize how this looks," Trent said. "No alibi for the time of her murder, and you have motive. I would have felt extremely cheated being dumped after my girlfriend made it rich."

Luis licked his lips, met Trent's eye. Unspoken, man to man, it had been a blow to his pride.

"She probably spoiled you with nice things, fancy trips..." Trent poked at the festering wound. "And all that was gone. Just like that!"

"Fine," Luis hissed. "It sucked all right, but I didn't kill her."

"Yet, you went right there," Trent volleyed back.

"That's been your implication all along. I mean, two cops—"

"Detectives," Trent corrected.

"Whatever. You show up at my door, asking where I was when my girlfriend was killed."

Amanda held back the urge to insert *ex*-girlfriend, letting Luis have that pass. "A question you can't apparently answer— or prove."

"Me. I'm the proof," Kaitlyn squeaked.

"And how do we know we can trust your word, Ms. Avery?" Amanda watched as her words impacted. They had Kaitlyn biting on her bottom lip and staring blankly across the room. "We were told you have a key to Felicity's house,"

Amanda picked up the questioning, directing these words to Luis.

"I used to. She had mine too, but when we ended things, we gave them back."

Again, Luis was sticking to the story that the relationship had ended mutually.

"You should stop wasting time on me," Luis pushed out. "I didn't kill her, but there are lots who could have."

She recoiled. "Like who?"

"Flick had some deranged fans, I tell you. But what do you expect? She did write about murder. Heck, some psychos are probably out there imitating her work right now."

Trent stilled his pen on the page.

Amanda was thinking on Luis's words too. *Imitating her work...*

The crime scene had been rather unique considering the stab to the heart and the Queen of Hearts playing card.

I didn't kill her, but there are lots who could have... Felicity Kelley's latest novel was a bestseller with a vast audience. Had Felicity's killer been trying to recreate a scene from it?

NINE

Amanda shifted her stance, wishing she had a place to sit. "Deranged fans. You think one of them killed her?"

Luis shrugged. "I mean why not? Just don't ask me for any names."

"Seems rather convenient in that case." Had he suggested deranged fans to take their attention off him? Much the same as the knife and playing card made it feel like the work of a ruthless repeat killer?

"I'm sure you can find out more from her agent or publisher. Some emailed all the time."

Felicity's phone might hold the names of the regulars. Then she and Trent could work with Detective Briggs in Digital Forensics to track them down through their IP addresses. They didn't need Luis to access her phone, but she was curious if he knew her passcode. "You wouldn't happen to know how to unlock her phone, would you?"

"Her fingerprint or a pattern." Luis drew it in the air with a fingertip. "No passcode that I know of."

There was no hesitation on his part in disclosing his knowledge. "Do that again, please."

Luis did, and she committed the action to memory. Trent was hunched over his notebook, likely recording the pattern in a diagram.

"Fantastic. That is a big help." Now Amanda couldn't wait to get her hands on Felicity's phone. She handed her card to Luis. "Call if you think of something or someone specific after we leave. Number's on there."

"Okay."

She wasn't sure exactly what to make of Luis's reaction to the news—genuine shock and grief or an act. With that said, she wasn't leaving because she thought him innocent, but rather, they had yet to build a solid case against him. The lack of an alibi certainly wasn't enough to get charges to stick. If they could establish a pattern to his behavior, possibly by speaking with Felicity's neighbors, they might find that he came around when Felicity hadn't welcomed his presence.

She and Trent left Luis and Kaitlyn. A quick talk to the neighbor across the hall confirmed she'd seen Kaitlyn last night. She had no idea whether Luis had been home.

Back in the car, Trent cranked up the air conditioning.

"Why are we leaving without that guy?" Trent said as he pulled his seat belt across. "He's guilty as hell to me. He certainly has motive."

"We need more."

"Sometimes the hoops we have to jump through are painful."

"Better to put in the work and arrest the right guy. We wouldn't want to put an innocent person behind bars."

"Guess we can't lock up the guy for being a douchebag." He looked over at her and smiled.

"Yeah, it doesn't work that way, unfortunately."

"Navarro brought up psychos imitating Felicity's work. It is possible the killer was recreating a scene from one of her novels.

We should probably start reading, beginning with the bestseller."

"I thought the same." Not that she was looking forward to it. Her phone rang, and caller ID told her it was Logan. "I've got to get this." She tucked in toward the door and answered with a smile. "Hey."

"Hey there, gorgeous. So, me and the guys just finished up, and we're thinking of going back to our place. You know, to have some beers, sacrifice meat to the altar, and just hang out. It's such a gorgeous day."

Our place... She was still getting used to that, as if she were betraying her late husband's memory by living with another man. Logan must still be adjusting too as it felt like he was running the evening's plans past her for approval.

"Mandy, you hear me?"

"Yeah. It's your place too. Why not?"

"I realize that. I just wanted to make sure you didn't have anything else planned."

Of course, he was just being considerate. "That's fine. Sounds good." How did she tell him she got herself wrapped up in a murder investigation during their vacation?

"I sense a *but* coming."

"I'm working a case." There was no sugarcoating this.

"I don't understand." Any excitement that had fired his voice was gone.

"You remember my mentioning a voicemail I got yesterday?"

"From that author who had procedural questions?"

"That's the one. Well, I called her back and found out that she was murdered."

"What?" Slapped out, loud enough she pulled her phone away from her ear, even though the damage was done. "Wasn't her sister murdered too?"

"A while back, yes. I can't get into details obviously, but I am investigating what has happened to the author now."

"Even though you're not due back until Monday?"

She bristled. Logan knew how important the job was to her, and he should realize that her connection to Felicity would trump her vacation and only strengthen her determination to get involved.

"I probably shouldn't have said that," he eventually offered, apparently reading the silence that stretched across the line.

"It's..." She couldn't say *okay* as it wasn't. She settled on, "I understand your side in this."

"What's going on with Zoe then? I know she was at Kristen's for the day, but aren't you supposed to pick her up for dinner?"

"I'll call Kristen and take care of it." She'd been so wrapped up in the case, but she also knew that Zoe was safe with Kristen and her family.

"If you want, or I can pick her up?"

"And what? Have her hang out with you and your friends?"

"She likes them."

"I'm not subjecting her to all that testosterone. Not to mention, I know how Chuck likes to toss back the beers. Speaking of, make sure he doesn't drive—none of them for that matter." It had been a drunk driver who took out Kevin and Lindsey. She certainly didn't want anyone else to suffer such unbearable pain when it could be prevented.

"You know I won't. All right. Need anything, call me." Logan blew a kiss over the line and hung up.

"Where to?" Trent asked bluntly, not looking at her.

"Let's pop over to the Sweeneys. We can ask them the few questions we still have, then we'll return to Felicity's and get our hands on her phone."

He put the car into gear without another word.

It felt like a cold front had moved in. Again, she got the

feeling it had to do with unrequited feelings. But was she putting it out there or was Trent? She loved Logan, but working so closely with Trent sometimes complicated things. After all, he was always there for her. He fully understood her and the job...

She cleared her throat. "So, we might need to read..."

"Possibly. You can't deny that the murder scene was unique enough to be fiction. Not saying it's some serial killer, could even be Navarro. Basically, anyone familiar with her books."

"And we could just be surmising all of this because of Navarro's comment about someone imitating her work. It could be what he wants us to think. I say we speak with her publisher and agent and see what they can tell us. We can't obviously disclose aspects from the scene, but we can dance around it and see where it gets us."

"If I was to place a bet on any novel, I'd start with the one being made into a movie. I mean, if I were a killer and wanted to cast a wide net of suspicion, that's what I'd do. Everyone would be familiar with it."

"I hear ya." And she did, even if she didn't want to. Until they had more facts though, she was determined to keep an open mind.

TEN

Amanda called Kristen as Trent drove them to the Sweeneys and talked with Zoe. Hearing her sweet little voice ignited an internal battle—continue working or go be with her daughter. The disappointment in Zoe's voice hadn't helped when she'd said, "I didn't think you had to work for several sleeps." As if Amanda didn't feel bad enough. She promised to pick her up as soon as she could, but it still didn't feel like enough. The phone call had ended with Amanda talking to her sister, who reassured her keeping Zoe for dinner was no problem at all.

Sometimes Amanda felt like everyone else was there for Zoe except for her. An unfair judgment she realized, but it didn't stop it from creeping in. As she'd advised a mother in a previous investigation, all anyone can do is their best. And Amanda was doing that; she just felt pulled in many directions and often away from Zoe.

Amanda looked at the clock on the dash. 4:32 PM. "I know we usually push late into the night with a fresh case, but I'll need to call it a day soon. Once we finish here and go back for Felicity's phone. I'll be ready to pick up first thing in the morning again."

Trent parked at the curb outside the address for Celeste and Barry Sweeney. A figure stood in the front window, and Amanda would bet it was Celeste.

"I understand, Amanda. Completely. Logan and Zoe are probably missing you, and it wasn't like they expected you would be working today."

"Well... Yes. But Logan's entertained with his friends, beer, and barbecued meat. Need I say more?"

"Not really." Trent laughed.

"Yeah, so he's not suffering," she added anyway. "And Zoe's at Kristen's, who has a swimming pool, and hanging out with her favorite cousin."

"Not suffering either."

"Thanks," she teased, mocking offense at the implication her absence wouldn't really be felt considering the circumstances.

They headed to the front door, and it was cracked open before they reached the top step.

Celeste was standing there, wearing a sweater, and hugging herself as if it were late fall or winter. "Detectives, do you have news?"

"Unfortunately, very rarely does it work that fast." It was tempting to offer an apology, but it would be hollow. An investigation took the time it took. "Can we come in for a minute?"

"Yes, of course." Celeste's voice was small, strained, husky as if taxed from heavy crying jags. Her face was red and blotchy, her eyes puffy.

The home was cold, the thermostat must have been set to "meat locker". No wonder Celeste was wearing a sweater. The chill of the air hit all of Amanda's bare flesh—arms, neck, and face—and she thought she should be able to see her breath. She shivered.

"Sorry, you're probably freezing. The air conditioner's busted." Celeste must have noticed Amanda's discomfort. "We've called someone in to look at it. That on top of..." She touched a hand to her cheek, her eyes glazed over, emotionally unable to finish her sentence. "We can sit out back."

"Might be nice," Amanda said.

Celeste led her and Trent through the house, past a galley kitchen where Barry was making tea.

He offered a cup to Amanda and Trent, but they both declined. It was easy for her as she wasn't a tea drinker. She liked her coffee—black.

Celeste saw them to a small patio area laid out with square concrete stone. A barbecue was off to one side, and a table with an umbrella and four chairs were at the other end.

"Sit wherever you'd like," Celeste said as she pulled out a chair for herself.

Amanda and Trent followed her lead.

"We won't be long," Amanda began. "We just have a couple of questions."

"Whatever they are, I'll do my best to answer them." Celeste released the grip she had on her sweater; the late afternoon sun quick at working its charm.

"You know that we investigated the murder of Felicity's sister," Amanda said, teeing things up. "When we notified Felicity, there were a lot of papers around her living room. Today, there weren't any. Should we find that strange?"

Celeste smiled, an expression that barely made its mark before disappearing into oblivion. "No. I helped her sort that out a long time ago. We organized all of it into totes."

Then they had been a new addition since their initial visit to Felicity's home, but that didn't explain why they were now empty. Amanda and Trent looked at each other.

Barry came out with two cups of tea. He set one on the table in front of Celeste and said, "Decaf for you." Then he retraced his steps to get the patio door.

"Oh, just the screen. Let some heat in," Celeste suggested.

He did that and then sat next to his wife.

"You guys were looking at each other a minute ago," Celeste said. "Like there's something I should know?"

"We found totes in the room near the kitchen," Trent said.

"Uh-huh. That's where she kept them."

"Only they were empty," Amanda pointed out.

"Empty." Celeste said the word as if she were trying it on, and touched a few fingers to her throat, lowered her hand.

Amanda didn't need to ask, but it was clear the absence of paperwork was noteworthy. She still wasn't sure exactly what it was supposed to be telling them or how it affected the investigation. "What was all that paperwork? Her books at various stages?"

"That and any research she printed."

"These books have since been published?" Trent asked. "Or were some new?"

"Most of them were likely already published, but she'd have WIPs around too. You really found nothing?"

Amanda shook her head.

"That is strange." Celeste blew on her tea and took a tentative sip. Barry followed his wife's lead.

They could have it all wrong—the paperwork wasn't all burned but some stolen. But why would the killer care about any of it?

"We don't know if it factors into her murder," Trent said. "Detective Steele and I were also wondering if Felicity rented anywhere, a space to do her writing?"

Trent's question presented another explanation for the absence of the paperwork that they had considered before.

"Not that I know of," Celeste said.

"Couldn't you just check her bank accounts to find out something like that?" Barry asked as he set his cup down on the table.

"We will. We just thought we'd ask." Getting their hands on

financials took time. "One more question before we go. Did Felicity have an area rug and long coffee table in the living room?"

Celeste blinked a few times, her brow wrinkled. "She did, come to think of it. What is going on? I don't remember seeing it when I looked in and saw her. But I was distracted by—" She swallowed roughly, and a rogue tear slid down her cheek. "Where would her rug and table have gone?"

"That we don't know. Yet." It was overwhelming to admit most of what happened in Felicity's house last night remained a mystery.

ELEVEN

Amanda expected the Sweeneys would give them answers. She just hadn't expected the ones they received. "We're assuming the killer burned all—if not most—of Felicity's work, but why?"

"It's hard to say at this point."

"We figure the killer turned up around five forty, and the early end of the time-of-death window was ten PM. Was Felicity subjected to literally watching her work go up in flames?"

"By a person who wanted to hurt her in that way? Someone jealous of her success?"

"Could be."

"It wouldn't have been easy for her to watch but surely she had backups of her work—a drive or computer. Not that we've found either."

"Presumably the killer took those."

"It almost sounds like this killer was trying to ensure something remained secret."

She didn't say as much but his words had her thinking about Felicity hiding her phone again. "We need to find out more. But if the killer burned all her paperwork, wouldn't there be more ash?"

"We don't know how long the fire burned, likely hours. As you just mentioned, Felicity was with her killer for hours before he killed her. It's also possible he took some of the papers with him, along with the coffee table and rug even."

"So, basically, the killer backed up a truck to Kelley's place." Amanda shook her head. "If that happened, you'd think someone would have seen something. Regardless, this all sounds very premeditated."

"I think the playing card alone tells us that much. It's not like most people keep a deck in a back pocket."

Amanda nodded.

Trent pulled down Felicity's street. The immediate area near Felicity's house was cordoned off, but the media was looming on the outskirts. Amanda groaned at the sight of Diana Wesson, a reporter with PWC News. She was standing at the edge of the barricade, her back toward Felicity's house, talking into a padded microphone, her cameraman filming away.

"She needs to go, along with the rest of them," Amanda said. Besides Diana, there were at least two other people she recognized as journalists, including Fraser Reyes, who'd written a damning piece about her and PWCPD two and a half years ago for the paper in the area, *Prince William Times*.

"I'm sure the officers will get them moving."

She resisted the urge to point out they were doing a "splendid" job of that so far. Getting out of the car, she hoped to avoid Diana. Thankfully, she must have been preoccupied with her narrative as she didn't run after Amanda. Normally, the reporter had a knack for sniffing out Amanda's presence and beelining for her. She failed to grasp the concept that Amanda would only ever direct her to the Public Information Office, a branch of the PWCPD. It was their job to work with the media.

Inside the house, CSIs Blair and Donnelly were still at

work.

"You're back," Blair said, sounding surprised.

"You know it," Amanda said. "Things are already failing to add up."

"No big shock there," Blair said.

"We have some findings for you, by the way." Donnelly headed toward her collection kit, beside which she had a few plastic evidence bags. The CSI handed one to Amanda and another to Trent.

"What do you have?" she asked her partner.

"Umm..." Trent held it in the air. "A bagful of confetti?"

Donnelly shook her head and rolled her eyes. "It's shredded paperwork, found in the office upstairs."

"We saw nothing in the shredder," Trent said.

"That was stuck in the teeth of the machine," Donnelly pointed out.

Amanda had seen the bin was empty, not thinking much of it at the time. Felicity could have dumped the bin herself, but in hindsight, maybe the killer had. He'd just missed checking the shredder closely as she and Trent had. "Can you piece it back together? It might give us a clue... What that is, I obviously have no idea."

"We'll do our best." Donnelly retrieved the bag from Trent.

Amanda looked at the one she held. Inside were three pieces of paper torn from printer stock. "'Beauty has always' and 'Case closed' in type, and this one is handwritten." Amanda looked hard and concentrated as she angled the page. "Looks like, 'Could it be?'"

"All of which might as well be gibberish." Disappointment marked its presence in Trent's tightened jaw and the downward turn of his eyebrows.

"It's possible Felicity's agent or editor may be able to help us. The printed words might exist in one of her books and aid with the investigation."

"Ah, one of her books. Did you hear that, Emma?" Donnelly was grinning and smacked her colleague on her upper arm. That got her a cold glare and a mumble.

"So I heard."

There must have been some previous conversation Amanda and Trent had missed. Amanda put her gaze on Donnelly. "You read her work?"

"Nah, not much of a novel reader. Not much time, but I often scan articles that Google feeds to my phone."

"Clickbait," Blair said. "And she's been going on about it."

Donnelly shook her head. "It's not always clickbait. Anyway, her latest book apparently rocketed to the top of the bestseller charts in a matter of days. Talk about luck." Her previous jovial expression disappeared at those words, as she looked where Felicity Kelley's body had been. "Or not so lucky."

"What's the name of the book?" Trent tucked the evidence bag under one of his arms and pulled out his phone.

"*The Romeo Killer.* You know, I might read it now." Donnelly nodded, her lips in a pressed straight line.

Trent pecked into his phone.

"Do you have any idea what it's about?" Amanda asked.

Donnelly shrugged. "Just that it's about a serial killer who targets women."

"A serial killer who leaves a calling card at every scene." Trent looked up from his phone, his face pale. "More specifically, a *playing* card."

Amanda's stomach swirled and clenched. "The Queen of Hearts?"

"Uh-huh."

"Is someone out there imitating that novel?" Donnelly asked.

Trent took a deep breath. "We might have been too fast to rule out a serial killer."

Amanda's mind was spinning with a hypothetical fear. Would there be more victims before this was all over, or was the scene only set to make them think copycat? Luis Navarro had pointed them to *deranged fans*. Was that an honest suggestion, or did he know more about Felicity's murder than he let on? Amanda hoped like hell if someone was copying the murderer from Felicity Kelley's book, it would stop with her death. But why kill the author herself?

Trent met her eyes, putting voice to her concern. "Are we going to have more dead bodies?"

"Let's just hope it's a tool the killer is using to throw off the investigation."

"Luis Navarro," Trent said. "He has motive. A rejected proposal, being cut off just when Felicity was in for a huge pay day."

"Acid to the wound," Amanda agreed. Luis Navarro topped the suspect list so far.

"Do we go pick him up? Push him more?" Trent asked.

She considered but ended up shaking her head. "Nothing has really changed since we last had this conversation. We need something more substantial against him."

"I think we have enough," Trent countered. "Felicity's rejection angered him, he decided to kill her and hide behind the ruse of a copycat. For the cherry on top, he points us to deranged fans."

"All conjecture. We can't put Navarro with Felicity within the time of her death."

"He doesn't have an alibi."

"Again, we need more than that. Which you know. And what reason would he have to burn her manuscripts?"

"To spite her for turning on him?" Trent hitched his shoulders. "He'd probably take sick pleasure in making her watch him destroy her work, or something similar happens in the book too. We need to get a copy and start reading."

"*Or* get the highlights from the publisher when we sit with them," she volleyed.

"Or that. Which is probably quicker." Trent's gaze drifted to take in the room. "Let's say the killer was trying to set up the scene to mimic the book—including the burned paperwork—did the one from Felicity's novel also run off with their victim's coffee table and rug?"

"What's that?" Blair asked, her brow furled.

Amanda walked to the section of discolored floorboards and drew her finger over the area. "There used to be a long rectangular coffee table right here. And it sat on top of an area rug."

"I'll play along. Where are they now?" Blair asked.

"A good question, but the better one is, why would the killer take them?" Trent paced a few steps.

Amanda considered his question, and an epiphany struck. "It must be about setting the scene. They likely didn't fit with what he was trying to create."

"We need to consider everything we see isn't giving us a clear picture of what took place." Trent stuffed his phone back into a pocket. "And if this isn't a serial killer, why did he imitate Felicity's work?"

There was no point in even taking a stab at answering that question yet, but she did hope Felicity Kelley's murder was an isolated incident and the method was just to muddy the investigation. Again, her mind returned to Luis Navarro. He had been rather quick to bring up deranged fans. She still held fast to what she'd told Trent though. While he deserved a more scrutinizing look, they needed more to justify bringing him in. She based that on knowing Malone would tell her just that. After all, Felicity's work was public, and a copycat could essentially be anyone.

"I have an alternate theory on the missing table and rug," Blair said as she grabbed a spray bottle.

Donnelly closed the curtains and flicked off the lights.

Blair sprayed the liquid on the floor in front of the couch. Donnelly pulled an ultraviolet flashlight out of a pocket and shone the beam over the area.

The results were as enlightening as they were devastating. Blood stained the floor from one end of the couch to the other. The trail revealed the killer must have flipped the rug back and pushed the coffee table out before dragging Felicity to her resting place.

The revelation was sickening. "The killer moved her. To set the scene or for another reason?"

Donnelly snapped photographs of the discovery. When she finished, Blair flipped the lights on and opened the front curtains.

Trent paced like a lion in a cage, left, right, left, right. The entire time his gaze was fixed to the floor. "She went down closer to the doorway. Maybe she was trying to get her visitor to leave. Then there was an altercation..."

Amanda turned to Blair and Donnelly. "Still no signs of forced entry?"

Blair shook her head. "None."

"She let them in, but didn't trust them. We assume that because she hid her phone. Then at some point—between ten and midnight—she wanted them to leave," Amanda said.

"After he'd been there for several hours," Trent interjected.

"Right..." It was one of those times Amanda wished she had the power to *see* things. It was hard enough trying to reconcile the timing. Felicity had called Amanda less than thirty minutes before the delivery driver failed to rouse a response. That suggested the killer had turned up within that time span. The call and her mystery visitor could have been a coincidence, but Amanda felt they were linked. If so, then wouldn't Felicity have been fearful for her safety? But she never said that much in her message to Amanda. She even sounded calm. And if she were scared, why order a pizza like it was any ordinary night? Why hadn't she called 911? Why let the man into her house if she viewed him as a threat? Then again, maybe she hadn't. Luis Navarro had a key to her house, which he'd claimed to have returned. Even if he had, it was possible he had copies made before turning one over to Felicity.

And around I go...

"Someone appears deep in thought," Donnelly said, breaking Amanda's concentration.

"I was just thinking the killer may have let himself in," Amanda said, glancing at Trent.

"Luis Navarro," he said.

"Yeah."

"Even still, we know that she was expecting pizza delivery. She could have easily opened her door thinking her dinner had arrived, only to be faced with her would-be killer instead. They could have talked themselves inside or coerced her into letting them in. Either way, the killer seems to have covered their tracks quite well."

"Speaking of..." Amanda recalled the shoe prints. "You said a men's running shoe, size ten?" They'd need to check if Luis Navarro was a match.

"That's right. And we found more while you were gone. There are several in the kitchen and dining room," Blair said. "Honestly, it looks like they went back and forth between the dining room and living room."

"They have to belong to our killer then." Her mind's eye could play this part out clearly. The killer grabbed a tote, hauled it to the fireplace, burned the paperwork, took it back. Then repeated the process. So much work, but for what purpose? If it was about setting the scene, why was that so important to the killer? And while he was making all those trips, where was Felicity?

TWELVE

Amanda played over how the sequence of events must have worked. In her mind's eye, the table and rug were in place when Felicity's unwanted visitor showed up. Presumably a struggle had taken place, during which Felicity was injured and dragged along the floor. Was it more than an injury though? Was this her true cause of death? "Is there enough blood to suggest she died in the original location?"

"There is a lot of blood, but it's hard to say," Blair said.

Amanda would follow up with Rideout at the autopsy on this. "We'd like to look at Felicity's phone."

"Have at it." Blair gestured toward the other evidence bag near the investigators' collection kits.

Amanda gloved up and pulled the phone out of its plastic sleeve. She traced the pattern given to them by Luis Navarro and was pleased when the screen came to life.

It was full of apps including the usual social media ones, the weather network, photo gallery, and email. As she sideswiped, there were several screens full of icons. She returned to the home page and opened the email. Two hundred unread messages, with many more grayed out from being read. A trip to

her Recycle Bin showed over five thousand. The settings
showed one email account, but the lack of organization fit the
Felicity that Amanda had met. She showed all the bulging
folders to Trent. "This is going to take far longer to work
through than I'd anticipated."

"Did you honestly think you'd find a prime suspect immediately?" he asked, a smile toying on his lips.

"Too much to expect, I know." Though she wouldn't have
turned up her nose at just one shining beacon to spotlight a
nutjob. "We're going to take this with us, if that's all right." She
held up the phone to the CSIs.

"You'll just need to sign for it," Blair said. "To protect the
chain of custody."

"You got it." She signed off and dropped the phone back
into the bag and was zipping it up when Officer Cooper came
inside the house, calling out ahead of himself.

"Detectives, I thought I saw you drive by," Cooper said.
"Officers have just finished talking with neighbors on the
street."

Life had taught her hope was for the foolish, yet here she
was... *hoping.* "Tell us you have something."

"Not a lot, I'm afraid. From talking with my fellow officers,
no one saw anyone here last night, aside from the pizza guy.
One person told us that much."

Which gets us nowhere... Amanda was thinking it might not
be a bad idea to have officers revisit the homes and ask if the
same applied to the wee hours that morning. It would have
taken hours if the killer burned all the paperwork, possibly
stretching well beyond midnight. But the likelihood was slim as
most people would be in bed.

"Wait. You said *not a lot.*" Trent angled his head. "Then
you have something?"

"Possibly. Neighbors three down, other side of the street,

said they were outside having drinks on their patio last night, listening to the radio."

"What time was this?" That bubble of hope was rising again.

Cooper consulted his notes. "They were up until three AM. Anyway, as I said, outside drinking and they smelled smoke. They figured someone was having a bonfire. It was a clear, still night and entirely possible, but I heard rumor the victim had a fire in her home. I was thinking the *bonfire* they smelled might have been coming from the vic's chimney."

Amanda hated that she was right. The killer had hung around to burn all of Felicity's hard work. Even as her dead body was lying there. "Great work bringing this to us, Officer Cooper."

He dipped his head. "Thanks, ma'am."

"I'm going to need you to do something else," she said.

"Name it."

"Can you revisit the neighbors and ask if anyone noticed a person around Felicity's house after midnight until her friend arrived at eleven thirty AM today?" She might be pushing it with this request. The department wasn't exactly flush with manpower to facilitate doubling up.

Cooper's face pinched in frustration. "I'll run it past our supervisor, see what he says. We still need to revisit those who weren't home or didn't come to their doors."

"All I can ask."

He dipped his head and left.

"We're heading out too." This from Blair as she and Donnelly set about getting their things together.

"And we're just ahead of you. Good night." Amanda led the way out of the house, Trent following closely.

"You need me to drop you at the station now? You said you were calling it a night once we got Felicity's phone. And I completely understand. You weren't even supposed to be working today."

She was torn now that she had Felicity's phone in hand. It was potentially brimming with leads, and the emails alone were far too much for Trent to handle on his own. That wasn't even touching on how they needed to talk with Felicity's agent and publisher. Though it would be after hours for them, and those conversations would be best in person. Amanda opened her mouth to reply when Diana Wesson called out.

"Detectives? Excuse me."

Amanda looked over her shoulder, and the reporter was rushing toward them. "Move it," she hissed to Trent.

"Do you have any information to share with the people of Prince William County? Are the rumors true? Is the bestselling novelist Felicity Kelley dead?" Apparently nothing stopped Diana from spilling out a rash of questions—not even jogging in stilettos.

"No comment." Amanda waved a dismissive arm in the air and slipped into the security of the car.

Trent turned the vehicle on and put it into gear but couldn't release the brakes as the reporter and her cameraman had pitched their tent in front of the hood.

"Just do it. For me, for the people." Amanda was only *half*-joking.

Trent laid on the horn, but neither of them showed any sign of moving.

"This is ridiculous." Amanda huffed and got out of the car. It worked to lure Diana and her minion to the sidewalk. Once they were in the clear, Amanda ducked back inside the vehicle and told Trent to floor it.

He did, a huge grin on his face. "You're a touch evil."

"Some people bring it out in me." She was smiling too. As the mouse in this little game with Diana, Amanda always intended to get away.

Trent took them in the direction of Woodbridge. "Going back to my earlier question...?"

"About dropping me off at the station?"

"That would be the one."

It shouldn't be that hard to answer. Zoe and Logan were waiting on her, but even though she'd been doing her best to focus on the case, guilt gnawed on her like a parasite. It scolded her for not being available to take Felicity's call or getting back to her right away. If she had, would things have been different? Amanda's flight had landed at 6:30 PM—three and a half hours before the early end of the TOD window. Amanda could have saved Felicity. *If only I had known she needed saving...*

"No one will think negatively of you, if you call it a day," Trent said, filling the expanding silence.

"*I* will." The confession was out in a flash.

"Doesn't surprise me to hear you say that. Knowing you, you've probably found a way to blame yourself in all this too. But you shouldn't. The only one to blame is the killer. If it helps make up your mind, know that I intend to keep working."

Was he a freaking mind reader? Sometimes it felt that he knew her better than she knew herself. The fact he made a point of saying he'd be putting in overtime didn't alleviate guilt, just stacked on a different kind. But at least the investigation wouldn't be put on pause. "While I've got my feet up, you'll be working. Is that meant to make me feel better?" She attempted to say this seriously but snickered and gave herself away.

"I see you're broken up at the idea. But if we're lucky, I'll make some progress tonight. Besides, we're partners, and do I really need to point out again that it's Wednesday, and you weren't officially due back until Monday? Go. Be with Zoe and Logan."

Logan was presented as an afterthought, but all the same, going home sounded great. "Okay, but you'll keep working?"

He smiled. "Yes, and I'm thinking I'll prioritize looking at her social media accounts and email."

"There's a lot there."

"There is, so it's best to get started. I'll just knock off what I can, one at a time."

She nodded, loving how his mind worked in such an organized manner. He had a way of breaking every task down into manageable steps. "May I suggest starting with the deleted emails?"

"Why?" Trent parked in the lot at Central, and they got out.

"If we are looking at a stalker or obsessed fan, she'd have deleted their messages."

"All right, I'll start there." He turned and clicked a button on the key fob twice, and the vehicle honked, confirming it was locked.

"Great. Keep me posted on what you find."

"Will do. First thing tomorrow morning. Good night." He saluted her before turning to walk toward the station's doors.

She stood watching, wanting to join him and get to work. *Seize control where I can...* It wasn't like she could reverse time and bring Felicity back to life, but she could find justice. To that end, she would do everything within her power. For the sake of her family, she'd pick up that quest tomorrow.

THIRTEEN

The water in her sister's pool felt incredible after a long, hot day, but it didn't wash away Amanda's guilt. Neither had Zoe's welcoming—and refreshing—wet hug. Amanda ended up borrowing a suit from her sister and joined everyone by the pool. Everyone being her parents, sister, and brother-in-law. Zoe and Ava too, who were busy splashing in the pool and squealing. It was a good spot to be. While it was seven thirty at night, the sun had lost its power, but humidity hung heavy in the air.

Was it selfish and short-sighted to allow herself such an indulgence? She'd left an active murder investigation to take time for herself. Felicity Kelley was dead, and if Amanda had responded sooner, if she hadn't been on the flight when she'd called...

"Iced tea?" Kristen set a tray down on the table near where Amanda was seated on a lounger. She came armed with a large glass pitcher and six glasses. Lemons and berries floated on top of the drink, and it swayed Amanda's answer.

"Yes, please." Her sister made the best iced tea—a perfect combination of sweet and tang.

Kristen poured some out and handed Amanda a glass. "Here you go."

"Much obliged."

Kristen laughed. She barely had time to pour herself some before Zoe and Ava rushed over from the pool. The girls were dripping wet, the water splatting onto the concrete patio. Zoe was licking her lips in anticipation of the iced tea, already knowing how delicious her aunt made it.

Kristen gave the girls full glasses but left Erik to serve up the rest and dropped onto the lounger beside Amanda. "You look like your mind's a million miles away."

"Probably because it is." She took a slow draw of her drink, savoring every drop as it passed over her taste buds.

"Talk to me."

"You know I can't do that." She glanced at her father. If she was going to open up to anyone here, it would be Nathan Steele. He knew the job and had been the PWCPD police chief before his retirement seven years ago. Astute as ever, her father looked over when she told Kristen she couldn't talk. He didn't speak, but his eye contact said all that was needed. He was there for her. And the offer was tempting.

"Hmm." Kristen kicked back on the lounger, stretching out her legs. "You can't or won't?"

"Both." Amanda smiled at her sister. Kristen was two years younger, and just one of her five siblings.

Zoe bounced up and down next to Amanda. "I need to go to the bathroom."

"Bring me your towel." Amanda set her glass on the stone next to her, and Zoe returned with her towel. Amanda dried her off as best as she could and wrapped the towel around her. "Okay, you're good to head inside. Just watch your steps on the tile floor."

"I'm not a baby." Zoe hustled off, and the patio door slid shut a moment later.

"Don't you just love this stage?" Kristen laughed. "They think they know everything but, oh, if they only knew how little they actually do."

Amanda smiled. "Honestly? I love the spark."

"By spark, you mean her defiant streak?"

"You call it defiant; I call it independent. It tells me I've done something right." Though Zoe's birth parents earned some credit too.

"Cheers to that." Kristen extended her glass toward Amanda for a toast.

Amanda reciprocated, but her gaze was on her niece, Ava. Three months ago, Ava had been kidnapped by a killer. She didn't show any signs that she was struggling with what she'd experienced, but Kristen had her speaking with a therapist once a week. Amanda had no doubt she'd bounce back though; she was one resilient kid and cop blood ran through her veins.

Zoe came back outside, and it was time to impart some bad news. Best to stop her before she jumped back into the pool. "Hey, Zoe," Amanda called out. "It's time to leave—"

"No." A huge groan of protest accompanied dangling arms and sagging shoulders.

"Yes. Get dried off. You can talk with Ava poolside for a bit more, but I'll be coming for you soon."

"Fine," Zoe huffed out and stomped toward her cousin, but so much for drying off more. She sat on the pool's edge and put her legs in.

"You're leaving so soon?" Kristen asked, disheartened.

"I need to get some rest. Tomorrow will be an early one."

"Aren't you on vacation until Monday?"

"Things change."

"Why do this to yourself, Mandy?" This from her mother, Julie aka Jules, an unabashed eavesdropper.

"Do what, Mom?" Amanda regretted asking the moment

the question left her lips. Besides, she already knew what the answer was going to be.

"Get yourself involved when you don't have to."

Amanda opened her mouth but snapped it shut. Her mother wouldn't understand that there wasn't always a choice—even after being married to a career cop. Unless she'd donned a badge, she couldn't get how some cases could suck her in, leaving her powerless to resist.

"Your mom is right, kiddo," her father said. "It seems to me you are involved. Possibly too much. You can't take cases on personally, or they'll topple your sanity."

"It is what it is." A blasé response, but it was accurate. She'd known when she signed up for this job there would be sacrifices. Following in her father's footsteps, she anticipated there would be cases that kept her up at night. She remembered nights he roamed the house in the wee hours like a ghost.

"Guess you could look at it like that, but it's best you allow yourself some separation between work and home."

She appreciated her father's words of caution and listened when he spoke. He'd been in her shoes. And despite some upsets, he mostly balanced work and play. She nodded, taking his words to heart, and flipped her legs over the lounger to get up.

Zoe looked over her shoulder then leaned in conspiratorially toward Ava's ear. "Oh, no, here she comes."

"And here she is," Amanda said. *Nothing like talking about yourself in third person...* "Time to skedaddle." She motioned with her arms for the girl to get up, which she did—reluctantly. Amanda fluffed the towel as best she could over the girl's damp suit and limbs, adding one big tussle of her blond locks for good measure. "Time to change." She pointed toward the house as if more direction was needed.

Zoe groaned but obeyed.

"How are you doing, Ava?" she asked her niece.

The teen's eyes clouded. "I'm doing pretty good. Still have the odd nightmare."

"It will get better. Remember you're safe now."

A subtle smile. "I know. Thanks to you."

Amanda's cheeks heated at the compliment, but she couldn't take all the credit. "It was a team effort. How are Nadine and her mother doing these days?" It was rather surprising that Nadine, Ava's best friend, wasn't there. Amanda had met the girl three months ago when her sister was murdered. It was also this same killer who had taken Ava.

"They're getting through. Just day by day, ya know."

"That I do." *Too well!*

"Well, I should probably change myself." With that, Ava headed toward the house.

Amanda was left standing there, looking out over the pool and at Kristen's beautiful yard.

"Mandy." Her father stepped up next to her, his hands in his pockets. "Do you want to talk to me?"

At his genuine offer, tears pricked Amanda's eyes. She could blame exhaustion, shock—*allergies*—as the culprit. Any of those would be a lie. She turned to her father. "How did you cope with..." She swallowed roughly, took a few beats. "Guilt? Knowing that you could have done something to prevent a bad thing from happening."

"*Knowing* is a strong word unless you're psychic. And just to be clear, the *bad thing* is murder?" Her father preferred his communication to be clear-cut with zero possibility for misinterpretation. Probably due to his time as police chief.

"Yes." She stared at the ground, avoiding her father's gaze.

"That one's pretty easy, kiddo. Did you wield the weapon? Take this life we're talking about?"

"No. Of course not." She met his eyes. "But it's not that simple."

"It needs to be. That's if you're going to keep your sanity."

She appreciated his words held truth, but applying them was much harder than accepting them. "This victim reached out to me just hours before she was murdered. I couldn't answer her call because I was on the flight home. If only I hadn't been on the plane, if—"

"Stop there. Nothing good comes from going down If Only Lane." Her father's face was stern as he held up a pointed finger.

"Easy to say. Surely, you had cases where you felt if you changed just one thing, the outcome would have been different?"

"Absolutely. I lost count of the times I almost left the force within my first few years in Homicide."

That confession froze the air in her lungs. "I had no idea."

"You would have no reason to."

"Why did you stay?"

"Probably for the same reason you keep doing this job—even when you should be on vacation," her father pushed back. "It's when we get the wins, when the bad guys get their due... it's a high like—"

"No other," she jumped in and smiled at her father. "But was that all that stopped you from leaving?" She sensed there was more.

"Ah, no. Not all." A strange energy surrounded her father, and she wasn't sure if he was going to confide in her. Just when she didn't think he was, he said, "Malone."

"Scott talked you out of quitting?"

"He did. Repeatedly. Just another reason he's a close friend of the family."

Huh. If Malone hadn't stepped in back then, what would that have meant for her career? She'd always admired her father and wanted to follow his path. In a way, she owed her badge—and her life—to her sergeant. Being a cop was in her blood, at the very pulse of her being. She couldn't imagine doing anything else.

"You need to find ways of releasing the endless what ifs and if onlys. The other option is insanity," her father emphasized. "Malone helped me realize that."

"What ways though?" *Is it too much to hope for one practical method I can apply?*

"It starts with the basics... The oath you took to serve and protect."

"Yes, but every time someone is murdered, I've failed."

Her father shook his head, smirking. "Look at it another way. You can't control everyone's actions. Surely you know that?"

"I do."

"And it's not your job to seize that control. Your job is to make sense of the aftermath and bring closure and justice. By doing this, and getting killers off the street, you protect the rest of the community from harm. You serve by your actions—one step at a time, one case at a time. Now, you can't solve them all, but you keep going because the fire to save the next victim keeps you going. You hold on to that and uphold your oath."

"Serve and protect." Her voice was barely above a whisper. The resolution was so simple in retrospect. She'd just never sat still with her thoughts long enough to break them down as her father just had.

"Exactly. Just remember, this job is never about you, kiddo. It was never about me. It's the much larger picture. Keep that in focus."

She nodded, unable to speak for the time being. Her father's words had struck her heart.

"I'm ready." Zoe came prancing toward her.

Amanda hugged her father and kissed his cheek, drew back and said, "Thanks, Dad."

"Anytime you need to talk, I'm here."

She nodded, holding back a flood of tears as some relief eased in. There was nothing humanly possible she could do that would turn back the clock and prevent Felicity's murder. Her power was closure, justice, and saving other potential victims. And if she had any say, no one else would suffer at the hands of the killer they currently hunted.

FOURTEEN

Amanda woke up refreshed and ready to make headway in the Kelley case. Her talk with her father last night had been what she'd needed to hear, and his advice was wise. While the guilt wasn't entirely gone, it had quieted. It was the logic of the matter. The past couldn't be changed, but the future was of her making. This thinking transformed the what ifs and if onlys into *even* ifs. Even if she had answered Felicity Kelley's call, she might not have been able to save her. *Fact.* And viewing Felicity's murder in this light had recalibrated her outlook. It gave her a renewed sense of purpose and determination.

Logan was spending the day with Zoe—tired and hungover, regardless. Sadly, it was just the beginning of his penance for last night's overindulgence. Zoe was expecting to go to a local place that offered an arcade, bowling, and glow-in-the-dark miniature golf. With summer vacation nearing its end, the place was going to be packed with screaming, rambunctious kids. She'd have mercy on him and exchange places if it wasn't for this case.

Amanda grabbed a coffee for herself and Trent from Hannah's Diner on her way to the station. It was the least she could do as he'd kept working last night. Despite his assurance it was no problem, she didn't want to take him for granted. She even added a chocolate donut—his favorite kind—to the order.

She entered Central and headed straight to his work area. Their spaces were separated by a low partition about forehead level. It afforded some privacy while making communicating easy as well.

Trent was at his desk, his head bent over Felicity Kelley's phone, or so she surmised.

"Here you go." She plucked one cup from the takeout tray and handed it to him, then the small brown bag.

"Ooh, what do we have here...?" He unrolled the bag and peeked inside. "This is a good day." He dipped his hand inside and took out his treat. He chomped off a bulging mouthful, leaving his eyes to do the smiling. "Thank you," he mumbled around the donut. "A *very* good day."

"Uh-huh. Now, after you've swallowed, fill me in on what you've got. I assume that's Felicity's phone?" She pointed to the device he'd set on his desk in favor of collecting his goodies from her.

"Mmm. Hmm." He nodded to accompany his mumbling.

She smiled at the sight before her. It was like her partner hadn't eaten before in his life. "Have you found anything helpful yet?" She couldn't be certain he'd have notified her last night, as he'd seemed quite intent on giving her space.

He held up a finger and swallowed a mouthful. It bulged in his throat, kicking out his Adam's apple. "Ah, no."

"Was wishing for a different answer..." She dropped onto the corner of his desk, perching there.

"Me too, but I barely scratched the surface. As for her email, though, unless Felicity has another email address that wasn't being delivered to the app, there's nothing concerning there. No stalker-type messages in her deleted folder either."

"What about in her inbox?"

"I started with the deleted ones as you'd suggested. That's as far as I got—you saw how many thousands there were."

"I did. Maybe her agent or publisher will be able to point us in someone's direction."

"We can always hope."

"No emails from deranged fans, but what did you find?"

"Lots of spam, messages from her publisher and agent, some from the media requesting interviews. The latter I'd suspect Felicity deleted after forwarding to her literary agent to handle, though I didn't verify this with the sent folder."

"She could have done that on a computer. Did you look up the agent? Justine..." Her mind was blank for the woman's full name, even though she knew they got it from Felicity's best friend yesterday.

"Justine Livingston," Trent replied, without consulting his notes. She needed her coffee more than he needed his. "When I searched for Livingston online, I found her agency's website and a contact form. But once I realized her office is in Washington—like Kelley's publisher, Garrison & Marrow—I found her cell phone number through police databases. I tried reaching her but had to leave a voicemail." He bit off another piece of donut.

"I assume you have an address for her though?"

He chewed, swallowed. "That was easy enough."

"Okay, let's hit the publisher first. If Justine doesn't call back by the time we're finished at the publishing house, we'll just drop in."

"Works for me. On the publisher front, I found out that Felicity's editor was Melody Schmitt."

She was pleased with all he'd accomplished, and it was clear the case hadn't suffered because she'd stepped away for the evening. Maybe striking a work–life balance wasn't impossible. After all, it wasn't up to her to right the world. Serve and protect—one case at a time. Today, she intended to do just that. "We'll start by speaking with her."

He nodded. "Just as a reminder, we still have Felicity's social media to look at."

"Let me scroll through that on her phone while you drive."

"You bet." Trent stood and stuffed the rest of the donut in his mouth just before picking up his coffee. She grabbed Felicity's phone, hoping it contained their next lead.

FIFTEEN

The drive to Washington was high traffic between the day of week, time, and summer tourists, atop the regular commuters. One benefit to the bumper-to-bumper traffic was it afforded Amanda more time to scroll through the mentions on Felicity's social media accounts. The same story applied to all of them. "No stalkers or haters replying to her posts."

"That surprises me." Trent glanced over but quickly turned his gaze back on the road. He slammed on the brakes to avoid colliding with the sedan in front of them, which came to a quick stop. "People need to learn how to drive." He slapped the wheel in frustration.

She let a few beats pass. "Going back to Felicity's socials... It comes as a shock to me too—especially given the size of her following."

"Agreed, and trolls aren't known for being quiet. It's possible her agent, her publisher, or someone else handles her public persona and makes sure it's kept clean."

Amanda's mind turned that over—the bit about someone handling Felicity's social media accounts. It was incredible how much her life must have changed with her newfound fame.

Trent pulled into the parking lot for Garrison & Marrow Publishing minutes after ten AM. The drive that would normally take about forty-five minutes had taken them an hour and a half. Still no call from the agent.

They pushed through the revolving door, entered the lobby of the grandiose building, and walked to the reception desk.

"Good morning." A young woman was posted there and smiling at them.

Amanda returned the greeting and added, "We'd like to speak with Melody Schmitt."

The receptionist's eyes narrowed. "Do you have an appointment with her?"

"We don't. We're detectives with the Prince William County Police Department, and her name has come up in one of our investigations." She pulled her badge, though it held no power here, jurisdiction wise. Still, it would give their presence some credit.

The woman paled in increments and licked her painted lips. "Let me see if I can get her."

"Thank you."

She tapped the piece on her ear, and it lit blue. "Melody, you have visitors at reception... Yes, I know. No appointment, but they are police... They didn't exactly say..." The woman's eyes danced over Amanda and Trent. "What is this about?"

"It's regarding an open investigation in Prince William County." If Felicity's murder hadn't hit the news yet, it was only a matter of time. Regardless, there was no point mentioning it to the receptionist.

The woman repeated Amanda's words, waited a few seconds, then said, "I'll let them know." She tapped on her earpiece again, and the light disappeared. "Melody will meet you in the eleventh-floor conference room. Take the elevator up, turn left, and the room is to the immediate right."

"Thank you."

"Uh-huh."

Amanda and Trent walked toward the elevators. She could feel the receptionist's eyes watching their every step and imagined what she'd be saying to her colleagues once they were out of earshot. Two detectives showing up from out of town would likely fuel gossip for some time.

They found the room. The lights were on, but no one was home.

"Okay, where the—" Amanda pivoted at the sound of footsteps padding toward them.

A woman—early thirties, round face, green eyes. Her brown hair was in a loose braid that was seated over her left shoulder. She was wearing a tan jacket over a peach blouse and black dress pants. "Detectives?" she said.

"Detectives Steele and Stenson," Amanda replied. "I assume you're Melody Schmitt?"

"That's me." Melody pinched a gold chain around her neck. Uncertainty leaked from her hesitant tone and body language, as if she wasn't sure she wanted to acknowledge her identity.

"We were told to speak with you here." Amanda gestured toward the open doorway of the conference room.

"Yes." The editor led the way inside.

A stately credenza held residence against one wall. Centered in the space was an oak table with ten leather chairs. Melody sat in one near the foot of the table. Amanda and Trent sat across from her.

"Ah, would you like any water or..." Melody said.

"We're fine, but thank you for asking," Amanda answered on behalf of herself and Trent, then said, "We're here with sad news, Ms. Schmitt. Unfortunately, Felicity Kelley was found murdered in her home yesterday morning."

"She... *she*... was what now?" The editor's face paled, and her mouth fell slack. Publishing crime fiction seemed to do little to buffer the impact of real-life murder.

"We are sorry for your loss," Trent added. "As Felicity's editor, I would assume the two of you were very close."

Melody nodded, but it appeared to take a lot of effort. "She was the first author I signed when I started at Garrison & Marrow three years ago."

"You bet on a sure thing." Amanda added a smile to her statement, and it sparked a mild one from the editor.

"I can't believe she's..." Melody put a hand to her neck and pinched her gold necklace again.

"We can imagine this news may come as a shock to you," Amanda started.

"Ah, yeah. I just saw her two days ago. There was a champagne lunch on the top floor on Tuesday."

"To celebrate the upcoming movie?" Trent asked.

"No, she came in to sign over international rights to her books."

"What time was this?" Lunch could be anytime from noon until three.

"It started at noon."

"And it was over when? Or more precisely, when did Felicity leave?" The contrast in Felicity's last day was incredible and extreme—from high to low.

"Around two, somewhere in there."

That allowed plenty of time for her to get home before all hell broke loose. "My partner and I have more questions, if you'll indulge us."

"I'll answer whatever I can, but I should probably call management to join us."

"We'd like to speak with you alone first, if that's all right." Amanda presented it as an option, knowing her choice of words would give the editor a feeling of power.

Melody tugged down on her blouse and sat straighter. "I'm sure that would be okay. What would you like to know?"

Amanda inched forward on her chair slowly, so as not to

spook Melody, but to insert some intimacy. A subtle cue to suggest she was safe with her and Trent and free to speak her mind. "We're in possession of Felicity's phone and looked at some of her email and social media profiles. It seems the world has nothing but positive things to say about her." This was when Amanda expected Melody to chime in with praise, but she remained quiet. Amanda added, "Usually when someone is in the limelight, as much as Felicity had been, it attracts a certain type of person—"

"A stalker?"

Tingles ran over Amanda's shoulders. Was the fact the editor went straight there a promising lead or logical progression?

"Could be," Trent said. "Do you know if she had any?"

Melody shook her head. "Not that I'm aware of. If she did, she never mentioned them to me."

"What about any deranged fans? Someone who crossed the line?" Amanda intentionally left out mention that Felicity's ex-boyfriend put them on this track.

"*Deranged?* Not sure about that, but some could be obsessive."

Amanda angled her head. "Help me see the difference."

"I suppose I see deranged as someone sending black roses or leaving a horse head in her bed."

That is quite the spectrum on the crazy scale...

Melody added, "An obsessed fan just means they love her work and can't wait for the next book to drop. Usually they're harmless."

It was the *usually* part that concerned Amanda. How much of a nudge did it take to go from obsessed to deranged? Amanda didn't imagine much. "Do you know if Felicity had any *obsessed* fans?"

"She had a lot, but none of them crossed a line. At least none that scared Felicity or caused her concern."

"That she mentioned to you, as you said." Amanda had laid out the cold fact that Felicity's not talking about them didn't mean they didn't exist.

"True enough. I'd suggest you speak with the marketing department as they handled her email."

Amanda was left to wonder how Celeste and Luis would have known about the messages they'd mentioned if they hadn't passed by Felicity's eye. Maybe someone here had mentioned them to her, and she told her friend and former boyfriend about them? Another possibility was they came in through direct messages on social media. "She had her email on her phone," Amanda pointed out again.

"Likely just her personal one. It wouldn't have been her public-facing one. Only G & M has access to that."

Amanda doubted this was the case for the publishing company's entire stable of authors, so she asked about that.

Melody shook her head. "It's only a service extended to A-list authors."

"Felicity wasn't always considered A-list though, was she?" Amanda asked.

"No. It takes the right book hitting at just the right time. No amount of marketing can supersede this."

Trent pecked notes into a tablet he had with him. He paused and looked up. "And that's what happened with *The Romeo Killer*? It hit at the right time?"

"Exactly. It's a formula we can strive to replicate—and do—but book marketing is not a rinse-and-repeat or one-size-fits-all."

"We will need to speak with the marketing person in charge of Felicity's email account," Amanda said.

"It's Kristopher, with a K, Black."

It would seem the *K* was worth being stressed, likely due to the marketer's insistence.

Trent finished tapping on the screen of the tablet and asked, "Does he also handle her social media?"

"We hoped that he would, but Felicity insisted on managing that herself. She said it was one way for her to stay in touch with her readers."

Amanda admired Felicity's intention, but surely that task would be overwhelming. Even more so with her recent success. Comments would have multiplied exponentially. "How did she keep up?"

"That I don't know." Melody frowned. "There's no one like her, Detectives. She was super to work with, and she always turned her manuscripts in on time."

"Then your overall assessment is she was great to work with?" Amanda asked.

"Yes, most of the time." Melody's lips twitched, and her eyes misted. "I just can't believe she's dead. I keep thinking that I'll wake up, and it will have been a nightmare."

Death has that effect... Amanda suffered for years, wishing the loss of Kevin and Lindsey was a bad dream. Ironically, it took accepting her dire reality was a *living* nightmare to move forward. "We wish it was, Ms. Schmitt."

Melody slid a strand of hair around an ear, and a few tears fell. Amanda looked around the room for a tissue box. She spotted one on the credenza, snatched it, and brought it back to the table.

"Thank you." Melody plucked a tissue, dabbed her eyes, and blew her nose. "I'm sorry to be emotional."

"No need to apologize at all. Your reaction is completely understandable." Amanda gave the editor a few moments to let her grief flow. They'd already touched on crazed fans, which needed to be explored more with the marketing department. Now it was time to delve deeper into the relevance of the Queen of Hearts playing card. They already knew it factored into the plot for Felicity's recent bestseller but not much beyond that. "You'll need to forgive me and my partner. Neither of us are readers. What is the killer's motivation in *The Romeo Killer?*"

"Wouldn't you prefer to read the book for yourself?"

Amanda appreciated spoilers didn't sell books, but the sooner they had a motive, the closer they might get to the killer. "If you would just tell us, that may prove quite helpful to the investigation."

Silence, then, "Oh. Don't tell me that—" Melody clamped a hand over her mouth, dropped it just as quickly. "Was she stabbed in the heart and a playing card put in her mouth?" She blinked slowly, her lashes wet with beaded tears.

The editor's response had Amanda going quiet for a few beats. The card *and* the knife to the chest was the fictional killer's method. "We're not at liberty to disclose details about the murder scene, but I will say that we believe there may be a connection between the book and her murder." She battled with making this confession, seeing the media headline: "Mystery Novelist Felicity Kelley Wrote Her Own Murder".

"Ah, I'm not sure what to say to that..."

"Let's start with the murder scene in the book itself then." It seemed motive was a touchy subject, so Amanda thought the switch in direction might help ground Melody's thoughts and establish a strong base for moving forward. "What can you tell us besides the fact the victims are stabbed in the heart?"

"Let's see... The Queen of Hearts playing card is placed deep in the women's mouths, folded into eight squares."

Amanda glanced at Trent, hoping to do so without Melody noticing. They had hypothesized before that Felicity's killer might have taken a page from her book. This tidbit gave the theory additional traction. It really was no longer a question of whether aspects of her bestselling novel were used in her murder—but why. The killer had premeditated and chosen this method for a reason, but to hell if Amanda could land on what that might be. Was it as simple as the killer wanting to muddy the investigation? Luis Navarro using it to cast suspicion on an obsessed fan? An obsessed fan wanting to *live* Felicity's work? A writer jealous of her success? "Ms. Schmitt, do you know of any authors or writers who were envious of Felicity's success?"

"You're kidding? Countless authors would want to be her, to have their books on the big screen. That's a big deal."

"Of course. Any stand out as being overly jealous?" She was hoping for a name, something that could serve as a solid lead.

Melody shook her head.

She and Trent were obviously missing pieces of this puzzle, but Amanda was determined to find them.

SIXTEEN

Amanda hadn't missed the fact the editor still hadn't answered her question about motive in *The Romeo Killer*. She circled back. "Can you tell us why the killer in Felicity's book was murdering people?"

Melody's mouth twisted, her lips curling down with uncertainty. "I'd feel more comfortable if I cleared that past management."

"Even considering the situation?" Amanda countered, applying some pressure. "The book is published."

"Our polices are quite restrictive, and I don't want to violate any rules. You could always read the book for yourselves."

Banging against this wall was frustrating, but it could be seen as a reminder to step back and think through all the angles. There were at least three aspects from Felicity's murder scene that aligned with the book—the knife to the chest, the Queen of Hearts playing card, and the fact it was folded into eight squares. It was possible the similarities ended there. What if they continued to press about the plot and their assumption was wrong? Rumor would have already spread like wildfire and be near impossible to douse. There seemed to be no fast workaround; she and Trent had to read the book. On the upside, it could enlighten them to a nuance that a retelling may not. Still, it would be good if they could gather a bit more information to confirm it was worth the effort. "Who do we need to speak to about getting a more detailed overview of the book?"

"The publisher, Ian Moss."

"We'll speak with him then. Before we go, though, was Felicity currently working on anything?" Amanda asked.

"She was due to turn in her first draft two weeks ago, actually."

"Thought you said she was on time with turning in her manuscripts?" Trent said.

"Normally, she was. I wasn't going to hold this one time against her record. Her schedule has been rather hectic since the movie news hit. Hey, I suppose you haven't since you're asking, but have you come across what she had ready?"

Amanda shook her head. She wasn't going to tell the editor about Felicity's missing laptop or hard copy versions either. Along those lines, they still needed to confirm Felicity backed up her work digitally—be that on drives or cloud storage.

"What was her latest project about?" Trent asked.

Melody winced. "That is definitely not something I have the authorization to share with you."

Amanda wasn't sure that pursuing this would get them any closer to the identity of Felicity's killer, but it was one more possible stepping stone. "Ian Moss again?"

"That's right."

Amanda wanted to address one more thing with the editor before leaving. "There were a few pieces of paper with printed text on them at the scene. I'm curious if you could search *The Romeo Killer*, or any of her other books for that matter, to see if they turn up in one of them."

Melody nodded. "I can look."

"Great. Trent, do you have those words close at hand?" She turned to her partner, trusting he'd come through for her.

"Yep. One second." He swept his finger around the screen of the tablet. "Here they are. The typed words were: 'beauty has always' and 'case closed.'"

"Hmm. The last one could have a place in any of her books. I'll have to search her manuscripts."

Amanda appreciated the editor's cooperation. She also realized even if she found the words, it might not advance the case. There was also a handwritten scribble that was barely legible. If she remembered right, it said 'could it be?' Amanda stood and thanked Melody for her time.

"Oh, before you go..." Melody opened a cabinet door in the credenza and pulled out two hardcover editions of *The Romeo Killer*. "Here is one for each of you."

"Thank you." Amanda hadn't much success with reading these days, but she had a feeling that trend had to change. Between the covers of this book might lie the key to solving a real-life murder.

Amanda and Trent parted ways with Melody when she got off the elevator on the eighth. They carried on to the lobby.

"A thought hit me while we were speaking with Schmitt," Amanda started. "Felicity must have had electronic backups of her work."

"We didn't find any drives in her house."

"Which I realize, and maybe the killer took them, but it's also possible she saved copies on web-based storage. I think it's worth looking into."

"Her financials could tell us, though sometimes those services are renewed yearly. We might have to look over a long period. Another option is we contact her internet provider, hope they confirm she had cloud storage through them, and go from there."

"Let's get it done as soon as we can."

The elevator dinged its arrival at the main floor, and they headed toward the front desk.

The woman there smiled. "Have a good—" She stopped talking when Amanda and Trent came to a standstill in front of her. "Can I help you with something?"

"We need to speak with Ian Moss." Amanda wanted to start with him. If he could summarize *The Romeo Killer* that would save some time.

"One minute." The woman typed on her keyboard, paused, squinted at the monitor, and dragged a finger across the screen. "He is here, but in a meeting until eleven. After that it looks like he has a fifteen-minute window."

"Put us in there," Trent said. "In the meantime, we'd like to speak with Kristopher Black from Marketing."

"Let me see what I can do." The receptionist tapped on the keyboard again, then clicked the mouse with flourish. "His calendar is showing all-clear. I'll call him now." She tapped her earpiece, and the blue light came on. She ran through a similar spiel to what she had when they'd requested an audience with Melody Schmitt. She pressed on the earpiece again. To Amanda and Trent, she said, "He can talk with you in his office. Seventh floor, off the elevator, turn left, third door on the left."

"Thank you," Amanda told her, and she and Trent headed back up.

"Well, if we don't accomplish anything else today, we got to ride the elevator at a huge publishing house." He was smirking when she looked over at him. She shook her head.

"Always you and the bright side." She smiled. "But in all seriousness, Trent, we're getting leads." She held up the hardcover edition of Felicity's bestseller. "We also have some reading to do."

Trent groaned.

She faced him as the elevator continued its ascent. Floor five... six... seven... A ding, then the doors opened. He unloaded, and she stepped out and caught his arm on a back swing.

"What was with the groan?" she asked him.

"I've never been good at required reading. In school, I'd pray to be assigned to groups, then hang back while the others carried me."

"And you actually got away with this?"

"Every time. I like reading when I have the time—even if it's not often—but the minute someone tells me I must read a particular book... Nope, no way. Not interested."

"Either a problem with authority or stubbornness."

"Both?" His eyes twinkled. "What about you?"

"Which is my issue—authority or stubbornness?" She touched a strand of her red hair. "I'll leave you to be the judge."

"You're being too hard on yourself, you're only a little stubborn."

"Jeez, thanks." Although, she did take possession of the trait as a compliment. At least that meant she knew her mind and what she wanted. "If it's really important for you, though, I'll do the reading."

"It would mean the world."

"Well, it's not like you'll have nothing to do while I'm reading."

"I wouldn't expect it any other way."

"Besides, depending on how much we're told, reading might not be our top priority." *I can hope.* She smiled at him and set off down the hall.

Trent knocked on the doorway for the third office on the left.

"Come in," a man called out from inside, and Trent got the door.

A man in his thirties, full beard and mustache, sat behind a desk. Pale complexion much like Amanda. Unlike her, though, his skin was milky smooth without a freckle in sight.

"What can I do for you? Cara said you were with the Prince William County Police Department?"

Cara must have been the lady at the front desk. "That's right. Detectives Steele and Stenson. You are Kristopher Black?"

"I am. Sit down if you'd like."

There were two chairs against the wall, and they positioned them to face Kristopher.

"We just spoke with Melody Schmitt. She told us you handled Felicity Kelley's email." Trent took his tablet back out and had the notepad app at the ready.

Kristopher narrowed his eyes. "What do you mean by handled—past tense? Was I fired and don't know about it?"

"Unfortunately, Felicity Kelley was found murdered yesterday," Amanda stepped in, laying it out as a basic fact without embellishment. Doing so made it easier to remain objective and distance herself.

Kristopher didn't say anything, but he leaned back in his chair. He rested his elbow on the arm and plucked at hairs in his beard. His eyes were blank and hard to read.

"You hear what I just said?" Amanda eventually prompted, anxious for him to respond, cautious of startling him.

He nodded and took a deep breath, blew out.

Trent said, "Mr. Black, we appreciate this must come as quite a shock to—"

Kristopher met Trent's gaze, then he danced it toward Amanda. "It's a shock all right."

It was in his words, his inflection, his physical reaction... Amanda had a hunch. "Were you and Felicity close?"

He licked his top lip. "You could say that."

"Could you elaborate?" Amanda was mostly in the dark as to how the relationship between an author and publisher worked, let alone author and marketing person. But she strongly sensed Kristopher and Felicity were more than simply colleagues of sorts.

"We rarely had to see each other, but we'd sometimes talk over Zoom. Mostly when she had questions about our marketing plans."

"I don't know much about publishing," Trent inserted, "but wouldn't her agent be responsible for sorting that out with you?"

"Typically, and Justine and I did consult often. But Felicity wasn't the type of author who was just about writing, if that makes sense. She was also a businesswoman. She wanted to be involved, to offer input, not just remain informed."

"Sounds like she was incredible," Amanda said.

"She was that. I had the privilege of accompanying her to many book signings. That's how I got to know her."

Amanda was interested in the depth of their relationship, and if it was romantic, whether that factored into Felicity ending things with Luis Navarro. Best to find out those answers. "Were you and Felicity seeing each other romantically?"

Kristopher nodded. "Not for long and nothing too serious. Say, just over a month. We weren't exclusive, but I was hoping to ask her about that this coming weekend. It just never felt like the right time, ya know? Her book blew up the bestselling charts, then the movie deal. I didn't want her thinking I was after her because of her money or fame."

Just over a month ago, Felicity still would have been with Luis. Had either man found out about the other one? "Felicity had a boyfriend. Did she tell you about him?"

"She did, but she ended things with him when we decided to start seeing each other."

"That's not how we heard it," Amanda said.

A flicker of pain crossed Kristopher's eyes.

"Then you didn't know she was seeing him up until three weeks ago?" Trent asked.

"Nope." A single word, but it carried a note of sadness. "I never took her for the cheating type. It was just one thing that I loved about her. I despise players and two-faced people."

He'd just denied knowing about Luis Navarro but how far could they take his word on that—and his relationship with Felicity? He could have exaggerated their connection, making it into something it wasn't. "Is there any way you can prove your involvement with Felicity to us?"

"Yeah, of course." Kristopher fumbled to get his cell phone out of a pocket and worked on it a few seconds. "Here," he said as he handed it to Amanda. "You'll see the string of text messages."

Amanda nudged closer to Trent, so they could both see the screen. The language was of a romantic nature, supporting what Kristopher had told them. She gave his phone back to him.

"Do you have any idea who might have... done this to her?" Kristopher's voice cracked partway through his question, and he massaged a temple.

Her mind instantly went to Luis Navarro. Did he know about Kristopher Black? Just because Luis was a cheater, that didn't mean he'd be okay if the roles were reversed. Though if Luis knew about Kristopher, why not send them here? Did he think that move too transparent and risky, that suspicion would immediately fall back on him? Whatever the case, he still had Amanda's attention.

SEVENTEEN

Amanda considered how to best proceed with Kristopher and decided to shift from the personal side while giving him a vague answer about their suspicions. "We have a couple of theories. We're hoping that you'd be able to help us sort out one avenue."

"Anything you need."

"In managing her emails, did you run into any fans who might have been obsessed with her, possibly crossing an inappropriate line in that regard?" Amanda asked.

"Thankfully, most were obsessed, as you put it or in love with her work. If not, she wouldn't have had the success she had. As far as any of them crossing a line, I don't think so... Well, unless you're talking about people trying to take liberties. She'd get emails from people asking for free autographed books or requesting their name be used for a character. Some were rather demanding, bossy even. Then there's a handful who think they know better than the author. They'll write in to say how the book should have been done."

That sounded similar to the messages Celeste had mentioned. Kristopher must have told Felicity about them.

"Was anyone in regular contact or give you the feeling something was off with them?" Trent asked.

"There are a few repeat offenders as I call them. They lay out all their personal details and ask Felicity to share hers. Some can get quite heated when their requests meet with a boiler-plate response. 'Garrison & Marrow Publishing and Felicity Kelley thank you for your readership and support.'" He prattled the latter off in a singsong voice.

"We're going to need their names," Trent requested.

Amanda glanced at her partner, back at Kristopher. "Actually, it would be even better if you could forward those emails to me." She produced her card, which Kristopher accepted.

"It might take me some time to ferret them out, but sure"— he lifted her card—"as soon as I can, you'll have them."

"Terrific." She and Trent would then get them to Detective Briggs in Digital Forensics to track the senders' IP addresses.

"Speaking about ardent fans, though..." He stopped there, his eyes widening. "There's one specific character that comes to mind. It wasn't anything he wrote, but rather, he showed up at every single one of her book signings. Just following her around across the country like a puppy."

The back of Amanda's neck tightened. That struck her as an obsessed fan starting the transition to deranged. "Do you know his name?"

"Sheldon Lowe. I saw her sign enough books for him."

"Do you know where he lives?" Trent asked.

"Unfortunately, no. I realize that probably doesn't help you much. I should have been more proactive, but he'd never struck me as violent. I guess that's why I'd just shake my head and roll my eyes about him."

"Did he ever email her?" Amanda asked.

"I will look."

"If you find any, forward them to me." This Sheldon certainly sounded like someone worth speaking with.

"I did overhear him talking to Felicity sometimes," Kristopher started. "She'd be signing, and he'd be going on about a book he wanted to write, looking for her advice. Felicity was always polite but guarded."

"All right, good to know." The theory of a jealous writer just moved up the list again. Combine wannabe writer with deranged fan, and that was one lethal combo. But one step at a time.

"Glad I could help, and I will get you what I can dig up. I just hope that you find whoever did this to her."

"You have our word that we are doing all within our power to that end," Amanda said. "We're very sorry for your loss."

"Mr. Moss." Kristopher sat up straighter and was looking past them to the doorway.

Amanda and Trent stood and turned around.

Presumably, *Ian* Moss, publisher, was standing there in a tailored suit. He was exceptionally good-looking with a Roman nose and blue eyes. He wore a gold pinkie ring on the right hand. No wedding band and any other jewelry she could see. She'd expect a person in his position to be in his late forties or fifties, but if he was, he'd cheated time. He looked closer to Amanda's age of thirty-eight.

He stepped toward them with an extended hand, and a smile that showed off bleached-white teeth. "Ian Moss, Publisher."

Trent shook first. "Detective Stenson."

"Detective Steele." She removed her hand from the man's clammy palm. Had he run to the seventh floor? Though he wasn't winded, and his physique testified to hours in the gym each week.

"I finished my previous meeting a few minutes early and heard you were here with Kristopher. What here in Washington has captured the interest of the Prince William County Police Department?" He clasped his hands in front of himself, and his eyes dipped briefly to the hardcovers of *The Romeo Killer* in their hands. He pointed at the book and said, "That's great reading right there."

He obviously had no idea that Felicity had been murdered. It was surprising that word hadn't reached him from Melody Schmitt already. Such news at Central would hit everyone's ears in a hot second—inherent of wagging tongues from small-town living and being a cop. Amanda picked up on something else that Ian had said, not so subtly. He sought to remind them they held no jurisdiction here. The question was why he'd felt the need to point that out. Then again, he was the top dog in a highly successful publishing house and was probably used to covering its ass.

"We were just finishing up with Mr. Black," she said. "How about we join you in your office, Mr. Moss?"

He fiddled with a button on his suit jacket, but left it in place. "Let's talk in the conference room down the hall. That's if it's all the same to you."

How many meeting rooms did they have in this building? "That would be fine." She offered him a pleasant smile and excused herself and Trent from Kristopher. His mind appeared a million miles away, his eyes glazed over and distant. It wasn't until she took a step to walk away that he spoke.

"I'll work on getting those emails right now."

"Thank you."

Amanda and Trent followed Ian down the hallway, and he showed them to a room that was a near replicate of where they'd spoken to Melody.

Ian got the door behind them and tugged down on his jacket. He undid its buttons when he took the chair at the head of the table. He exuded confidence and authority, but he would have earned both. Amanda couldn't imagine the journey to the top of the publishing ladder would be an easy one to navigate—and he'd reached it before the age of forty, by the look of him.

She and Trent sat next to each other across from Ian. That way they'd both be able to read his facial expressions and body language. And those two things always had something to say. Like now. Ian was sitting with his shoulders squared and he appeared stiff, as if he were holding his next breath. The package told Amanda he was guarded.

Amanda set her book on the table and said, "I'm assuming you don't know why we're interested in speaking with you?"

"I do not." Ian looked back and forth between them, quirked an eyebrow.

Trent put his hardcover on the table and turned on his tablet.

"Your author, Felicity Kelley, was found murdered yesterday," Amanda said matter-of-factly.

Ian didn't say anything but leaned back in his chair, rocked slightly. His eyes became glassy. "Well, that's a tragedy, if ever I heard one. Wow... I can't believe..."

Amanda was curious if the tragedy was Felicity's loss of life or his loss of a lucrative author. Cynical, but the thought entered in all the same. Blame it on being witness to so many selfish people who were more grieved by how another death affected their lives. After several seconds passed in silence, she prompted, "Mr. Moss, are you okay?"

"I am. It's heartbreaking is all. Her career had just skyrocketed. The bestseller lists, the movie..." He flicked a finger toward the hardcovers. "We just had an intimate gathering a couple of days ago."

"We heard about that," Amanda admitted.

"She's going to be a tough one to follow. *The Romeo Killer* was by far her best work. The world is fortunate she gifted us that before she left."

Amanda bristled. "She didn't exactly leave of her own choice, Mr. Moss."

He held up his hands. "Not what I meant by any means."

His strong reaction calmed her some. "What can you tell us about *The Romeo Killer?*"

"What? Why would I ruin it for you?"

Again, she was presented with the opportunity of admitting that Felicity Kelley's murder had elements that seemed undoubtedly connected to the book—but did she want to advertise that fact? As she'd thought before, she wished for more plot points before edging there. "If you could just answer the question, however you wish."

Ian tugged on his jacket again and angled his head. "Do you believe it's connected with her murder?"

"Please just tell us a bit about the book—the killer's motive, for example." Amanda hoped he'd oblige.

Ian rubbed his forehead. "He's a bleeding heart... the killer. He had his heart broken by a beautiful woman and essentially set out on a killing spree targeting other successful and beautiful women."

The victimology suited Felicity Kelley on both scores, and the publisher's words had just moved Luis Navarro up to prime suspect. They had to push him more, find out if he knew about Felicity's budding relationship with Kristopher Black, for a start. "Thank you for sharing that." *It's more helpful than you know*, she resisted the urge to add.

"Right. Of course, of course." He waved a hand of dismissal now, as if his divulging that part of the plot hadn't bothered him. "You can find the highlights on the back cover, even, but he'd stab the women and leave a Queen of Hearts playing card in their throats."

A few beats of quiet, which Ian broke.

"You knew that much?"

"We did," Trent said.

"Do you have any idea who may have done this to her?"

"The investigation is still young, Mr. Moss." Though her mind was screaming Luis Navarro's name and begging that this man would tell them more about the book. She had this feeling that wasn't going to happen. She preemptively tried another tact. "Can you think of anyone who might have had an issue with her?"

"She was adored, well, obviously. Look at her success. This attracted some questionable characters. Kristopher said he was getting some emails for you, and I am assuming it's those types of messages he's pulling together?"

"You're rather intuitive, Mr. Moss. It has crossed our minds we may be looking at a fan who became a stalker and escalated from there. Any names come to you?" Amanda asked.

He shook his head. "Kristopher would definitely be the best point of contact in that regard."

"Before we go, we understand Felicity was working on a new novel for Garrison & Marrow," Trent said, taking his eyes from the tablet. "Can you tell us what it was about?"

A slight grin, then, "Certainly not off the top of my head."

"Even though she was probably one of your highest-grossing authors?" Amanda countered.

"We've been blessed with many, Detective. It's why our house is one of the largest in the world."

Amanda wasn't in the mood to hear the promotional brochure. "Would it be all right with you if Melody Schmitt, Felicity's editor, told us what it was about? She was concerned about violating confidentiality."

"Do you think it might help you figure out who killed her?"

He certainly was a curious man, but that likely came with his position. He'd be expected to have all the answers. "We're just covering all the bases." She pressed on a smile.

"Hmm. I suppose that given the circumstances, an exception can be made. Though, of course, we'd still require you both to sign a confidentiality agreement."

"We would be happy to read it over, decide from there." The striking similarities to *The Romeo Killer* didn't mean the work in progress didn't factor in somehow, though it felt like a shot in the dark.

"All right, then. I'll get the lawyers on preparing the paperwork."

"When should you have that?" Amanda had no intention of hanging around waiting. Her entire body was quaking with the desire to move on Navarro.

"A few hours, give or take."

"Is this something you could send electronically and us sign and return the same way?" she asked.

"I don't see why not."

"And once that's out of the way, Melody can fill us in over the phone?" She'd prefer not to drive back out to Washington, if it wasn't necessary.

"Yes. I am sure you'll find that Garrison & Marrow will cooperate fully with this investigation, Detectives. Felicity Kelley was a true talent, and she'll be missed."

"That she will be," Amanda said, adding her voice to that sentiment. She hadn't known Felicity well, but from the little she did, the mystery author struck her as a shining light. Where she earned Amanda's respect was her seeming dedication to getting the facts right. After all, she had sought out a detective to help with police procedure. Not everyone put that effort into their work. But Amanda was committed to putting her all into finding out why someone killed Felicity Kelley.

EIGHTEEN

Amanda stepped into the hall ahead of Trent. "We need to bring Navarro in immediately."

"Agreed. A bleeding heart as motive for the killer in Felicity's book? That can't be a coincidence. Felicity rejected Navarro's proposal and ended things."

"Uh-huh, just as she reached a pinnacle of success."

"Successful and beautiful women," Trent reiterated what Moss had told them about the Romeo Killer's targets.

"Navarro would be well aware of all of it."

"He might have known about Kristopher Black too."

She considered and shook her head. "I'm not sure whether he did or not, but Celeste didn't mention Black."

"Felicity could have kept their relationship quiet," Trent added. "Either way, Felicity dumped Navarro. But then he decides to mimic Felicity's method? Why do that?"

"It points to him, while at the same time, it's subliminal. He makes us think we're after a serial killer, not looking at an isolated incident. It also lights up a bunch of suspects. Everyone who has read the novel knows the plot."

"Like the *deranged fans* he directed our attention to. All this makes him feel removed and free of suspicion."

"Though that's where he's wrong." Amanda had her phone out and was calling Malone. She filled Trent in on her plans. "I don't want another minute passing with Navarro on the streets. It's going to take us a chunk of time to get back to the county, and I want him at Central when we arrive."

Trent's phone rang. "It's Justine Livingston, Felicity's agent," he said before answering. "Hello, this is Detective Stenson..." He stepped away so they both had some distance to manage their calls.

Amanda filled Malone in on their suspicions about Navarro.

"I see why you'd have your doubts about this guy's innocence," Malone told her. "Enough to bring him in?"

"Yes, I don't see the harm. We'll just talk to him, feel him out more. He never did give us an iron-clad alibi."

A brief pocket of silence, then, "All right, I'll have officers bring him in. You headed right back?"

Amanda glanced at Trent, and she could tell from the odd word hitting her ear that he was trying to arrange a meeting with the agent. With them already in Washington, it made sense to tend to that before returning to Woodbridge. At least with Navarro in holding at Central, he wouldn't be free on the streets. It would also give him time to sweat things out. "I think Trent and I have one more stop first."

"Okay, well, he'll be here waiting unless you hear from me. You might know already, but Kelley's name and her murder have hit the news."

"That was bound to happen." She was shocked it had taken as long as it had. The media had been crawling outside her house yesterday evening.

"You know it." Sarcasm in full force and, with that, Malone ended the call.

She pocketed her phone, and Trent was looking at her—raised eyebrows and pressed lips. If his facial cues weren't enough, his pointing at his phone told her he wanted to know when to set up the meeting with the agent.

"Right now," she said, speaking lowly.

Into his phone, Trent said, "How does within the next half hour work?... Yes, I know where your office is located... All right. I'll see you soon." He put his phone away and brought Amanda up to speed. "She's good to meet at her office right now."

She smiled, having gathered as much from his side of the conversation.

"What about Navarro?"

"Malone's going to have officers bring him in."

"Huh. He'll have some time to stew." A smirk passed his lips.

"How did Livingston strike you?"

"Strange and noncommittal."

"Then she doesn't know about Felicity's murder yet. Malone just informed me it's hit the news."

"She didn't give me the impression it had reached her. On the upside, she could give us information on the book Felicity was currently working on. Then we'll be able to avoid the confidentiality agreement with G & M."

"I'm not sure she'll be any more open about it than the publisher."

"I suppose. Her confidentiality is likely already contracted."

"Most likely."

They made it down to the lobby and headed toward the car, and Trent took them to Livingston's agency, which he informed her was called the Living Word.

"It sounds like the name of a church."

He smiled. "Great minds... I thought the same."

. . .

Amanda looked up the website for the Living Word on the way there. It was a boutique literary agency with one agent—Justine Livingston. The site boasted a small stable of authors, but some even Amanda recognized. Apparently, Justine Livingston was highly sought after in the publishing industry, just as Celeste had told them.

When they got there, Trent had to pay for street parking.

A man was sitting at the front desk, and he smiled broadly as Amanda and Trent walked toward him. "How can I help you?"

Given the posh energy coming from the pages of the website, Amanda would have expected a cooler reception. After all, he served as Justine Livingston's gatekeeper.

Trent held up his badge. "We're Detectives Stenson and Steele to see Justine Livingston."

The man barely glanced at Trent's gold shield. "Do you have an appointment?"

"Good heavens, Jeremy." Justine Livingston swept into the reception area, bringing with her a cloud of cloying perfume. It was likely expensive as it was a blend of layered fragrances. "Did I not tell you I was expecting people?"

Jeremy's cheeks flushed. "Sorry, ma'am."

Justine rolled her eyes and turned her gaze on Trent and took him in from his shoes to his forehead. "You, I spoke with on the phone but, you, I don't know." She turned her attention to Amanda.

"Detective Steele," she said.

"And I'm Detective Stenson, if you don't remember my name," Trent said.

"I remember," Justine said coolly.

"Do you have somewhere private we could talk?" Amanda asked, prompting the woman to stop with her judgmental glances.

"Certainly." She snapped her fingers at Jeremy.

"The conference room is ready, Ms. Livingston."

"Let's go, then, shall we?" She pivoted on her Jimmy Choo heels and motioned with a hand for Amanda and Trent to follow.

She saw them into a room with a meeting table and seating for eight. Enlarged prints of book covers were in frames around the room with gold-embossed plates beneath them noting the units sold. It was much like a person might expect from a music company with high-grossing albums.

"Please, sit." Livingston's tone was impatient, and she made a broad motion with her hand to indicate any chair was available, except for the one she lowered herself into. She drew back from the table and crossed her legs, clasping her hands on her knee.

Trent and Amanda took chairs to the agent's right, and Trent got his tablet ready.

"If you'd like water, please help yourself." Justine gestured toward a water pitcher and three glasses. That must have been what Jeremy meant by the room being ready.

"I'm good, but thank you," Amanda said.

"You said this was regarding Felicity Kelley," Justine directed at Trent, as she picked at the hem of her skirt. It was a nervous tic, telling Amanda the assured agent was more anxious than she was trying to let on.

"You might have heard the news...?" Amanda wagered the agent hadn't just as Trent had suspected after speaking on the phone with her.

"What news?"

"Felicity Kelley was murdered Tuesday evening," she said, laying it out factually, keeping emotions at a distance.

"No. That's not possible." Justine shook her head. "I just saw her. That day."

Such a common fallback in denial of death, as if recently seeing someone made it impossible for them to die. She was guilty of the same when Fred Hudson had told her about Felicity. "We're sorry for your loss."

Justine's eyes welled with tears, and her chin quivered. The self-assured literary agent was disintegrating in front of them.

"This is no doubt quite a shock," Amanda empathized. "But we need to ask you some very important questions."

"Yes, of course. Whatever they are." Justine pressed her lips, nudged out her chin, and squeezed her hands tightly.

"To start, how did she seem to you on Tuesday?" Amanda regretted not thinking to ask this of Melody Schmitt and Ian Moss. "Did you see her at Garrison & Marrow's event?"

"Yes, and she was excited. She got another payday. We drank champagne, laughed..."

"We understand she didn't hang around long," Amanda pointed out.

"She left a bit early, but she's a lightweight and said she wasn't feeling well."

"And how did she get home?" Trent asked.

Justine smiled though the expression quickly fractured. "In a limo that I hired for her."

It sounded like Justine took good care of her authors. "We believe her recent rise to fame might have factored into her murder," Amanda said, pleased with the line she towed. It gave question to there being similar elements from the crime scene to *The Romeo Killer* while not directly stating their suspicions of a copycat.

"How so?" Justine pinched the collar of her shirt, the huge diamonds adorning her fingers twinkling under the fluorescent lights. She sought out Trent's gaze. "How was she killed?"

"All we can say at this time was she was stabbed," he told her.

"In the heart?" Justine countered.

"Yes," Trent said.

"Just as in *The Romeo Killer*." Justine's face shadowed, and she stared across the room.

Amanda gave it a few beats, then said, "It's clear that you cared for Felicity and would want her killer apprehended. Whatever you can tell us about the book may help in that endeavor." While she was speaking, her mind was on Navarro. Were officers at his door right now, or was he already at Central?

"I take it neither of you have read it?" Justine said, as if she were appalled by the possibility they hadn't.

Both Trent and Amanda shook their heads.

"Unfortunately, the job doesn't leave us with much spare time," Trent added.

"You two might be the only ones in the world." A slight lift to Justine's lips, falling short of an actual smile.

"We might be," Amanda said, playing along.

Justine uncrossed her legs and wheeled in toward the table, where she set her elbows. Her hands unclasped, and her posture leaned forward—all the body language was indicating an openness to talk. "What is it you'd like to know?"

Finally, Amanda thought. They might not need to use valuable time reading after all.

NINETEEN

While questioning Luis Navarro had to wait, this meeting with Justine Livingston could prove quite enlightening. "All we know so far is the killer in the book was a bleeding heart, who targeted successful and beautiful women after being hurt by one."

"That barely scratches the surface," Justine said. "I might best start at the beginning. Do you know about the Queen of Hearts playing card?"

"Know of it, not much of its role in the book," Amanda said.

"The killer is a professional poker player who travels the circuit. He meets his victims at hotel bars, chats them up, and they go back to the woman's room. Beautiful, successful, as you were told. Also, self-assured and worldly."

Amanda would circle back to the playing card in a minute. "What did they do for work?" *Surely, they weren't crime authors...*

"Entrepreneurs, saleswomen on location for meetings, that type of thing."

"Career-oriented," Trent said.

"That's right."

Trent was swooping his fingertip around the tablet's screen, letting the quick stroke app do its thing.

"What happens once they're back in the women's hotel rooms? Do they have sex?" Amanda didn't assume this was a given.

"Sex, for sure. It sells books." Justine winked at her, and for a brief moment the dark cloud of grief dissipated. "He'll order room service and have a bottle of champagne brought up. He'll pour it out, seduce them. Afterward, he lures them back to the living area. These women are wealthy and all staying in suites. He pours out more champagne and turns on the gas fireplace. Then, once the women are fully relaxed, he stabs them directly in the heart with a knife."

Trent shifted in his chair and passed a side-glance at Amanda. "To testify to them being heartbreakers."

"Precisely. And he takes the power into his hands, ending things before they can."

So much of this was eerily similar to Felicity's murder scene. Had the fire been lit to set the scene, the manuscripts and research merely collateral damage? Despite the fact Felicity was found long after the fire burned out. "Just the one stab wound?"

"That's right. No hesitancy at all either."

"Does this poker player have a medical background, so he knows exactly where to strike?" Though the lack of hesitancy could also indicate experience at killing.

Justine shook her head. "It took him practice. As it comes out toward the end, his first two victims took a few stabs to die."

How lovely, Amanda thought. It amazed her that such violence qualified for entertainment. Though it wasn't a new concept. Look at the gladiators of Roman times. Crowds packed coliseums to witness human bloodshed. But glorifying murder wasn't limited to the Romans or that point in history.

"How are they found?" Trent asked.

"Lying on the floor in front of the fireplace, the knife he

used to kill them still in their chest. They're wearing robes provided by the hotel, over lingerie."

The more they learned about this book, it was indisputable Felicity's killer was influenced by *The Romeo Killer*. Now, they could add location of the body to the list of similarities between fiction and real life. Maybe that was why the rectangular coffee table and the rug were removed. As for her clothing, that was in sharp contrast to the book. Why, if the killer was so eager to copycat the fictional one? Surely, he had plenty of time to dress her after he'd killed her. But the lack of lingerie would work to lessen suspicion against Luis Navarro. If they had arrived on scene and Felicity was dressed for a romantic evening, he'd certainly have jumped right to the top of the suspect list. And speaking of a romantic evening... "You mentioned that the killer and each victim shared a bottle of champagne. Does he leave that and the glasses behind?"

"Yes."

That was another way in which Felicity's murder scene differed from fiction. "He wasn't concerned with leaving trace?"

"He wasn't in the system."

"Still, he left a part of himself at every murder. If he was caught for one, he'd go down for them all." Amanda was thinking of fingerprints and DNA.

"Which is what ends up happening."

Time to return to the playing card... "Why was the Queen of Hearts folded into eight squares?"

"The number eight is representative of several things. It can denote power, victory, and strength, but it's also a statement of love and devotion."

Amanda considered what that might mean in the scope of Felicity's case. Had Luis Navarro staked his claim on Felicity Kelley by killing her? If he couldn't have her, then no one else could. Was it also his morbid way of proving his love for her? As she'd thought before, he would be familiar with the plot of *The*

Romeo Killer. It would be rather genius of him to copycat that killer. But Amanda also had to follow other possibilities. "We understand Felicity was working on a project up until her death, that it was due to be turned in two weeks ago. What can you tell us about that?" She wasn't confident Justine would be any more forthcoming than the publisher, but she had to try. As Amanda's father had drummed into her, the only stupid question was the one left unasked.

"Hum. Not much, I regret saying. I am bound by contractual confidentiality." Justine hugged herself and rubbed her arms as if fending off a chill.

"Please tell me what you're thinking," Amanda prompted.

"It's probably nothing..." The agent met Amanda's gaze.

"Let us determine that." She put it out there delicately.

Justine nodded, slowly. "Felicity took inspiration from real life—solved cases, which she'd apply twists to, of course. But sometimes she liked tackling cold cases, putting her own creative spin on them, and writing the ending."

"What do you mean by tackling?" Trent asked.

"Playing armchair detective, if you will."

The back of Amanda's neck tightened. "Tell me that she stayed in her armchair." Were they too fixed on Luis Navarro re-enacting a scene from the bestselling book? Had Felicity dug into a real-life murder case and cornered the killer? This doubt alone made it even more imperative to gather all the facts they could.

"I would hope so, but— Do you think her research may have gotten her killed?"

"We're still exploring numerous angles," Amanda replied.

A slight bob of her head, and Justine volunteered, "Felicity was devoted to her research."

"Her best friend described her as being obsessive lately," Amanda pointed out.

Justine smiled. "That makes sense. She was behind making her deadline with her latest book."

"Which we heard from her editor was unusual. Why was she running behind?" Amanda asked.

Justine shook her head. "She never got into it with me, just assured me she was almost finished."

"This latest book that Felicity was working on... Did she take her inspiration from a real-life murder case?" It was hard to let this possibility go, even with Luis Navarro at the top of her suspect list.

"I wish I could tell you. I don't ever read her books until the first draft is finished, and she never got into the specifics of where the idea came from. Not with me."

In that case, Luis Navarro remained their main suspect.

TWENTY

Amanda and Trent left Justine Livingston with their condolences. But before that, they asked specifically about Sheldon Lowe. Justine was very familiar with him and had her assistant look into him online some time ago. He had gathered the basics, including his home address, which Justine shared with them. His residence was conveniently located in Dumfries, and Amanda and Trent would follow this up if it became necessary. The fact Justine had felt the need to gather intel on Lowe only disclosed she viewed him as potentially dangerous.

Trent's stomach was grumbling voraciously enough, it might as well be against a loudspeaker, and Amanda suggested they stop for a bite to eat. Despite wanting to return to Central and start questioning Navarro, she hadn't heard if he was there yet.

They were settled in a booth at a restaurant in Washington. A sign on the window announced, "All Day Breakfast" and it had Trent sold. He had the omelet special, and she had their skillet with a Greek flare, which included thin slices of gyro meat and chunks of feta.

Her phone chimed, and she checked the message. "It's from Malone. Navarro's at Central, ready for us." *Like the sarge read my mind...*

"Love to hear it. Everything seems to be pointing us in his direction."

"I agree, and now that we've learned more about *The Romeo Killer*, it's apparent he used that as his guidebook on murder one-oh-one." She put a forkful of her meal into her mouth.

"I'm not disagreeing, but there are differences too." Trent took a bite of egg.

"I gathered those too—no champagne bottle or flutes, her clothing was casual not indicative of a night of romance. But it's not enough to let him off the hook. Same goes for the location of where she was murdered—in her home, not a hotel room." She stabbed a piece of gyro meat but didn't lift it to her mouth.

"If we are wrong and Navarro isn't the killer, where will it leave us?"

"We still have other avenues to explore, including that Sheldon Lowe character." She toyed with her food, moving it around with her fork. "But we're going to push Navarro, see what he says. Then if he checks out, we'll go from there."

The server came to their table and collected Trent's plate and looked at Amanda. "Are you still eating, or would you like a box?" Her gaze traveled to Amanda's barely touched meal and then met her eyes.

Amanda set her fork on the table. "I'm finished, and there's no need to pack it up."

The server took Amanda's dish, a look of disapproval on her face. And, yes, Amanda should feel bad about wasting food when some people in the world were going hungry. But it wasn't going to be edible after baking on the rear seat of the car for countless hours.

The server returned and slapped the check on the table.

One would think Amanda had rejected food that the woman herself had prepared.

"The PWCPD is picking up this tab," Amanda told Trent, grabbing the check folder. She scanned the receipt to make sure it was right and slipped a department credit card in the appropriate slot. She set the folder, so it slightly overhung the edge of the table to notify the server it was ready.

"Well, I'm full up." Trent patted his flat stomach.

"They don't exactly go small on serving size here." She'd never say so, but her partner was looking leaner these days. Not in an unhealthy way, but rather like he was exercising more.

About five minutes later, they were back in the car and Trent was taking them back to Woodbridge. While he drove, Amanda used the time to call Celeste Sweeney. She had a few things she wanted to ask her.

"Hello?" Celeste came across as tentative and leery, understandable as Amanda's number, registered to the PWCPD, would show as unknown.

"It's Detective Steele. Is this Mrs. Sweeney?" she asked even though she recognized her voice.

"It is."

Two words, and Amanda sensed apprehension. She was probably braced for an update, and Amanda was regretful she didn't have one. It was probably best that she get right to the point of her call. "I just have a few questions, if you have a minute."

"Of course."

"To start, did Felicity ever work out points of her plots with you?" This question would lay the groundwork for where Amanda was headed.

"Sometimes."

That's promising… "But not with the most recent one she was working on?" When they had first spoken to Celeste, she said that Felicity was uncharacteristically tight-lipped about it.

"All she said when I pushed was she should never be discussing her books with me, and she was going to stop."

Amanda was curious if it was just a simple change of heart or indicative of something else. On another topic, she asked, "Did Felicity do extensive research for her books?"

"Oh yeah. She got anal about it, if you ask me."

Justine Livingston's term *armchair detective* wasn't far from mind. Felicity may have pried into a cold case and caught the attention of a killer. Yet another option to explore if Navarro wasn't guilty. And thinking of Navarro... "Does the name Kristopher Black sound familiar to you? Did Felicity ever mention him?"

Trent gave her a thumbs up, and Amanda smirked and shook her head.

"Kristopher," Celeste said as if trying out the name to see if it struck any sort of memory. "I don't think so."

There was the chance if she didn't know about the budding romance there, neither had Luis Navarro. Amanda gave Trent a thumbs down. He frowned and put his focus back out the windshield.

"Thank you very much, Mrs. Sweeney."

"Not a problem. Call if you have any other questions. I'll be here."

"Will do." Amanda ended the call and filled Trent in on her conversation with Celeste.

"Sounds like whatever Felicity was working on took a lot of her focus."

"Or obsession," Amanda countered. "But not just that, why all the secrecy? She'd talk her plots out with her friend in the past. What if Felicity poked around a cold case and got close to the real killer?"

"I was thinking the same."

"Yep. Justine's *armchair detective* and Felicity picking real-life cases causes me concern."

"But without knowing what she was working on, we're nowhere on that front."

"Nope. And Celeste never heard of Kristopher."

"Which I'd gathered from the thumbs down. But it doesn't mean that Navarro didn't know about Kristopher."

"In agreement there." Amanda exchanged her phone for Felicity's and looked at her message history, specifically interested in the thread in which she communicated with Kristopher Black. "Huh. So, there are texts between Felicity and Kristopher, but they only go back three weeks."

"Did someone delete the previous ones? Navarro? He told us how to access Felicity's phone."

"And they did break up around three weeks ago. If he deleted previous texts, he was aware of the relationship Felicity had going with Black."

"More motive. He's cheating but not about to tolerate being cheated on."

She pointed at the speedometer. "Can't you go any faster?"

"Only if you want me to risk getting a ticket."

"Let's try our luck."

"All right, if you say so." The car surged ahead, and Amanda gladly watched the world go by in swatches of color. It was time for Luis Navarro to come clean with them.

TWENTY-ONE

There was no way either of them could have spotted that cop with the radar gun until it was too late. He'd been perched on a bridge, hunched down.

"I told you," Trent said to Amanda as they walked to their desks at Central.

Amanda had a feeling she'd never hear the end of it. "I'll cover it."

"The least you can do." He handed her the ticket.

She'd look at the hundred bucks as a necessary expenditure to move things along. "I'll get Navarro pulled from holding and brought to an interview room. You want to pull up his background for us?"

"No problem."

They entered their respective cubicles and got to work. She called the officer in charge of the holding cells, and Trent tapped away on his keyboard.

The officer managing the desk groaned. "That guy."

"What about him?"

"I'll be happy to hand him over to you. He's a broken record, going on about his innocence. I told him I've heard it all before. Had to start tuning him out. Give me ten minutes to get him to Interview Room One. He's not working with a lawyer that I'm aware of."

"Good to know. Thanks." She ended the call and joined Trent in his office space.

"Just getting it up now," he said.

"Ah, take your sweet time. We have ten minutes." She was teasing him, but he didn't seem to find her jest amusing. She held up her hands. "Apparently your goat is easy to get."

"If you got a goat, it wasn't mine."

She snickered, and the screen filled with Luis Navarro's background.

"This isn't looking good." Trent pointed toward his monitor.

She leaned in and saw that Navarro had a record. "Add this to the list of things against this guy."

"I'd say. History of assault and battery five years ago."

"Who did he assault? Did he serve time? If so, how long?" She assumed he'd have spent some time behind bars.

Trent consulted another database. "Looks like he was given two years' probation. Slap on the wrist, but it wouldn't seem it was enough to teach him a lesson, especially if he graduated to murder."

"That's light. What are the details?"

"Looks like it was a domestic. Police were called to the scene, and a woman claimed he'd hit her."

"This is the first time hearing this guy beats women."

"It's not like these assholes announce themselves."

Amanda let the comment slide because she knew it had come from a very personal place for Trent. His aunt had married an abusive man and cut Trent and the rest of his family out of her life.

"Steele? Stenson? Glad to see you're back." Malone was standing in the doorway to Trent's office space. "I asked the officer in Cells to notify me when you had Navarro brought up for questioning. Anything you care to update me on?"

Amanda met Trent's gaze and blew out a breath that had strands of her hair fluttering up. "Where to start?"

"Anywhere. I'm not picky." Malone put his hands on his hips.

She let him know about their talk with Felicity Kelley's agent, leaving out the break for lunch afterward. It would also be best to skim over Felicity being pegged an armchair detective. They didn't have a clear connection between her latest work and her murder; they did when it came to *The Romeo Killer*. Sticking to the facts would get them in front of Navarro faster. She filled in Malone on how the book played out, the killer's motive, the scene itself, the reason for the Queen of Hearts playing card, and the meaning of it being folded into eight squares.

"You've got to be kidding me." Malone shook his head. "I can't buy into all this symbolic crap."

That fact didn't surprise Amanda, having known the man all her life. His belief system was based upon teachings from the Catholic Church, and he didn't venture much outside traditional views. "Some people do, Sarge. In this case, the killer did, and I believe it's also why that aspect was replicated at Kelley's murder scene."

"Elaborate." Malone's brow wrinkled as he crossed his arms and angled his head.

"As I just told you, it was to symbolize power, strength, love, devotion..."

"And this fits Navarro, how do you figure?"

"Felicity had turned down his proposal," Trent said, stepping in. "And she ended things. We have yet to establish if Navarro was aware that Felicity was moving on with another man. But if he did, that would be another hit to his pride."

"All well and fine, but playing devil's advocate here, you

have aspects lining up with the book, what's steering you away from Felicity's murder being the start for a copycat killer?"

"Are you asking whether we've considered it the work of a serial?" Amanda was shocked at Malone's suggestion as he was always the last person who wanted to go there.

He hitched his shoulders. "Keeping an open mind."

"Well, there are distinct differences," she said.

"Which you also told me."

"Let's start with the lingerie. In the book, yes; not with Felicity Kelley. There was a fire burning for hours in the fireplace, and Navarro had more than enough time to dress her in something lacy. But he didn't."

"I have a feeling you're going to tell me why."

"I am. He knew that it would point her murder to him immediately," she said nonchalantly.

"Yet, he lands in the spotlight anyhow."

"No one said criminals were smart, boss," Trent interjected with a smile.

Malone bobbed his head. "True. But if you're going to pluck apart one difference between reality and what hit the pages of Kelley's book, you should do the same with all of them. Why no champagne bottle or glasses?"

And there is more to consider... "Were the anomalies an oversight or intentional? One could only guess at this point. But, regardless, it doesn't make Navarro appear any less guilty."

"I'm not saying he doesn't have marks against him."

"And we just found out he has a history of assault," Trent advised Malone.

"You guys should get in there."

She dipped her head, and her cell phone rang. "Detective Steele," she answered before the second ring. As she listened to her caller, she could hardly believe what she was hearing. "And you're sure?"

Malone and Trent were looking at her, obviously eager to know what she'd been told.

"You have any doubts about Navarro's guilt, Sarge? I'll help eliminate them. That was Officer Cooper. He was out following up not-at-homes in Kelley's neighborhood. The woman across the street witnessed Felicity Kelley in her driveway a week ago, having a screaming argument with a man. The cherry on top? The man's description matches Navarro."

Malone stepped aside, and she and Trent hurried out—a tablet in his hand—headed to the interview room.

TWENTY-TWO

Amanda dropped into the chair across from Luis Navarro. "We meet again."

"You didn't need to send officers to come drag me in here. I'll talk openly with you."

"What we like to hear." She bobbed her head at Trent, who sat beside her. "Then you won't mind telling us what you and Felicity Kelley were arguing about last week in her driveway."

Luis slumped back and sighed. "It's not what you think."

"We're not thinking anything," she said casually. "We're asking you to tell us about it."

"All right..." Luis shifted his butt in the chair and sat up straighter. "She was being hysterical for no reason."

"Enlighten us," Trent said.

"I tried to tell her how good we were together. That just because she didn't want to get married, it didn't mean we had to end things. She started yelling, saying I never listened to a word she said, and that I must be mental."

"And you yelled back?" Amanda countered, building on what she already knew—that the confrontation fired both ways.

"I did. Who the hell wants to be called a mental patient?"

"It's not easy letting go, I get that." Trent pressed a hand to his chest. Amanda was buying his performance, and a part of her wondered if it was more authentic than she cared to admit. Those two kisses, from over a year ago, continued to complicate things between them and there were times she wished they had never happened.

"It wasn't about that," Luis pushed out and crossed his arms. "We were good together."

It would seem that was a hill he was willing to die on, but didn't he see that it didn't help his cause while under suspicion of murdering Felicity? Was he delusional enough to think this was some friendly conversation? "Felicity obviously disagreed with you. How far did this argument go?"

"We just yelled, and I ended up leaving. God, she had a way of pushing my buttons."

Amanda remained quiet, just observing the man in front of her. He really seemed obtuse.

"I can see that," Trent pointed out. "She told you it was over and done, not easy to handle. Did she tell you why?"

Amanda resisted the urge to glance at Trent as he led Luis to the guillotine.

Luis flailed a hand. "She said she'd moved on."

"With another guy?" Amanda feigned surprise.

"Yeah. She wouldn't tell me who."

"Ouch! Seeing the woman you care about with another man..." Trent winced. "That had to hurt, drive you a little insane."

Again, Amanda sensed that Trent's words were more personal than just for Luis Navarro's benefit. She was with Logan and in a happy, committed relationship. Trent kept quiet about his dating life, and she had no clue if he was seeing anyone special.

"It did piss me off, especially while she was standing there accusing me of cheating while she was doing the same thing."

Amanda resisted a smug smile. "So, you knew about Kristopher Black?"

Luis shook his head, not in denial, but clear aggravation.

"Is he why you were screaming in her driveway? Did you leave matters at that?" Her question was loaded with the implication that he'd taken things further.

Luis paled, and his mouth gaped open. He looked from her to Trent and back. "You really think that I killed her?"

Amanda shrugged. "I mean it's possible, right? You had motive."

"I didn't have motive!"

"She didn't want to be with you, she wanted to move on. *You* couldn't take no for an answer." Amanda laid out the accusation and watched it strike.

"Listen, I didn't kill her. You have to believe me."

"Not in the habit of extending blind faith," she kicked back, crossing her arms.

"Well, you need to prove I did it. I don't need to sit here and prove my innocence."

"You told me how to access Felicity Kelley's phone, didn't you?" she asked him.

"You know I did."

"You haven't denied knowing about Kristopher Black, and you could have easily read the messages between him and Felicity."

Luis shoved back into his chair and grimaced.

"There are a lot of texts missing from a conversation between Felicity and Mr. Black. Did you delete them?"

His charade melted from his expression. "Fine. I knew about him."

"It must have made you crazy." Amanda sat back slowly and gestured toward Trent.

"Assault and battery, five years ago. Two years' probation," Trent said evenly.

"Shit." Luis raked a hand through his hair. "I wasn't guilty then either. That bitch hit me and was gearing up to take another swing when her drunk ass lost balance and she fell down, hit her head on the ground."

"Blaming the victim, that's how you want to play this?" Trent seethed. "Though it is what abusers do."

"I'm not an abuser, and I'm not a killer either. Maybe I need a lawyer."

"Up to you." Amanda gestured with open palms.

"No, nope, I don't need one. I didn't do anything wrong."

"All right, then. Let's continue," Amanda stated calmly.

"Is it because of my record that you think that I... *that I* killed Flick?"

"We wouldn't presume to know, even if we have our theories," Trent said.

"Let me guess... All because she broke my heart, I wanted her to feel the pain I was going through? I wanted to hit her where it hurt."

Tingles laced down Amanda's arms as she absorbed his last statement. Burning Felicity's work would have certainly hit where it hurt for her. "Is that why you burned all her books and research?"

"Her— *What?* I didn't do that. The killer burned her books?"

His reaction to Amanda's question was level-headed, and she bought his surprise, but there was a far worse crime to discuss. "More importantly, someone killed her." With Amanda's words, the stark reality moved in like a storm cloud. A young woman was ushered from this world against her will.

"I know. It breaks my heart." Luis's eyes glazed over as he looked into space.

"Just like her leaving you," Amanda said softly, and he met her gaze. "You may not have intended to hurt her. The situation simply spiraled out of control. Just talk to us, clear the air." *And your conscience...*

"You should stop wasting your time on me and find her killer." His fight seemed to have left him.

"That's what we're working to do, Mr. Navarro, but there is evidence against you. Motive we've covered. She wanted to end things, you clearly didn't. Something which you just admitted to us." She paused there but, smartly, Luis remained quiet. She added, "Your prior relationship with her made it feasible she'd let you inside her home."

Luis let out a snort. "After our fight, she told me she never wanted to see me again."

"Ouch." This from Trent, and it had Luis glancing at him.

"All I'm saying is there's no way she'd let me inside."

"And it's the way she was killed," Amanda proceeded as if the previous volley didn't happen between Luis and Trent. "She was stabbed in the heart." On their first visit they hadn't shared where, just that she had been stabbed.

"She was..." Luis looked at the table. "Like in her book."

"Yes."

"Was there a Queen of Hearts playing card in her..." Luis opened his mouth and pointed inside.

Amanda nodded.

"Folded into eight squares?"

"You tell us," Trent said.

"Eight means power and is a statement of devotion."

"What makes you say that?" Amanda asked, pretending to be oblivious.

"It's from her book. Was she in lingerie? Her boy toy could have been over."

"No reason to believe he was." Everything that Luis was asking or saying confirmed that he was familiar enough with *The Romeo Killer* to imitate the killer.

"She wasn't in lingerie. Then what, shorts and a tee?"

"Yes," Amanda admitted.

Luis's eyes squinted. "That doesn't make sense."

"What doesn't?" Trent asked.

"Everything else you've told me lines up to the plot of *The Romeo Killer*, but not what she was wearing. And, oh, was there a champagne bottle and glasses?"

Amanda was tiring of participating in this back-and-forth dialog. "We think you refrained from dressing her in lingerie so we wouldn't immediately suspect you."

"Yet, here we are."

"Is that a confession?" she countered.

"Hell no, I didn't kill her. Never raised a hand to her."

"You never did give us a satisfactory alibi. Nothing we can verify," Trent pushed out.

Luis worried his bottom lip.

Amanda bounced on his obvious discomfort. "You lied to us. You weren't home for most of the day and didn't slip out for a burger. Where were you? I wouldn't suggest you make me ask again."

"Courtney's place."

"Who is Courtney?" she asked through clenched teeth.

"I'm not proud of this, but—"

"Don't tell us she's your sister," Trent cut in. "And don't lie to us and say you're not proud. Your stripes give you away as a player."

"Fine. It's who I am. Can't a man be himself?"

"Sure. Nothing wrong with that." Amanda's insides were churning acid. Luis Navarro was a dirtbag, but was he a killer? "How long were you there?"

"From six until eleven."

Another question was why had Kaitlyn lied to protect this guy? Was she trying to save face? "We're going to need Courtney's information to verify what you're telling us."

"If it gets me out of here." Luis prattled off a phone number. "We never got around to last names."

Of course you didn't...

Amanda and Trent stood to leave.

"Wait," Luis called out. "I can go, right?"

"Not until we've had a chat with Courtney What's-Her-Name," Amanda said. Out in the hall, she told a uniformed officer to escort Luis Navarro back to the holding cells.

"This guy has more women than a Saudi prince has in his harem."

"Do I sense jealousy?" Amanda shot him a side-glance.

"Not in the least. I'm a one-woman man and prefer a meaningful relationship."

"Huh." She wished she hadn't uttered a sound, but there it was... And did she tell him she had a feeling he was still hung up on her? How egotistical would that come across? And her mind might be more the issue than his.

"Don't tell me that surprises you."

She sensed he was slightly offended that she might think he was into recreational dating. "Not really," she backpedaled.

He didn't say anything more, but an awkward tension lay in the silence. Again, it might just be her feeling it. Either way, there were more important areas to focus on—primarily finding Felicity's killer. And one step toward that goal was meeting up with Rideout for the autopsy—which he would be starting within the hour.

TWENTY-THREE

Amanda called Courtney's number but had to leave a message, which was unfortunate for Luis Navarro. Until they had his alibi sealed up, or their time for holding him without charges timed out, he was a guest of the county. She brought Malone quickly up to speed on the interview before leaving Central.

On the way to Manassas for the autopsy, Amanda checked Felicity's phone. No hateful or inappropriate comments or messages on her social accounts, just a boatload of sympathies. Even with all they'd checked off their list today, she and Trent were walking into the morgue at about four—an hour after Rideout would have gotten started on the body.

"Just when I didn't think you were going to show." Rideout was wearing a white jacket, scalpel held midair, protective shield in place over his face. He must have been about ready to cut the Y-incision.

Amanda and Trent approached the gurney where Felicity Kelley's dead and naked body lay. Seeing her like this—a pale bluish white beneath the unforgiving overhead lighting—was painful. Amanda resurrected Felicity's voice to mind. To think her message was left just two days ago. It felt much longer than that.

Rideout set down the blade on a nearby table with other tools of his trade. That he was putting his work on pause told her he must have big news to share.

"You have something." Not a question.

He lifted the face shield and draped a sheet over Felicity's body. A respectful gesture. "That I do. Where do you want to start?"

"How about cause of death?" Trent asked.

"Felicity Kelley died due to blunt-force trauma to the back of her head."

"Then the knife was just there for us to see and make assumptions," Trent said. "Window dressing."

Amanda nodded. "All about setting the scene. We believe the killer copied the murders from Kelley's book, *The Romeo Killer*," she added for Rideout's benefit.

"We have some killer out there imitating a fictional serial killer? Not good, folks." Rideout's lips set in a thin, straight line. "Though, there are certainly unique elements to this case that would work well within the pages of a novel. As I was saying, it was a strike to her head that killed her."

"You didn't notice the injury on her head until you got her here?" Amanda asked, slightly surprised if that were the case.

"I didn't move her around a lot at the scene, but you'll recall that I would have expected more blood for the stab wound?"

"I do remember that. Well, it must have been the coffee table. We've just been running with things as if she'd injured herself from striking her head on it, not dying due to it. The CSIs discovered a blood trail from one end of the couch to the other..."

"I was informed about the blood, but I don't remember seeing a coffee table," Rideout said, puzzled.

"That's because it wasn't there by the time all of us showed up." She met Trent's gaze. "The killer did all he could to right the scene. He destroyed the table, burned it in her fireplace with all her papers... Or took it with him."

"And we're still left to decipher the killer's motive in doing all that," Trent said.

"More specifically, *Navarro's* motive. Was it to set things up to make us think we're after a serial killer? After all, if we're busy exploring that, he's in the clear."

"You have a suspect?" Rideout asked.

"Yep, and he's looking pretty good for it," Trent replied.

"There are things stacked against him, to be sure," Amanda added. "Though he did give us an alibi. We have yet to verify it."

"Let's hope you've got the guy, because I don't want to see this on my table again." Rideout's voice was dry.

"Makes three of us," Amanda said, speaking also on Trent's behalf.

"I do have more to tell you, if you're interested."

"Of course." Amanda smiled at the ME. "Please, go ahead."

Rideout took a small bow. "There was epithelium under the victim's fingernails."

Good girl, Amanda thought, but she wouldn't expect anything less from a crime fiction author.

"Possibly from an altercation that ended with her hitting her head on the coffee table," Trent said.

"Sounds quite likely," Rideout agreed.

"It's clear Felicity's killer had gone to her house with the intent to kill her. The playing card," Amanda said. "What about the knife? Had it belonged to Felicity?"

Rideout shook his head. "It would seem the killer brought it with him. It was a chopping knife, likely part of a nice set but nothing special."

This was just more proof of premeditation. "Were any prints pulled from the card or the knife?"

Rideout perched his gloved hands on the edge of the gurney. "No, ma'am. Not so much as a partial on either."

"Anything unique about the card?" Trent asked. "The deck it came from could mean something, or even confirm a suspect."

"You'd have to talk with the CSIs for more information there," Rideout told them.

She nodded. "Is there evidence of consensual sex or rape?"

"None."

That was yet another way the scene didn't perfectly align to the book. The Romeo Killer seduced the women he killed. If Luis Navarro was Felicity's killer, consensual intercourse would have been off the table. At least he hadn't raped her to set the scene. "And no champagne bottle or flutes," she said more to herself than the others.

Rideout's eyes narrowed. "Now, I'm out of the loop."

"Goes back to Felicity's bestseller," she told him. "Any more confident on time of death?"

"Definitely between ten and midnight, as I had surmised on scene." He picked up his scalpel, a not-so-subtle cue for them to settle in for the show or leave.

"We'll go," Amanda said. "Call if you find anything else we should know."

"You know I will."

Amanda and Trent cleared out of the morgue. It would be about five thirty when they got back to Woodbridge. There was time to salvage the evening to be with Logan and Zoe, and whoever else happened by the house.

Still no call from Courtney What's-Her-Name. It looked like Luis Navarro should be getting comfortable for an overnight stay in the cells. The thought was appealing, and she was even somewhat at peace with Luis locked up tight.

She checked her email as Trent got them on the highway. At least it held some highlights. "I received the email from Ian Moss with the confidentiality forms, and one from Kristopher Black with the emails we were interested in as attachments."

"Terrific. Guessing you'll fire those over to Briggs?"

"You betcha." She took care of that and returned to the email from Ian. The confidentiality forms were sent as a PDF and could be signed electronically. She forwarded one to Trent, and his phone immediately chimed.

He tilted his head. "That from you?"

"Uh-huh. You're starting to become a mind reader like one of your sisters."

"Not exactly. And she's not a mind reader as much as she's a clairvoyant... or so she says." He smiled over at her and took the exit for Woodbridge.

"Isn't that the same thing?"

"Not according to her. Anyway, I'm guessing it was the confidentiality form?"

"Right again. When you hit a red light or once we get back to the station, just sign off on it and flip it back. Then the gates of the kingdom will open," she jested, trying to insert some joviality. It was hard to shake the images from the morgue, of Felicity's lifeless body... Death was so very final. Full stop.

"I'd like to read it first, if that's all right with you." He turned down the street for Central.

"I suppose that's probably a good idea. We might as well run it past Malone too." She wasn't enthused about the delay, but reading before signing was the responsible thing to do. Besides they wouldn't get anywhere flipping it back today as the publishing house would already be closed.

Trent parked, and they went into the station. Before heading to talk to Malone, they swung by their desks and printed two copies of the confidentiality form for reading through. Amanda also made a call to Logan, which he answered on the second ring.

"Hey, beautiful."

"Hey." She wondered how *beautiful* he'd find her when she relayed that she was running a bit late.

"You're going to be home really late, aren't you?"

All it took was one word for him to assume that. Not that she blamed him, given the time. "Not too late. I should be home within the hour."

"You'll be able to have dinner with us. Wowie," Logan teased and laughed.

"You and Zoe have fun today?" Until hearing Logan's voice, all thoughts of them playing hadn't even occurred to her. She'd been so focused on the investigation.

"That we did, and we'll tell you all about it. Later."

"Can't wait." She puckered a kiss across the phoneline, said, "Love you", then ended the call.

When she and Trent got to Malone's office, they found that his office door was closed and he had company. Through the glass, she saw that Chief Buchanan was with him. His deep baritone traveled into the hallway, but his words were muffled.

The chief was gesturing rather emphatically, and it was apparent that something had him worked up. Usually, Buchanan was rather cool-tempered and level-headed.

Malone's gaze dipped to the door, and Buchanan turned too. Then he started walking toward it. He opened the door, mumbled greetings to them, and left.

Okay...

She entered Malone's office with Trent behind her. He closed the door, and she jacked a thumb over a shoulder. "What was that about?"

"Don't you worry about it."

His saying that had the opposite effect. It also didn't help that Malone's cheeks were flushed, and he wasn't looking her in the eye.

"What's up?" He leaned back in his chair, clasping his hands over his lap.

"We just wanted to bring you up to speed on the case." Amanda sat down in one of the chairs facing his desk, and Trent leaned against one of the filing cabinets in the room.

"You want to join the conversation, Stenson?" Malone waved for him to sit next to Amanda.

"Yes, Boss." Trent did as he'd been told.

"Lay it out. Let's go." His gaze dipped briefly to the papers in Amanda's hand.

"We're still waiting to firm up Navarro's alibi," she said. "I left a message for his girlfriend, lover, whatever she is to him, and haven't heard back yet."

"All right. He gets comfy for the night in holding. What else?"

"We just returned from Manassas. Cause of death wasn't what we'd expected," she said.

He leaned across his desk and angled his head to the left. "It had nothing to do with the knife in her chest?"

"Nope. Blunt-force trauma." She told him about the missing coffee table and rug, realizing she'd skipped over that with her last briefing. "Other than minor differences, the murder scene presented much like the ones in Felicity Kelley's novel, *The Romeo Killer*."

"Still thinking the ex is responsible?"

"He has things stacked against him. Whether they hold up, we'll have to wait and see. It comes down to his alibi." Amanda wasn't close-minded when it came to Navarro; there were other avenues to explore. Like Sheldon Lowe, obsessed fan. "One thing hanging over us is that all of Felicity's manuscripts and research were likely burned in her fireplace. It feels like there's more to that than simply recreating a scene from a book. Either way, Trent and I have talked about seeing if she backed up to a drive or cloud storage."

"You tell me that you think Kelley's murder was an isolated

incident, and you peg her ex-boyfriend. What reason would he have to destroy her books?"

"Hurt her where it would cause the most pain," Trent said.

"Kill her and figuratively destroy her legacy." She wondered if they'd get a satisfying answer for why her work was destroyed.

"Reach out to her internet provider about any cloud storage. Get it done."

"We will. And speaking of paperwork..." Amanda lifted the confidentiality form she had in hand.

"I was wondering what that was."

"The publisher at Garrison & Marrow requires us to sign a confidentiality agreement before they will enlighten us about Felicity's latest project."

"Let me see it." Malone reached out, wriggling his fingers.

She handed the printout over, and he scanned the two-page document.

He looked up, raising his brows. "You read this yet?"

"I glanced at it just before coming in here," Trent said.

Malone looked at her. "You?"

"Haven't done that. Yet. But I trust Trent."

"You should trust your partner and, honestly, I don't see anything too alarming about it aside from the fact I don't like it."

"Why is that?"

Malone handed the pages back. "By signing it, you're making a personal commitment to keep it quiet from the press. If this project somehow ends up factoring into the investigation, do you really think you can control the media?"

Amanda glanced at Trent, who was frowning. The last thing she wanted was a lawsuit. "What do you suggest?"

"I think there should be a clause added that would protect you. Some fancy wording that essentially excuses you if anything winds up in the news."

Amanda slumped back in her chair and chewed on Malone's words of caution. Would it be taking unnecessary personal risk by signing the document as it stood? But who knew how long it would take lawyers to land on acceptable lingo? Maybe they'd just put a hold on signing—for now. After all, Luis Navarro could very well be the killer and it would be case closed.

"I see you're thinking it over. Continue to, and let me know. I have no problem shooting this up the chain of command and getting department lawyers involved. I suggest you sleep on it. See how things pan out with Navarro."

Amanda looked at Trent, who was nodding.

"I agree with the sarge," he told her.

"We'll decide in the morning." Amanda led the way from the room. With the investigation at a natural pause, it was the perfect time to take a break and she planned to make the most of it. Still, there was the gnawing in her gut. There was always the chance they were wrong about everything, and there was a serial killer out there stalking his next victim.

TWENTY-FOUR

Last night had been awesome. Amanda had gotten home by six thirty. Based on Logan's and Zoe's smiles and laughter, they'd both had fun on their day's adventures. It had her wishing that she could have been with them. Even with the dawn of a new day, regret at missing out burned in her heart.

She snuck out before either of them woke up, letting them sleep off yesterday. Her first stop was a gift to herself—Hannah's Diner for an extra-large coffee.

The parking lot was mostly full and, inside, she had to get in line. Highly unusual. In fact, this was a first. She stepped out to see around a large man in front of her and saw May Byrd, who owned the place, and her niece, Katherine Graves, bustling behind the counter.

Katherine caught her eye, smiled, and waved at her as she set down a to-go cup on the counter.

One served, a million to go... Amanda was anxious to get into the station and start working. She returned Katherine's smile, struck by how much things had changed.

She and Katherine hadn't exactly gelled when she'd been interim sergeant for Homicide during Malone's recovery from surgery. Their different approaches to cases had them blending about as well as water and oil.

Since she had a few minutes ahead of her, Amanda pulled out her phone and checked her messages and emails. Logan had told her he'd read somewhere that checking one's phone before getting out of bed or just after could affect the flow for the entire day. Not that she was sure she bought into it, but she gave the concept a try and it seemed to have merit. By this point, she was wide awake. Her mind had her up hours before she'd even got out of bed. Add to that, she'd had a coffee before leaving home.

She still hadn't heard a peep from Courtney, which left Luis Navarro in limbo—or more precisely, in holding. Meanwhile, the case was also redirected. Instead of trying to cull out suspects, she and Trent would work to build the case against him. The fact Courtney hadn't returned her call may be a message in itself.

There were no text messages, but she had an email from Briggs confirming receipt of her email. He told her he'd track down the IP addresses and likely be able to have an answer next shift, which would mean tonight.

"Amanda?" Katherine was calling her name and waving madly for her to approach the counter. She'd been so absorbed in her phone that she hadn't noticed the customers ahead of her had been served and left.

She looked over her shoulder. The line still went to the door, and she was holding it up. "Sorry," she offered a blanket apology, to which no one responded, and prattled off her order to Katherine. "Two extra-large black coffees to go." She'd get one for Trent. Somewhere along the line it had become a bit of a habit. He'd pick up for her too some days.

"Hard at work, I assume." Katherine smiled at her before turning to fulfill the order.

"That girl's always hard at work," May piped up and flashed Amanda a huge grin that had the skin crinkling around her eyes.

"Looks like business is booming," Amanda said to May.

"That's due to this girl." May nudged her head toward Katherine. "She got the diner a website and invested in some online advertising."

"Impressive." It certainly wasn't something May would have done in a million years. Amanda didn't even think May advertised —beyond fostering loyal customers who got the word around.

Katherine returned and set the cups on the counter, and Amanda handed over payment. "It was nothing, Aunt May." Katherine touched May's shoulder—a brief connection but even Amanda could feel the transfer of affection there. But she was also privy to their background story. For most of Katherine's life, May hadn't been a part of it because she and her sister—Katherine's mother—were estranged.

"Well, I don't want to hold you up." Amanda collected the coffees, wished them a good day, and got on the road to Central.

She found Trent at his desk, his head bent over Felicity's phone.

"Good morning," she said as she came up beside him and set down the coffee that she'd brought for him.

He looked from it to her. "You spoil me."

"I try." *Why did I say that?*

"Thank you." He dipped his head and set Felicity's phone down and picked up the coffee cup. Cradling it in both hands, he took some eager sips.

"Don't mention it. Rough night?"

"A bit."

"Want to talk about it?"

"Not really."

All right then... "Anything exciting there?"

"Yes, actually. Not in the way you might be thinking. There

still hasn't been any hateful things posted to her social media or messaged to her privately, but Garrison & Marrow made an announcement this morning."

She glanced at the clock on the wall. It was just eight thirty. "They woke up early."

"Honestly I was surprised something didn't hit yesterday."

"Garrison & Marrow likely brought lawyers in to come up with the best way of wording it. After all, a company making their money from the written word wouldn't want such an announcement done without grace."

"True enough."

"What surprises me is how early in the day it was issued, though I suppose their audience is global."

"The news has certainly gotten out though. There are thousands of condolences on her social feeds and on the one belonging to G & M. She meant a lot to many people."

"I have no doubt. I say we continue to monitor them and her social media." Her phone ringing stopped her there, and the caller identity showed *C. Buikema*. She answered, "Detective Steele."

"Hey, ah, this is Courtney. You left a message for me."

Amanda stood taller. "Yes, thank you for calling me back."

"This is the first chance I've had."

Slightly defensive, but Amanda let it go. "Courtney Buikema, is that right?" She wanted to confirm for the record.

"That's me." Two words spoken with the burden of hesitancy.

"Luis Navarro mentioned you are a friend of his. Is that right?"

"Yes."

"Were you with him this past Tuesday night?"

"Uh, yeah, but he left for home about midnight."

Which would have left Kaitlyn hanging around Luis's

empty apartment, also proving her a liar. "What time did you start hanging out?"

"About six that night."

"Are you willing to sign a statement to that effect?"

"Sure, no problem. Where would I do that?"

She told Courtney to go to the front desk at Central and give them her name. Amanda would leave an envelope there for her with paperwork to sign. "When should we expect you?"

"I can be there in fifteen minutes."

Won't Luis Navarro be a happy man... "Thank you."

Courtney hung up without a goodbye, but it was the conversation that shook Amanda's world. She made eye contact with Trent. "We'll need to cut Navarro loose."

"That was Courtney What's-Her-Name, I take it?" He smirked.

"Courtney *Buikema*, as it turns out, and she's alibied him."

"And we believe her?"

"She's willing to put statement to paper, and it's not like Navarro was free to contact her and tell her to lie."

"Very true. Back to ground zero."

"Not exactly. We have Sheldon Lowe to look into. How about you pull his background while I type out Courtney's statement for her to sign?"

"Do you want me to pull one on Kristopher Black too? For all we know his relationship with Felicity turned sour."

"I didn't get that feeling from him, but a look at his background wouldn't hurt."

"All right, consider them both done."

She drafted the statement and handed it over to the officer at the front desk. When she returned, Trent flagged her over.

"Not a smudge on Black. Not one on Lowe either."

"Except for what we've been told about his behavior in following Felicity to all her signings."

"Exactly. The lowdown on Lowe... He's forty-two and lives

in a house in Dumfries—that we knew from Felicity's agent. From what I could tell he holds the mortgage and doesn't rent. He lives alone."

The vague picture potentially painted someone with an isolated existence with time on his hands. "Employment?"

"It's Criminal."

"What?"

"A bookstore called It's Criminal."

She didn't remember seeing any by that name in Prince William County, but she couldn't profess to know the local hotspots for buying books. She'd picked up hers at the grocery store. "Where is that located?"

"Woodbridge."

"Did they open recently or...?"

"Don't know. I take it you haven't heard of them either?"

"Nope, but I'm not exactly a bookworm."

"I did check with the database for the Department of Motor Vehicles, and he has a current-year BMW X5 registered to him."

"Makes sense the guy has money to burn. He did follow Felicity all over the country for her book tours."

"You're surely not knocking the Beemer though?"

"Wouldn't dare." Though, she'd never been one for the flashy show of material success, and BMWs certainly qualified. "Let's go have a talk with Lowe."

TWENTY-FIVE

Before leaving Central, Amanda and Trent signed the confidentiality agreements as they were and sent them back to Ian Moss. They'd run this move past Malone, who okayed it, even if he wasn't entirely thrilled by the idea. She had convinced him that it was one way of possibly getting ahead of the game if things didn't pan out with Sheldon Lowe.

The bookstore's website noted it opened at nine, so they headed there instead of Sheldon Lowe's home. The one thing she noticed immediately was the home page had a slider advertising signed copies of Felicity's *The Romeo Killer*.

It wasn't too hard to guess how he came into possession of them, since he had followed Felicity around to all her signings. She turned to Trent before getting out of the car. "I'd like to ask this guy where he got his signed copies to sell. Kristopher said he remembered Sheldon's name because he'd watched Felicity sign it enough times. He wouldn't have the books personalized if he wanted to sell them."

"What are you thinking, then? Felicity would sign some and ship here, or drop by the store?"

"Possibly." If that was the case, she hadn't feared Sheldon. But would she let him in if he showed up at her door?

Trent parked in a spot in front of the store. Its Criminal was in a narrow storefront, along the main street in Woodbridge, wedged between an appliance store and a laundromat.

The bookstore was painted bright teal, and a large window with black trim showcased a variety of books atop blue silk. Hardcovers of *The Romeo Killer* were stacked amid twinkle lights, with one copy sitting in a brass holder on an actual pedestal.

Trent got the door for them, and a bell chimed overhead. Smack dab in front of them was a grandiose display of Felicity's bestseller that put the window display to shame. There must have been a hundred hardcovers. It was hard to believe a small store like this would move that many copies—bestselling book, regardless.

A woman in her sixties was reading the back of a romance novel, and a man was browsing the cookbooks.

"Good day." A man was walking toward Amanda and Trent, smiling broadly. The expression struck as genuine. He was wearing black-frame glasses, and the overhead lights cut a glare across the lenses.

"Mr. Lowe?" Trent likely recognized him from the licensing database when he found out about the BMW registration.

"That's me." The smile disappeared, and he crossed his arms, narrowed his eyes. "You are?" He glanced at Amanda, back to Trent.

They both held up their badges, and Sheldon let out an audible sigh.

"I'm sorry, but if you're not here to, at least, browse, I will have to ask you to leave."

Amanda took a step toward him. "Unfortunately, it doesn't work that way. Detective Steele, and this is Detective Stenson. We have questions about your relationship with Felicity

Kelley." She considered *relationship* a diplomatic way of phrasing it even if it was stretching things.

He unfolded his arms, started to tuck his hands into his pant pockets, but stopped mid-motion. A flicker shot across his eyes, and then he bolted for the front door. He pushed Amanda in his haste to get away, and she collided with the Felicity Kelley display and crumpled to the floor.

"You all right?" Trent offered to help her to her feet, but she waved his hand away.

"Just get Lowe." She struggled to get to her feet. Getting jabbed in the ribs by the corners of hardcovers wasn't exactly a pleasant experience. *Ouch!* She rubbed her sides as she left the store.

The bell that had added an ambiance of charm before now grated.

She stepped outside and looked left and right. No sign of Trent or Sheldon. No footsteps or voices to alert her which direction they were in either. Nothing until a BMW sped by with Trent running along behind it, yelling.

"That's Lowe! He's getting away!"

"He won't get far." She pivoted for the department car and held out her hands for Trent to toss her the keys. They got in, she flipped on the lights, and pulled out in pursuit of Lowe. "Call it in, Trent."

She'd push the gas harder, but there was only so much she could do for the safety of everyone around. The fact they were on his tail might motivate Lowe to turn himself in, though it probably wasn't going to work out like that. For a scared rabbit already on the move, it was usually all about flight.

Trent gripped the dash as she took a sharp right, having spotted that Lowe's Beemer had turned down that street. Closer now, she saw him looking in the rearview mirror. There was no question, he knew they were following.

Lowe sped up more, and Amanda barely taxed the engine

of the department car. He sped through an orange light, and she breezed through the red, getting honked at by another person for her trouble.

Amanda overheard Trent talking on his phone in the passenger seat, notifying Dispatch they were pursuing a murder suspect. He gave their location, make, and model of Lowe's vehicle, his license, his name, and advised he was unarmed as far as they knew.

Sirens started around them as PWCPD cruisers joined the pursuit.

"Can't say I had a high-speed chase through Woodbridge pegged for today." Trent palmed his phone.

"Neither did I, but we go where the day takes us." She torqued the wheel, swerving to avoid a car inching into a left-hand turn.

That was close!

Her heart was pumping with adrenaline. "He's guilty of something."

"Yeah, killing Felicity Kelley."

That may very likely be the case. Otherwise, why run at the mere mention of her name? He certainly wasn't letting up on the gas, and he was headed toward the highway.

Trent's phone rang, and he answered on speaker. It was an officer sharing the same observation she had just made and confirming they were calling state police to lay out a spike strip.

This is getting real!

Lowe merged onto the highway with Amanda and two cruisers following. They traveled for about ten minutes when another call to Trent's phone confirmed the location of the strip. It was an additional ten minutes down the highway from their current position. The state police certainly didn't waste any time.

They'd have Lowe if he didn't take the next exit ramp. She breathed easier when he breezed past it.

As they neared the strip, state police cruisers were at the side of the road.

The rear brake lights on Lowe's BMW lit. He came to a complete stop before damaging his tires.

Smart choice, as they would cost a mint to replace. But concern over his vehicle would be the least of his problems.

Amanda parked their car and got out with Trent to apprehend Lowe. He was inside his vehicle, and without knowing for certain he was unarmed, they couldn't take any chances. They approached with guns raised.

"Mr. Lowe, put your hands on the wheel!" she yelled at him.

Lowe complied, and Trent opened the driver's door.

"Keep your hands where we can see them," Amanda said. "And get out of the vehicle."

Lowe did as directed, and Trent patted him down to make sure he wasn't concealing a weapon. Once he gave the all-clear, PWCPD officers cuffed him and loaded him into a cruiser.

Trent tapped the trunk as they left, knowing he and Amanda would soon catch up with Lowe at Central.

One state police officer worked on lifting the spike strip, while two others came over to Amanda and Trent.

"Thanks for your help, guys," she told them.

"Don't mention it. Glad we were able to help," one of them said.

"We'll call for a tow truck to pick that up too," the second officer added, with a nudge of his head toward Lowe's BMW.

"Great." Lowe wouldn't be happy about it, but too bad. He was the one who decided to run.

She and Trent cleared out. This time, Trent was behind the wheel.

"Lowe has a lot of explaining to do," she said, stating the obvious. Her entire body was still quaking from the flush of adrenaline.

"There's an understatement."

Amanda had Sheldon Lowe set up in Interview Room Three. She even saw to it that he had a bottle of water—whatever it took to set the man at ease. She even offered him something from the vending machine, but he'd turned it down.

While he sat in there, she and Trent watched in silence through the two-way mirror from the neighboring observation room. If Trent was like her, he was contemplating how things could have turned out much differently. Thankfully, no one had been hurt.

Malone slipped inside the room. "Luis Navarro's been released, but you're already looking at someone else. Talk about line 'em up, rack 'em up. I also heard you two had a bit of an adventure."

"And the day's still young," Trent muttered.

"Happy that it all ended well." Malone flicked a finger toward the glass. "That the man responsible for the high-speed chase?"

"That he is. Name's Sheldon Lowe, and he's now our prime suspect in the murder of Felicity Kelley," Amanda said.

"Fill me in..."

Amanda told Malone how Sheldon had come to their attention.

"He ran at the mere mention of her name? Guy sounds unhinged for sure." Malone rubbed his beard. "Good call bringing him in."

"He didn't leave us any choice after he took off like he did," Amanda countered.

"True enough."

"We're going in now, but feel free to watch." Amanda brushed past Malone, and Trent followed.

Amanda cracked the door to the interrogation room, and Sheldon called out, "I need to get back to my bookshop."

"That's not going to happen, Mr. Lowe," Amanda said coolly, as she dropped into a chair across from him. Trent sat next to her.

"I'll be robbed blind." Sheldon groaned while sweeping his hands nervously through his hair, the chain on the cuffs he still wore dangling.

She was short on empathy for the man who could have gotten them killed. At the same time, her job was to serve and protect the people of Prince William County. She couldn't exactly stand back while one of its citizens was robbed. "No one else is working there right now?"

"No. Please, just let me call Cynthia. She'll take care of things. Please."

"Who is Cynthia?" she asked.

"She works for me at the store."

"We can call her. She in your contacts?" Amanda held up his phone, which they had confiscated when they brought him in.

"Yeah, she's in there." Sheldon gave her a passcode to unlock the phone, and Amanda selected Cynthia's name.

Soon after, the line was answered by a woman with a young-sounding voice. Amanda put the call on speaker.

"Ma'am, this is Detective Steele with the Prince William County PD. Are you Cynthia—" She looked at Sheldon for the last name.

"Barkley."

"Sheldon? Is that you?"

"It is. Please just get to the bookstore ASAP," he said.

"Where are you?" A good mix of concern and curiosity marked her voice.

"Mr. Lowe is helping us with a case right now, Ms.

Barkley," Amanda said. "But if you could get to the store, as he asked."

"Ah, sure. But, Shelly, when will you be back?"

"Just lock it up for now," Sheldon told her.

"Okay," Cynthia dragged out.

Amanda ended the call. "Now that's out of the way, Mr. Lowe, let's have a real talk."

TWENTY-SIX

Amanda opened a folder that she'd brought in with her and took out a promotional photograph of Felicity Kelley.

Sheldon leaned forward, his eyes dancing over the glossy image. The glimmer of a smile touched his lips. But as if just becoming aware that she and Trent were watching him closely, he pushed up his glasses and sat back again.

"She's beautiful, isn't she?" Amanda decided she'd play this interview a little differently than most. Instead of leaping right to their suspicion, she wanted to lay the groundwork for their interest in him. For that, she intended to prove his infatuation with the author. She was sure his obsession extended beyond showing up at all her book signings. Given the way his pupils dilated upon seeing Felicity's face, she concluded Sheldon Lowe had romantic feelings for Felicity Kelley. Dangerous and volatile territory, especially when one builds up a nonexistent relationship in their head. "Mr. Lowe? She's beautiful?" she prompted when he hadn't responded.

"Yeah, she... *she* is." He seemed to be having a hard time tearing his gaze from the photo. Eventually, he did, but his eye contact wasn't steady.

He was clearly hiding something, and she was determined to find out if it was Felicity's murder. "Why did you run?"

"I'd rather not say." Sheldon bit his bottom lip.

She could approach his reluctance one of two ways: head-on or circle back. The former could cause him to request a lawyer, while the latter might allow them to learn a lot more. "I noticed you sell her books in your store," she said, choosing option two.

"If you want to talk about Flick, can you at least remove these?" He wriggled his hands, and the cuffs jangled.

It was rather unsettling that he referred to Felicity by her nickname, but Amanda considered the request. Sheldon struck her as bookish, but the fact remained they deemed him a strong suspect in a murder case. "I'm sorry, but we can't do that."

Sheldon pursed his lips and let out a ragged breath, but then spoke. "Of course I sell her books, I'd be stupid not to. Felicity Kelley is an A-list author. *The Romeo Killer* will be a box-office hit."

"It sounds like you're a huge fan of her work." She tagged on a smile.

"You could say that."

His response was dry and reserved. Was he guarding himself because he was guilty of her murder? "What is your favorite book?" She refused to ask outright if it was *The Romeo Killer* for the reason of building the case against him on firm footing. If it came down to prosecuting Sheldon Lowe, she didn't want some defense attorney claiming she'd led his statement.

"It's hard to choose just one." His shoulders relaxed, no longer hunched forward, they lifted higher. "Which would you pick?"

"*The Romeo Killer* hands down." She turned to Trent. "My partner's a fan too."

Sheldon grinned. "Your favorite?"

"I'd have to say the same," Trent said.

"It is the one with all the buzz, but even her early stuff was good."

"What did you like about *The Romeo Killer?*" She was curious how his answer might tie back to Felicity's murder.

"All of it, I guess. Completely believable."

Amanda nodded, while a churning in her gut alerted her to the implication of his blasé answer. It was avoidance but also possible admission. *Believable?* Was that relatability why he'd copied Felicity's work? She cleared her throat. "Have you been a fan of hers from the beginning?"

"Pretty much. She's local too, as you would know."

"That's right. She lives in..." Amanda let that hang out there like she had no idea. It was honestly incredibly noteworthy they had talked this long without him bringing up Felicity's murder.

"Triangle," Sheldon volunteered.

"Oh, you know that? You really are a fan." Good Cop was on notice but was needed just a little longer.

"I follow her to all her signings—some books I get for myself, others for the store. It's Criminal has carried her titles from the start. She even signs copies in-store or drops them off for me to sell. Quite sure she did this because she likes me."

Kristopher Black hadn't mentioned this, but he might not be aware of the arrangement. Even if he was, he might not have seen a point in sharing it. But if Felicity had gone out of her way to sign books for the store, it would have been professionally motivated not indicative of personal feelings for Sheldon Lowe. And it also made it unlikely she had feared Sheldon—as Amanda thought before—meaning she may have let him into her home. There were more facts working against him too. His seeming obsession was just one. "Then you were close? That's why you feel comfortable calling her Flick?"

"She told me to."

"You helped make her who she was then." She tossed out

the sentiment, building on one of his earlier statements, tagging on a smile in an effort to lure his pride.

"I don't know about that. Maybe I helped."

Modest rejection, but it struck Amanda as shallow. And if anyone was helping anyone, it was the other way around. Kristopher Black had told them Sheldon sought advice from Felicity on his own book idea. "You said she lived in Triangle?"

"Yes. In a nice, historical two-stor—" He stopped talking and snapped his mouth shut.

Amanda tensed. "By all means, continue."

"No, I don't think I will."

"Huh. See, her home—that 'nice, historical two-story'—is right where we found her body." She took a photo of Felicity's face, as taken at the crime scene, out of the folder and slapped it onto the table. Good Cop was gone.

"No!" Sheldon cried out, and tears pooled in his eyes but didn't fall.

"How does it make you feel seeing her like that?" Amanda resisted the urge to say, *faced with your own work*. There was a reason Sheldon ran, and it was obviously dark enough he hadn't wanted to tell them why.

"Heartbroken... devastated." He rubbed his cheeks with the back of one hand, while the other continued to hold the image of Felicity's lifeless face.

Amanda wasn't buying his bereavement act. If the picture was so upsetting, why did he keep hold of it? An innocent person wouldn't look a second longer than necessary. She'd had suspects flip pictures of victims over and push them back across the table to her. "Is there something else you want to get off your chest, Mr. Lowe?"

"About?" His voice was hesitant.

"Her death. Is it why you ran from us when we wanted to talk to you about Felicity Kelley?" She purposely didn't say *murder*, not wanting to spook him into silence. To catch this gopher, she had to employ a tactful strategy.

He lowered the photograph but continued to stare at it.

She snapped her fingers, and he flinched and dropped the picture. "Did you hurt her, Mr. Lowe? Even by accident? You didn't mean to do it..." It took all her acting ability and patience to pull this off. There certainly had been nothing accidental about Felicity's murder scene. It had clearly been premeditated.

"No, no, I'd never harm a hair on her head." He ran his hand over the photo as if caressing Felicity's face. "Who did this to her?"

"We were hoping you could tell us." She let that statement sit, expecting he'd get the implication that she and Trent deemed him responsible.

Sheldon remained silent and shook his head repeatedly.

He was clearly uncomfortable, but she had to figure out if it was for the reason they suspected. "What were you doing this past Tuesday between five thirty PM and midnight?"

"I was..." He swallowed roughly, his Adam's apple temporarily bulging.

"It's all right, you can talk to us," Trent prompted, stepping in and taking position as Good Cop. "Just tell us whatever you can remember."

Sheldon traced a finger around the photo where it sat on the table. His gaze was set on the image. "I was watching her."

Goosebumps sprouted down Amanda's arms. He knew where she lived, as he'd confessed just moments ago. Had he watched her house and then killed her? "From where?" she asked, calmly, levelly, impressed by her ability to remain cool, given the circumstances.

"I should probably get a lawyer."

"No need for that," Amanda said. "We're just talking." *Let him think that anyway...* Though the cuffs and their conversation should have made the reason for their interest in him abundantly clear. Their chief concern wasn't the fact he led a car chase through the streets of Woodbridge onto the highway.

"It won't look good for me... What I have to say next." He sniffled and rubbed a finger under his nose.

"As my partner said, you can talk to us." Amanda's tolerance for this man was quickly waning. He was twitchy and certainly looked guilty enough. And if Sheldon Lowe did kill Felicity, she wanted to lock him up as soon as possible. He didn't deserve another second as a free man.

"Sometimes, I sneak into her backyard." He spoke quietly, almost in a near whisper as if it made his stalking less creepy.

She stuffed down her discomfort, focused on the job. Whatever was necessary to get this guy to talk. "What would you do there?"

"I'd watch her through the patio door or her kitchen window. You probably won't understand."

"Try us," Trent tossed out nonchalantly.

"She was amazing. Beautiful. Talented. But she never saw it. She was so down-to-earth." His eyes flicked to meet Amanda's. "I swear I never hurt her."

"All right, and that's where you were Tuesday night? In Felicity Kelley's backyard, looking through her windows?" Amanda asked.

"For a bit, yeah."

Now that Sheldon had gotten past the initial admission, he seemed to have gotten over his fear of speaking freely. *Good for us...* "For how long and when exactly?" she asked.

"I hung around from eight until ten thirty, but I didn't see anything. Her curtains were closed."

"And they usually aren't?" Amanda asked.

"No."

If Sheldon was telling the truth, then he was unlikely Felicity's killer. At the early end of the TOD window, that only left half an hour to burn all her books and set the scene. But, again, that was hinging everything on the word of a stalker. She wasn't in the mood to extend him a pass. As for the curtains, they could ask the CSIs about the ones in the back of the house. If Sheldon wasn't the killer, the man who was may have closed them at some point in the evening. Felicity could have too, for that matter, even if out of character. But the drapes in the front living room window were open. "Here's the thing, Mr. Lowe, what you're telling us doesn't completely rule you out for her murder."

Sheldon paled. "I swear, I didn't hurt her!"

"As you keep telling us," Amanda said. "Did you love her, Mr. Lowe?"

He remained quiet.

"Mr. Lowe," she prompted.

"Yeah, sure, but it's not what you think."

"And what's that?" she volleyed back.

"That she rejected me and I got revenge."

"Did she did reject you?" Amanda latched right on to that aspect of his statement.

"I asked her out *once*, she turned me down, and that was that."

"That must have hurt." Amanda's intention was to hook an emotional reaction. Sheldon gave her nothing.

"It just was."

His response left her questioning if he really was laid-back about her rejection, especially considering how much support he gave her. "It doesn't sound like she valued you."

"Most people misunderstand me. Been an issue all my life." He pushed his glasses up his nose again.

"Did Felicity find fault with your big book idea?" It had to be asked.

He met her eyes. "No, she was very encouraging."

Given his steadfast eye contact, Amanda believed him on this point. She circled back to his earlier comment. "Why did you leave at ten thirty?" Effective interrogation often involved a little back and forth, a whisper of trust then a withdrawal. It kept the suspect guessing where they stood and served to rattle some into confessing their crimes.

"I got a call from my mom. She needed me."

Trent leaned forward. "For what?"

"She was trying to get her new computer set up."

"Rather late at night to be doing that," she said, and it earned her a glare.

"I'm telling you the truth."

"Then you wouldn't mind showing us your phone so we can see this call," she countered.

"You still have my phone. Go ahead and check the call history, I have nothing to hide."

She took the phone from the table and headed straight to the call log. Scrolling back to Tuesday night, she saw an incoming call from *Mom* that lasted a minute. She put the phone back down. "All this tells me is your mother called you. Not that you left Felicity's property."

"Please. I swear..."

"I know. You wouldn't hurt her," Amanda parroted, pulling from his tired defense.

"Call my mom, and she'll confirm what I told you. Please."

Amanda wasn't so sure what his mother's word might do for him. Blood could be strong and defend in blind faith. "We'll speak with her."

"Just call her. Right now." Sheldon's face flushed.

"We'll get there, but we have more questions. You might be able to help us." She presented this as if she were coming around to his side. She really just intended to cover as many bases as she could with this initial interview.

"Whatever you need." Sheldon shifted up straighter in his seat, hope seeming to lighten his spirit.

"In the time you were at Felicity's house, did you see

anyone else lurking around?" She revisited his claim that he hadn't seen anything a moment ago. "Perhaps a different vehicle in her driveway?"

Sheldon pressed his lips and seemed to give the question serious thought. A few moments later, he was shaking his head. "Not that I recall. And I would; I have a sharp mind."

She doubted tendencies toward stalking and obsession were an indication of strong mental health. "We're going to leave you for now, Mr. Lowe, while we look into what you've told us."

"What? No, let me go! I'm innocent here."

"You might be when it comes to Felicity Kelley's murder, but you are facing charges for evading arrest and street racing that endangered the lives of others."

"Oh, please. I just ran because—" He snapped his mouth shut.

"I think it's quite clear to us why you ran, Mr. Lowe," Amanda said. "If we have more questions for you, we'll bring you back in here."

Sheldon had dropped his face into his hands and was sobbing when she and Trent left the room.

"Hardened killer is a crybaby?" Trent said once in the hallway.

"Killers can experience strong remorse. I'm not putting anything past this guy, and neither should you."

TWENTY-SEVEN

A quick call to Sheldon Lowe's mother confirmed his statement. He had arrived at her house just after ten thirty and fallen asleep on her couch about two in the morning. Then again, that testimony was contingent on whether the mother's word could be trusted. A second call to CSI Blair confirmed the curtains in the back of Felicity's house were closed. Sheldon had told the truth about that. And a third call that she made to Celeste confirmed she knew Sheldon Lowe. She also said that Flick tolerated him and was nice to him because she felt sorry for him.

Trent made a call to Cynthia from the bookstore and confirmed that Felicity Kelley dropped off signed copies of her books and never acted strange or afraid of Sheldon Lowe.

Regardless, Amanda wasn't releasing Sheldon from suspicion that easily, and given that he was facing unrelated charges, it wasn't like she and Trent had to scurry to build their case. This had her mind returning to an avenue they'd started down but never explored.

She called Garrison & Marrow on speaker at her desk and asked for Ian Moss. She was given a slight runaround, but nothing that wasn't expected for a man of his position and importance within the publishing house. She drank some coffee while on hold and listened to sales pitches for several novels. That certainly made better use of a captive audience than meaningless music.

Then a soft click.

"Mr. Moss, speaking."

"Detectives Steele and Stenson here. Did you receive our signed forms? We sent them over this morning."

"One minute." He put her on hold and returned several seconds later. "I have them here. All appears to be in order."

"Excellent. What was Felicity Kelley working on?" she asked, wasting no more time.

Her question was met with silence, then, "I have several meetings today, and it would be best if you spoke with Melody Schmitt regarding this. I will let her know she can talk with you freely about the project and have you connected with her."

"Thank you."

"Just hold the line," he added, unnecessarily, just before the promotions started up again.

"Hello, this is Melody Schmitt." The editor prattled off her greeting almost robotically.

"Ms. Schmitt, it's Detectives Steele and Stenson. We spoke yesterday." *Even though it feels so much longer ago...*

"Of course."

Amanda didn't think she should need the reminder, considering the circumstances that necessitated their visit. "Mr. Moss told us you would be the best person to fill us in on the details of Felicity's latest project."

"She was working on a book she pitched about a murdered intern at a publishing house," Melody told them without hesitation. "As I believe I mentioned yesterday, she was due to turn it in two weeks ago. I now feel more comfortable telling you the reason she was delayed. She said she'd devised the perfect twist and wanted to do some rewrites before sharing the manuscript with me."

"What was this twist?" Trent asked, beating Amanda to it.

"No details, just that she changed who the killer was."

Amanda figured a publisher would prefer to be more hands-on in this regard. "You were okay with her holding back the details?"

"I trusted her. She's repeatedly proven herself a superb storyteller."

"Was it normal for her to change things up last minute?" Amanda imagined it would be unlikely, given that Felicity typically met her deadlines.

"Not really. Her first drafts usually closely modeled the original pitch."

"How detailed are the pitches?" Amanda asked.

"That depends on the author. For Felicity, the pitch itself was rather vague, more a concept. She fleshed it out just before she began writing and would send that over to me."

"Could you send us a copy of that?" If it was as they'd considered before and Felicity's inspiration from real life fueled her fiction, it might help. It could even strengthen their case against Sheldon Lowe in a way they didn't see yet.

"I would have to run that past Mr. Moss. As far as I know, I'm only cleared to verbally discuss the book, not provide written content."

Amanda figured that would likely be her response as she recalled a clause in the confidentiality agreement that allowed for a verbal accounting of the synopsis. But her mind returned to what Melody had said a moment ago. "Did Felicity tell you why she was changing the killer's identity?" Knowing what they did from the agent, that Felicity often played armchair detective and took inspiration from cold cases, had she gotten too close to a killer? And was that Sheldon Lowe?

"She thought it would make the book stronger. She sounded

very convinced of that fact and inspired. What she decided, my guess is we might never know."

"Without sending us anything in writing, will you recap the points of the plot, including who the killer was originally supposed to be?" Amanda asked and took a sip of her coffee.

"Ah, sure. Let me think a second here. I have so many story-lines running through my head. Actually, just give me a minute, and I'll pull up the document from the company server."

The clicking of keys traveled the line. Then there was silence during which time Amanda suspected Melody was reading.

"Here it is. In the original pitch, rough synopsis, I guess you could call it, the killer was the victim's ex-boyfriend."

"Motive?" Trent asked, again beating Amanda to the same question.

"He was jealous of her newfound success. The victim, the intern, was one of those people who possessed an attractive quality. Things came easily to her. Not so much with the boyfriend."

Amanda and Trent looked at each other. She couldn't be sure what he was thinking, but her mind slipped to Felicity's ex-boyfriend Luis Navarro. He was cleared of her murder, but Amanda wondered if Felicity took inspiration from her relation-ship with Luis and the situation of her rising fame. "When did she first pitch the book?"

"Two years ago."

Long before her relationship even started with Navarro...

Melody added, "Felicity wasn't a fast writer. She liked to edit as she went along, research some too."

"We heard she did a lot of that," Amanda admitted. "Do you know where she got the idea for the book? Even the original killer?"

"She didn't share that with me."

"Her agent told us Felicity often took her inspiration from

real life," Amanda began. "Do you know if she loosely based the plot for her latest project on a cold case?"

"I'm sorry, but I don't."

"That's fine." They could revisit Justine Livingston, tell her they had signed a confidentiality agreement, and see if she *suddenly* remembered Felicity's source of inspiration. That's if she hadn't told them the truth before when she said she didn't know. Regardless, Amanda had a feeling this was worth taking a closer look at—especially with Felicity's insistence to change the killer's identity just two weeks ago.

TWENTY-EIGHT

The call with Melody Schmitt had lasted shy of fifteen minutes, but it had topped up Amanda's determination. While Sheldon Lowe wasn't completely ruled out as a suspect, her mind was open to other possibilities. They owed it to the case—to Felicity —to follow through and get more information on the murdered intern book, starting with what had initially inspired Felicity. As a side note, Melody had searched Felicity's manuscripts for the random words found on the scraps of paper and didn't turn up anything for her trouble.

"Trent, why don't you follow up and see if Felicity had cloud storage? While you're doing that, I'm going to give Justine Livingston a call about this intern book. She might be able to tell us more than she originally let on knowing about."

"You got it." He left her cubicle, and she made the call.

The receptionist answered partway through the second ring. Amanda announced herself and was patched right through to Justine.

"Detective? Do you know any more?"

"We're still working on the case, but there's something you could probably help us with."

"Anything. You name it."

Her husky voice suggested she'd had a rough night though that was completely understandable considering a client had been murdered. "Garrison & Marrow shared some about Felicity's latest project with us, the one she was working on before she died." She paused there, but Justine inserted nothing. Amanda continued. "It was about a murdered intern at a publishing house." That should prove they were privy to details about the book. "You had told my partner and I that Felicity often based her books on real life. I'm going to ask you again, but do you know what case inspired her current project?"

"No. As I told you before, I don't. I really wish I could tell you, but Felicity kept that from me."

"She normally didn't?" Amanda pounced on something in the agent's voice, a hesitance, leeriness... Just something was *off*.

"Usually she was very forthcoming about such things."

"Any idea why that wasn't the case this time?"

"Honestly, no, I don't."

One guess might be the case struck close to home for Felicity. The most personal thing would have been her sister's murder, but it was solved and Eve hadn't been in publishing. And as far as Amanda knew no one else in Felicity's intimate world had been murdered. "All right, if anything occurs to you, please call."

"You have my word."

Amanda thanked her and ended the call. Trent was still in his cubicle and currently on the phone with a local internet provider. By the sound of it, he was caught in an automated purgatory.

Speaking of the internet... She brought up a browser window and searched *murdered publishing intern*. Twenty pages of results came back.

She added *Prince William County Washington DC* to the

search tab, hoping to narrow down the results. It reduced them to three pages.

Not ideal, but better.

She scanned the titles of the articles, dismissing any that struck out the words *intern* or *publishing*. She was still left with several and started reading. Most covered a fatal home invasion that had taken place fifteen years ago. To this day it remained unsolved.

The victim was Naomi Chapman, twenty-one, resident of Woodbridge. Shot three times to the chest.

Felicity had lived only fifteen minutes down the road in Triangle. Did she have a personal tie to Chapman, or was it more about an unsolved murder in the world of publishing that had caught her attention?

Sympathy poured through the articles, lamenting Chapman's age and that her future had been taken from her. She had just graduated from Harvard University and was on the fast track to advancement where she worked at a publishing house by the name of Between the Pages in Washington, DC. Apparently, the company had made an official announcement of Chapman's promotion from unpaid intern to commissioning editor on the day she was killed.

The timing sounded hinky, somehow convenient. Felicity's original pitch had the victim killed by her boyfriend, who was jealous of her success. But she'd decided to change that two weeks ago for an unknown reason. Was there any correlation between fiction and real life?

"Amanda?" It was Trent, and he was looking at her over the low partition.

"Ah... yeah?"

"You look deep in thought."

"I am, and you need to know why."

"All right. But me first. You look like you have a lengthy update."

"I think I do."

"I was able to confirm that Felicity had cloud storage. The internet provider has requested a warrant to release access."

"Which I would expect. You want to handle that?"

"Sure. After you tell me what you have." He got up and joined her.

She leaned back in her chair and indicated the article on her screen. "I have a strong feeling this murdered intern case may have inspired Felicity's latest project." She shared the highlights she'd gleaned, and when she was finished, Trent's mouth was gaped open.

"Sounds like you might have hit a bull's-eye. How far do you want to pursue this?"

"I think it's like we considered before. What if Felicity Kelley poked her nose into this case and got the attention of the killer in the process? Could still be Sheldon Lowe, might not be..."

"She really might have taken the whole armchair detective thing too far," he said.

"I have a bad feeling she did. You get the paperwork for the warrant, and I'll dig more into this case, starting with finding out who handled it fifteen years ago."

"Sure." He went back to his space.

Amanda looked up Naomi Chapman's name in the PWCPD system and swore at her discovery.

Trent popped his head up. "Do tell."

"The lead was Dennis Bishop."

"Huh. Well, his name was bound to surface again at some point." Trent returned to what he was doing.

At some point... She let out a puff of air. Dennis Bishop had left the PWCPD two years ago January—not by choice as much as the result of disciplinary action. He'd held back integral evidence in a murder investigation. When Amanda had uncovered that, she'd also found extenuating circumstances were at play. As a result, Dennis wasn't held legally accountable, nor did the PD see fit to withdraw his pension, but he had walked away from his badge.

She still felt the burden of exposing his wrongdoing. And to see him would be like taking a time warp to another lifetime. She had changed so much since then. When Dennis had known her, five and a half years had passed after losing her husband and daughter and she was all-consumed by grief. And even though she had done the right thing by reporting Dennis, her purpose and drive back then were almost nonexistent.

She opened another screen and searched for Dennis Bishop's information. She had no idea where he'd ended up after he left. For all she knew he could have moved to China.

His record came back and told her he was living in Lorton, Virginia. Lorton was a small town, a mere fifteen-minute drive from Woodbridge, with which she was very familiar. It was charming and idyllic and could be the backdrop for any Hallmark Christmas movie. Of all the places in the world, she wouldn't have seen Dennis Bishop making his home there. Though, he did have a sister. It could be where she lived.

There was nothing listed for Dennis's employment, and she wondered how he filled his days. The more she thought about speaking with him and seeing him, gunk from the past regurgitated. It had been around that time when she'd first uncovered an operating sex-trafficking ring in Prince William County.

But she might be able to avoid contacting Dennis. After all, his notes and evidence would be in storage. But they didn't account for one thing. If Felicity based her latest project on this case, she wouldn't have had access to all this. She would have gone directly to the source. In the least, Amanda needed to ask Dennis if he had spoken to Felicity Kelley. And, if so, what he may have told her.

She called the number on file for him, and the line rang several times. Just when she expected to land in voicemail,

Dennis answered. She recognized his voice. "Dennis, it's Amanda Steele."

Silence stretched out as if it were elastic.

"How are you doing these days?" As soon as the question was out, she regretted asking. She had wanted to set the stage for a friendly conversation. Instead, she'd prepped the launch pad for confrontation. Not that his leaving the PWCPD had been her fault, but if she hadn't exposed his past, he'd likely still be on the payroll.

"Just get to the point, Amanda. What do you want?"

And there's the hostility... But could she blame his sharp reaction? He'd seen through her veiled inquiry after his well-being. Too much time had passed for it to be genuine. "Very well. One of your past cases—"

Dennis groaned loudly. "Don't tell me that you're doing this again. My conscience is clear, Steele, so whatever it is, check with evidence lockup."

"Wait!" She imagined he had already pulled his phone back, preparing to hang up on her.

"What?"

"It's a case from fifteen years ago. A home robbery where a twenty-one-year-old woman was murdered."

"What about it?"

The quick turnaround in his attitude had her speechless for a moment. She had expected he'd repeat his directive to pull the evidence files and leave him out of it. "The victim was—"

"Naomi Chapman. Shot three times in the chest, and she was found by her maid the next morning. Ruled a fatal armed robbery."

The picture forming of Naomi Chapman was unfolding. She was a wealthy young adult, who lived alone in a house, had graduated from Harvard, and apparently had a maid. Money hadn't been an issue. "You remember all this after fifteen years?"

"Don't make anything of it."

It was hard not to. She wouldn't be able to provide all this about a past case on instant recall unless she'd recently re-familiarized herself with it. With Dennis, she'd have to watch how she played this—a frontal attack wouldn't be effective. "Have you heard of Felicity Kelley?"

"Yes. What about her?"

"She was murdered three days ago in her home."

"She was— *What?*" The question was hurled out several decibels louder than the rest of his words.

"It's been in the news."

"I do my best to avoid it."

"She was killed in her home. Cause of death was blunt-force trauma, not gunshot wounds. Nothing to indicate it was a robbery or home invasion either."

"I'm still stuck on what you said. She was murdered?" His reaction was one of shock, as if he were trying to make sense of her death. That typically happened when a person knew the deceased.

Tingles danced on Amanda's arms. "You knew her."

"I did. Felicity came around asking questions about the Chapman case. Though it was a long time ago... I'd say a year and a half ago even."

There was her confirmation. Felicity's inspiration had come from the Chapman case. The question remained, did her poking around lead to her murder? But there was a dark cloud over the revelation that Dennis had spoken with Felicity. If he hadn't, would she still be alive? "Let me get this straight, you briefed a civilian on a police investigation?"

"A cold case. And I didn't reveal sensitive information."

"Jeez, Cud." She snapped her mouth shut and closed her eyes.

"Not Cud, to you or anyone. I gave up chewing gum. The dentist told me it was cracking my back molars."

She didn't know whether to find the personal offering amusing or surprising. Honestly, it was a blend of both. But it told her his walls were coming down. He was probably feeling guilty. "What did you tell Felicity? What questions specifically did she ask?"

"We had a number of conversations."

"You had a number—" She clenched her jaw. Being judgmental wouldn't get her anywhere. And they needed to find out exactly what Felicity knew.

"I'm going to overlook your attitude and talk to you on two conditions."

"What?"

"One, the judgment stops."

"Fine." Hard to promise. Chalk it up to ethical reasons. "And the second?"

"Leave me out of this, Steele."

"How can you expect me to—"

"Nope. I've gone through enough grief, and I don't want any more trouble."

Amanda opened her mouth, and almost broke promise one by asking how he could expect her silence when he had violated the integrity of a police investigation—cold or otherwise? If she withheld this and it made it back to Malone, even as a family friend, there would be hell to pay.

"Steele? What's it going to be?"

"My lips are sealed."

"Good. Then I'll see you at my place in an hour? I assume you have the address?"

She read off the one showing in the database, and he confirmed that was right just before ending the call.

The conversation left her drained and angry. The nerve of Dennis, thinking he could call the shots in this, was maddening.

"Guessing that didn't go well." Trent crept around the opening of her cubicle.

"Someone's a genius."

"Well, the warrant paperwork's with a judge to review."

"There's some good news." She closed all the search windows and turned off her screen. Though if Malone was interested in watching her every move, he'd be able to see that she searched Dennis Bishop. If that were to happen, she technically never would have broken her promise to Dennis. It still wouldn't exempt her from Malone's wrath.

"Are we going somewhere?" Trent asked her.

"Yep. I'll fill you in once we're in the car." She got up and passed Fred Hudson. She mumbled a brief greeting, but he didn't bother to reply or even look at her or Trent. *What is his problem?*

Detective Hudson had never given her the impression of being warm and fuzzy, but a cold front had passed through. With it, Amanda got the feeling he might be why the police chief was in Malone's office the other day. If she was right, and he had expressed some grievance about being bumped from the case, shit could be about to hit the fan.

TWENTY-NINE

It was a short drive to Lorton, but Amanda still found time to think about what they might be in for with Dennis Bishop. Would he hold the past against her? And did it matter if he did? Any discomfort was worth suffering to find out what he had told Felicity about the Chapman case.

Trent parked in the double-wide driveway of a yellow brick two-story house. The place had seen an addition, but it matched closely to the original structure.

"Here goes nothing," she said, getting out of the car.

The front door was dark blue with shiny brass hardware. She rang the bell, and footsteps pounded toward the door.

It was flung open, and Dennis Bishop was standing there with a drooling toddler on a hip. Dennis appeared a bit frazzled, but somehow more relaxed than she'd ever known him to be when he was a detective. At first assessment, retirement from law enforcement looked good on him. He barely acknowledged her or Trent but stepped back to let them inside.

"Who is this little guy?" The child had the largest baby blues she'd ever seen, and he was watching her with avid curiosity.

"My nephew, Darren. He's my sister's kid." Dennis took the child to a playpen in the living room, off the entrance, and set him in it. "Could one of you grab the door?"

"Sure." Trent shut it and joined Amanda and Dennis.

"It's nice that you help her out." Amanda hadn't meant to be insulting, but Dennis's face scrunched in a mild scowl as if he took it that way.

"Yep, just a glorified babysitter. Not much else to do."

What could she say to that? He obviously held remnants of a grudge. She just hoped that it wouldn't affect his openness with her.

"Either of you want a coffee or water?" Dennis tossed a stuffed toy from a puffy chair into the playpen, barely missing his nephew's head.

"I'll take a coffee, if it's not too much trouble," Amanda said. "Just black."

"Not a surprise. And you?" Dennis turned to Trent, and he asked for one too. "I'll be right back." He left the room to see to that, and the second he had left his nephew's sight, Darren let out a wail.

Amanda sat there, conflicted, her internal motherly instincts wanting her to jump up and soothe the boy. The other part feared overstepping. But since when was she so concerned about how her actions would be taken?

Dennis didn't return to tend to Darren, and Amanda almost wondered if he'd made a run for it. She went to the playpen and ran her fingers along the bars, making a *thump, thump, thump* noise as she did so.

Darren stopped crying, his soaked lashes beaded with tears, and he looked at her hand as it moved. He then glanced up at her. His chin quivered like he was considering whether to let loose again. Amanda kept doing her thing. The kid's eyes twinkled, and his frown turned into a smile. Then a giggle.

Amanda relished it for a few beats. The sound of a child's laughter was something that nothing else could come close to touching. So light and innocent... *healing. And I can never have another baby...* The thought struck—unexpected and paralyzing. She was left gasping for air and put a hand on her stomach.

"I should have known when he quieted down..." Dennis was back with the coffee, and he extended a mug to her.

"Ah, thanks."

Dennis gave the other cup to Trent, dipped back into the kitchen, and returned with one for himself. He dropped into the chair that he'd cleared of the toy.

Amanda and Trent sat on a couch across from him.

There was a span of silence. Again, Amanda found herself very much in her head, thoughts of her infertility aside. What was the proper etiquette at seeing someone after this long? Someone whose fate you may have altered. She'd best focus on the bigger picture. She got comfortable and sipped some coffee, letting it calm her. Behold the ironic powers of a stimulant... "What did you tell Felicity Kelley about the Chapman case, Dennis?" she asked, getting right to the point of their visit.

He took his time drawing a few sips of his coffee, then set his mug down on a side table. "Nothing that she couldn't have found out from scouring the internet."

She doubted that, but calling Dennis out wouldn't serve their purpose. They needed him to talk freely. "Can you just tell us what you told her?"

"You said that she was murdered?" Regret and sadness were buried in his tone, but it wasn't touching his expression or body language.

"She was. In her own home," Amanda added.

Dennis let out a deep breath and raked a hand through his hair. His gaze was directed on his nephew, but his eyes were blanked over. "She was a smart kid. And talented."

"Did she tell you why she was interested in the Chapman case?" Trent asked, earning eye contact with Dennis.

"You must think you have part of that answer, considering you're here. Do you think her poking around got her killed?"

Amanda stiffened. He had known Felicity's intentions and how dangerous it was for a civilian to get involved with chasing a killer, yet he'd spoken with her. "Was she poking around?" Tossed out nonchalantly, sucking her reserve of diplomacy.

"Well, yeah. She was like a dog with a bone. She had all sorts of questions and even cornered me where I volunteer."

Thought you were just a glorified babysitter with nothing else to do... "Where is that these days?"

"Gunston Hall, twenty hours a week. My early retirement from the force honestly turned out to be a blessing."

Then why so much bitterness toward me? The thought struck, and she kicked it out.

"The free time allowed me to think about what I really enjoy," Dennis added. "I've always loved history, and so volunteering at Gunston Hall feels like the perfect fit."

Amanda was happy that he had found peace but was curious about something else. The articles she'd read about the Chapman home invasion never mentioned Bishop at all. "How did Felicity come to talk to you? How did she even find you?"

"She was a resourceful person. Too smart for her own good, possibly."

Amanda angled her head. "Come on, Dennis."

"Fine. She told me she had a contact within the PWCPD—didn't name them or say whether they were a man or woman. But they told her I had been the lead on the case."

Dennis told her on the phone that Felicity had come to him easily a year and a half ago, which would be about a month before Amanda had met her. Prior to Felicity asking Amanda if she could call with procedural questions. But whoever this cop was that had shared case information needed to face disciplinary action. Worse consequences if their loose lips had factored into Felicity's murder.

"You never pressed the matter? This cop not only violated sensitive information but also his or her oath by endangering a civilian," Trent said.

"I couldn't make her tell me."

"No, but you could have turned her away," Trent pushed back.

"Get off your high horses, or there's the door." He jabbed a pointed finger, and Amanda recalled her promise not to be judgmental. Guess Trent hadn't agreed to that.

"How did she find out you volunteered at Gunston Hall?" Amanda asked, redirecting.

"Through my sister's social media. I tell her to stay offline, but she's addicted to letting the world know her every move. You'd think being related to a cop, she'd have wizened up."

Once a cop, always a cop. She wasn't going to correct his tense and drank more of her coffee.

Dennis added, "My sister took my picture one shift and tagged the location. I told Felicity to go away, that it wasn't something I could discuss. But she was persistent, and it started to feel like if I just spoke with her, she'd leave me alone. That's the path I chose. Not that it worked. She returned a few times. Obviously, looking back, knowing what I know now, that was a short-sighted decision. But is there proof her murder is linked to the Chapman case?"

"It's just a lead we're following," Amanda stonewalled.

"Right, so I talk while you don't. As much as things change, they stay the same," Dennis said in a huff.

"Do you know why she was so driven to find out more about the Chapman case?" Trent leaned against the arm of the couch, propping up his elbow there.

"She told me that it involved the history of her publishing company."

Amanda thought back to the articles she'd read and didn't remember any mention of Garrison & Marrow. "I thought Chapman worked for Between the Pages."

"She did before Garrison & Marrow took them over."

Now, that didn't feel like a coincidence.

THIRTY

What Dennis had just told them was a revelation that certainly explained why Felicity Kelley had been so interested in the Chapman case. It touched close to home. "Garrison & Marrow bought Between the Pages?" Amanda asked.

"Uh-huh. Between the Pages was a small publishing house that offered small print runs for their authors. Their business tanked in 2011 when the e-book revolution began because they refused to evolve with the times. G & M took them over, acquiring their authors and staff." He rattled that off, devoid of emotion.

Amanda sat with that insight for a bit, unsure what to make of it. "Tell us a bit about the Chapman case. Did you have any reason to think it was anything but a home robbery that turned fatal?" She was grasping because it would seem something about the case held Felicity under its spell. But did it factor into her murder? A question that kept bouncing around in her head and might soon drive her crazy.

"You tell me. All of Chapman's jewelry was stolen. The parents held an insurance policy on a few pieces and the combined value was nearly three hundred K. There was also a string of home robberies at the time, and no one was ever caught. But before you ask, none of the other break-ins resulted in murder."

Darren was motorboating his lips while he swept a toy car through the air as if it were flying. Amanda wondered what adventure his young mind was taking him on. He was a happy and content little boy, that was for sure.

"Go on... So, Chapman was killed in her home," Trent prompted.

"Shot three times. She was found face up on her kitchen floor. The burglar came through the back door, which is off the dining room to the back of the kitchen. The window in the door was broken. That made it easy enough for the perp to reach in, twist the lock, let himself in."

Perp, short for perpetrator, and cop talk for bad guy or suspect. "*Him?* Are you sure it was a man?" Amanda asked.

"That was never in dispute. Shoe prints in the garden bed told us that much. Some led in the direction of the back door. Others that matched were found beneath another window in the back of the house, off a main-level office."

Amanda never read those things online, but she was stuck on one nugget. "What size were the prints?"

"Size ten, I believe. A very common size for a man. It wasn't exactly groundbreaking for the case."

She supposed he had a point, but was it a coincidence the ones left in Felicity's living room were the same size? "Did you share this with Felicity?"

"I might have told her some of this. But, please, I didn't think it would hurt anything."

Amanda clamped her mouth shut. *Except that now she's dead!*

Trent tapped the arm of his chair. "Did you consider stalkers or ex-boyfriends?"

Amanda nodded at her partner. She'd been wanting to ask

about top suspects in the case, but the conversation had taken a detour.

"No stalker, but we questioned the ex-boyfriend at length. He had a solid alibi, and it landed us nowhere. It really looked like it was connected to those other home robberies. The trail went cold."

It seemed apparent why Felicity had chosen the ex-boyfriend as the killer in her initial proposal. "I take it you told this much to Felicity... about the ex?"

"I did, not feeling it was too much of a secret."

Amanda could argue the point, but let it be. Dennis was talking. "Tell us more about Chapman's life." Her cheeks heated from suppressing her anger.

"She had everything going for her, a real daddy's girl, and hers just happened to have gobs of money. He spoiled her, bought her the house in Triangle, set her up with a Mercedes."

"And paid for her Harvard education," Amanda chimed in, recalling that fact from a news article.

"That's right. Chapman just received a promotion at Between the Pages the same day as her murder. Before coming home, she had celebrated with her fellow interns at a local bar."

"The name of the place?" Trent asked.

"It's all in the file, but Taps and Cocktails. They're in Woodbridge. Just a small place."

Amanda had been there before, but if she was going to pick a bar in Woodbridge, it would be the Tipsy Moose Ale House, hands down. It was also where she'd met Logan.

"Chapman left after everyone else, so it's a little unclear the exact time she got home," Dennis said. "Her time of death was pegged between midnight and two AM and was never narrowed down."

"You shared all this with Felicity?" This amount of detail wouldn't have made the news.

"I didn't see the harm. The case is how old, Amanda?"

She kept her mouth shut, resisting the urge to argue. They needed Dennis on their side. But just because the investigation dated back fifteen years, it didn't mean it was open season to spill all. Even more so because the case was technically still unresolved. The mystery cop who sent Felicity to Dennis was at fault, but Dennis should have turned her away. Amanda hoped like hell this case hadn't been what led to Felicity's murder.

"You should know that she didn't seem completely in the dark when she came to me," Dennis offered, as if reading Amanda's mind.

"You think this contact she had in the department told her a lot?"

"Yeah, I don't want to say much more, and I'm not about to push anyone under the bus." He drained the rest of his coffee and set his mug back on the table. "I really don't know what more I can tell you."

"You said Felicity was insistent," Amanda began. "Did you get the impression she doubted it was a home invasion?"

"She made no secret of the fact. That's why when you told me she was murdered, I honestly wondered if she did stick her nose in this too far. Did she attract the attention of Chapman's killer and set him on edge?"

"We are considering the same," Amanda admitted now. "And the more you tell us, the more I'd say it's quite possible. Did she happen to ask about a Sheldon Lowe, by chance?" It was a shot in the dark, but he was an avid fan who might have secrets to protect. It just may be that his past had transected with Naomi Chapman.

"Not that I remember, and I've never run across him. Who's this Lowe guy?"

"Someone who has our interest," she said, keeping it vague.

"Well, pretty much anyone could have killed Felicity Kelley. She was in the spotlight."

"Before we go," Trent started, "were there any aspects of the case she seemed especially fixed on?"

"She didn't like the timing, which I think I mentioned. That really bothered her. Promoted and murdered the same day. She also mentioned that she found out Chapman's front light came on the night of the invasion. Guess it was around midnight when that happened. I'm not saying it didn't happen, just that I don't remember that tidbit."

"Where did she find that out?" Amanda prickled, assuming it had something to do with the flapping jaws of the officer.

"From the next-door neighbor. A Shirley Morton. She lived there with her husband, who is deceased now, but she's still there."

"She spoke with the neighbor?" Amanda said.

"Guess so."

Just how actively was Felicity looking into the Chapman case? What had started off as a hunch was becoming a far more valuable lead than she could have imagined. It would seem that when Felicity set her mind to getting facts, nothing could stop her—unless something had. "Did she ever tell you who she suspected killed Chapman?"

"No, but I could see that she was becoming obsessed. I warned her to step back, go home, and leave playing detective to her books."

Too little, too late... It also hit a sore spot for Amanda. Her niece had recently poked her nose into a murder investigation, and it had almost gotten her killed. Dennis's assessment was that Felicity was obsessed; Felicity's friend, Celeste, had commented on how focused Felicity had been, more than usual. Was it simply because the cold case had distant ties to her publisher, Garrison & Marrow? Or was she honestly trying to solve a murder with the skill set of an armchair sleuth?

THIRTY-ONE

Amanda thanked Dennis for his cooperation to which he grunted. They'd never gelled, and that was more obvious than ever, but at least he had spoken with them.

The car was a humid, stagnant cesspool by the time they returned to it. Trent turned the vehicle on and got the air conditioning running. He lowered all the windows and looked over at her. "You said one of Bishop's conditions was we keep him out of it. How can we do that if Felicity's nosing around Chapman's murder factors into hers?"

"We'll deal with that if it comes down to it." Amanda hadn't heard enough to convince her Naomi Chapman had been intentionally targeted, murdered, and the invasion staged. Though currently, her knowledge of the case was limited. But there was the fact Felicity had shown excessive interest in the case and now she was dead. Was that merely a coincidence?

"You don't believe the Chapman case is connected in some way to Felicity Kelley's murder?"

"Not saying that. We just need to learn a lot more. I suggest we sign out the evidence from lockup, read the interviews and case notes, look at the crime scene photos, and go from there."

"Seems reasonable. We should also see if there's any link between Sheldon Lowe and the Chapman case." He shrugged. "Just while we're at it."

"Logical to me. There's something else weighing on my mind. If Felicity already had a contact in the police department, then why did she ask if I'd help with procedural questions? And why did she call me the day of her murder?" She suddenly linked the two questions. "Did Felicity find evidence that the cop killed Chapman? It would explain why Felicity called me and not nine-one-one. She trusted me. Or am I seeing killers everywhere now?"

"I think you're just trying to think through all the angles. Killer or not, we definitely need to find out who this cop is."

Fred Hudson immediately popped into her head. After all, he certainly wasn't too happy to hand over the Felicity Kelley investigation. Tag on the cold shoulder he was giving her and Trent, that only backed that up. He'd also made a huge deal about Amanda knowing Felicity as if her working the case would be a blatant conflict of interest. Was it because he was trying to take the attention off his own connection? She wasn't going to share her suspicions with Trent, but she said, "We can check Felicity's call history to see if we can ever put Felicity in touch with any officers working with the Prince William County PD."

"And short of that, considering it sounds like she had this contact some time ago, Felicity's agent might know this officer's identity."

"She could. As you mentioned, their contact dates prior to our meeting, before she sought out Dennis a year and a half ago. Felicity and this cop could have fallen out of touch. They could have retired or moved on..."

"That might help us narrow things down within the department."

"Only thing with that is we'll need to clear such an inquiry past Malone. We'd need to mention Dennis Bishop."

"So be it, Amanda."

She hated breaking her promises as much as she hated being in this position. But a person's word was paramount. That's what her parents taught her; it's what she tried to instill in Lindsey and now Zoe. "Just think of it this way, Dennis technically isn't an officer of the law anymore—and, yes, I realize that's a loophole. If the Chapman case does factor into Felicity's murder, that will stay on Dennis's conscience for the rest of his life."

"Little good that does Felicity."

"Agreed, but I'm not sure what can be done within the confines of the law. It's not like he's on the department's payroll." She balanced her words with her own internal judgment. Dennis should be held accountable. Same too for this mystery cop. "Dennis's possible role aside, I can understand Felicity's draw to write a story based on Chapman's murder. She was wealthy, had it all, and was taken down just as her life was really starting..."

"Laid out like that it does sound convenient... orchestrated. And Dennis mentioned that one of the things that hadn't settled with Felicity was the timing. How it came the same day as her promotion."

"Right, and then there's what she found out from the neighbor. The woman told Felicity she saw Chapman's front light come on that fateful night. I really don't think it's a lead that Dennis followed up on."

"It didn't sound like he even knew about it."

"Or he didn't remember."

"It sounds like it's time to get back to Central and work our way through the evidence."

"Soon enough, but I have another stop in mind first. I'd like to talk to this neighbor for myself."

"Before we read the files?"

"Why not?" She desperately wanted to get a feel, boots on the ground, whether it was worth their time to continue pursuing this avenue. Either this cold case factored into Felicity's murder or it didn't, but the sooner they figured out that answer the better.

Trent got the address from the onboard computer and got them on the road. He looked over at her. "You know what's eating me is Felicity had a killer in mind for her novel but then switched it up. Did she plan to expose the real killer's identity?"

Amanda hadn't considered Felicity would go that far, but had that been her intention? "I've got another question for you. If all this led to Felicity's murder, how did the killer find out about her sleuthing?"

Shirley Morton's house was the one on the east side of what had been Chapman's place—not that one could tell them apart. All the houses on the street looked alike. The development would have been new fifteen to twenty years ago, but it wasn't aging well.

The neighborhood was bustling with activity. Peals of children's laughter and talking rang through the air. Some bicycles lay abandoned on front lawns, while some kids pedaled fast down the sidewalk. A man was washing his car in his driveway.

Shirley's house was dark, and Amanda didn't think they'd find her at home until a shadow crossed the front window and proved her wrong.

Amanda rang the doorbell, after already knocking once. The chime was a standard *ding-dong*, and it had footsteps padding toward them. The door swung open.

The woman didn't look older than mid-sixties but had a head of gray hair and deep-green eyes. "Hello?"

"Shirley Morton?" Amanda asked, holding up her badge, as

did Trent beside her.

"I am."

"We're Detectives Steele and Stenson," Amanda said and tucked her badge away.

"About time I'm being taken seriously."

The woman's reaction took Amanda off guard. She angled her head. "About what, ma'am?"

"That poor young woman who was murdered." She pointed next door to what had been Chapman's house. "I assume that's why you're here. Can't concoct any other reason you'd be interested in talking with me. Come in. Just wipe your shoes on the mat."

Amanda and Trent stepped inside and did as Shirley had requested.

Shirley's house was cluttered with bric-a-brac and the color palette consisted predominantly of dusty rose and hunter green. She seemed to be stuck somewhere back in the nineties. "Please, sit wherever you'll be comfortable." She gestured into the sitting room full of antique furniture, predating the color scheme. The cushions on the couch were thin and scalloped wood accented the back and arms.

Amanda sat in a chair, as did Trent. Shirley took up residence on the couch.

"You weren't surprised to see us, Ms. Morton," Amanda said. "Why is that?"

"I heard about that crime author, Felicity Kelley, being murdered. She came around asking questions several months ago now. Just showed up at my door one day out of the blue."

Amanda glanced at Trent. She wasn't sure if his hackles were raised like hers, but it was unsettling that this woman seemed to link both murders. "May I ask why you think the two incidents are related—her murder and us being here?"

"Not so much your being here, but she pushed her nose in. From what I know, Naomi's case was never solved, and Felicity was a nosy little thing. I've learned in all my years that the past is often best left alone."

"Would you be willing to tell us what you told her? It could be very helpful in assisting our investigation," Trent said, tacking on a gentle smile.

"Well, she asked if I remembered that night. I assured her, it's not one I'll ever forget. Bet your ass."

Amanda smirked at the mature woman's spunk.

"Police lights, sirens, the whole works... Oh, and forensics people. I still remember seeing her body going out in a black bag and being loaded into a van."

"That must have been hard to witness," Amanda empathized, though she noted it hadn't scarred Shirley enough to pull up roots and move.

"It was. She was so young, pretty little thing too. Her whole life really had been ahead of her before someone saw fit to kill her."

Amanda stiffened. It was the way Shirley put it that had Amanda suspecting she never considered Chapman's murder the result of a robbery. "Did you see anyone stalking outside her house that night? Even earlier in the evening?" She was tiptoeing around, curious if Shirley would share the bit about the front light with them. And she certainly wasn't going to be the one that brought it up.

"Nope, and I said the same to detectives that had come around back then. I told them I saw the light on her front porch turn on."

Amanda wasn't sure how much faith she put in that meaning anything. Exterior lights could be set up with a motion-sensor and triggered by movement. But she and Trent were here because this point seemed to have mattered to Felicity, and Amanda wanted to find out why. "Did you see anyone at her door?"

"Actually, I didn't, but there's a good reason for that. The window in our bedroom faces the house next door. It was late, and both of us—that's myself and Paul, my late husband, may he rest in peace—were already in bed with our lights out. But our curtains weren't exactly blackout ones and when Naomi's front light came on, it would glow around the edges and bleed into our room."

"Then you were aware it had come on but didn't get out of bed to see what was going on?" Amanda pieced together what she believed the woman was trying to say.

"That's right."

"Do you know if the light was set up with motion sensor?" Amanda asked.

Shirley shook her head. "It wasn't. Thankfully, or Paul and I would have gone insane. Though more me, I suppose, as I'm a rather light sleeper."

"Did you happen to hear anyone knock?" This came from Trent as he settled back in his chair.

"I don't think so. But we all have doorbells."

It sounded like Chapman may have had a guest the night she was murdered. Robbers don't typically ring the doorbell—and there was the broken window and prints in the back to consider. But it was hard to ignore that the timing of the visitor fell right within Chapman's time-of-death window. "When you told the detective about the light, what was his reaction?"

"He thanked me, but I don't think he made much of it. I mean he mustn't have. Naomi's killer was never caught. At least that young woman, Felicity, was actually paying attention to me. You don't think she put her nose in too far and got herself killed?"

"We're still investigating," Amanda said. "You said that Felicity just showed up one day. When was that?"

"A few months ago. She fudged the truth though. Told me she was an investigative reporter revisiting the case. Guess I can't blame her. She just wanted answers. Now why she cared so much, I don't know. What happened to her? The author? The news only says so much."

"We can't disclose those details." Amanda had no qualms about shutting out civilians from police matters.

Shirley shuddered, pressed her hands together, and looked up toward the ceiling. Her lips moved, as she spoke in a quiet undertone, uttering words to herself, possibly her deity. A few moments later, she let her hands relax and placed them in her lap.

Amanda waited a few beats, then asked, "Did you and Felicity speak about any other things relating to Naomi?"

Her green eyes danced from Amanda to Trent and back again. "Yes. One thing. I shared my suspicion with her."

"Which was?" Amanda asked.

"Naomi's maid was bad news."

The maid had been the one to find Naomi Chapman. Was it a coincidental or planned discovery?

Trent edged forward in his chair. "Can you elaborate?"

"I tried to warn Naomi, but she wasn't listening to a word I said. She was young and thought she knew everything. But I knew the maid from my past."

Tingles spread on Amanda's arms, just anticipating what Shirley might tell them and suffering from the suspense.

"She worked for a friend of mine, and she had things go missing. The maid, Faye Douglas, swore it had nothing to do with her, but my friend is smart as a whip. She set up a hidden camera and caught her red-handed, taking cash off her dresser. Confronted with the video, Faye returned the money and other trinkets she had stolen. My friend still fired her ass."

Amanda wanted to know more about this maid. Had she stolen from Naomi? And if so, had Naomi found out and confronted her about it? Faye's sticky fingers had extended to *trinkets*. Did it stretch further to include valuable jewelry? The jewels could even have been gone before the supposed home invasion. Had Faye killed Naomi and simply pretended to find Naomi? Dennis Bishop hadn't told them the maid was even considered suspect, just that Chapman's ex-boyfriend was questioned. "Did you share this information with the police at the time?"

"I didn't."

"And why's that?" Trent asked.

"There's a long leap from stealing some things to killing a person in cold blood, but people are capable of anything."

Shirley had said she'd shared her suspicions about the maid with Felicity. Had it further sparked Felicity's interest and landed her in trouble? But Amanda couldn't completely ignore that they already had a suspect in custody for Felicity's murder. "Just one more question before we leave," Amanda started. "Does the name Sheldon Lowe mean anything to you? Maybe he was a friend of Naomi's...?"

Shirley seemed to give it some thought, but a few seconds later, shook her head. "The name doesn't sound familiar."

Amanda gave her a brief description of his current looks, though they could have been far different fifteen years ago. Still, it didn't bring anyone up for Shirley. Amanda stood and handed Shirley her card. "If you think of anything else, either from your time with Felicity, or from when Naomi Chapman was killed, please call."

After Shirley assured Amanda that she would, Amanda couldn't get out the door fast enough.

They loaded into the car, and as the vents belted out cool air, her heart was racing.

"We need to speak with this maid, Trent. Feel her out, see what she has to say. Even if it's just to rule her out from suspicion."

"Agreed. She may very well hold the key to the entire investigation."

"To *two*."

THIRTY-TWO

Amanda and Trent grabbed a bite to eat before heading to speak with Faye Douglas, Naomi Chapman's maid. A quick call to Justine Livingston hadn't given them a name for Felicity's police contact, but it had been worth a try. They still had Felicity's phone records to look at.

"There is one thing starting to really gnaw on me," Amanda said once they got back on the road. "It's that front light coming on. It wasn't motion triggered, so it stands to reason Chapman had a late-night visitor."

"Or she just simply turned it on because she thought she heard something." He hitched a shoulder. "Just playing devil's advocate. And typically, burglars don't knock."

"I realize that. I'm just saying, from the standpoint of considering that the home invasion and subsequent robbery was staged *after* the murder, she could have known her killer and let him in."

"Just like Felicity did."

"Uh-huh." Amanda's mind went to the value of the stolen goods. Those close to Chapman may have been aware that she had money and jewels worth taking. Then again, how prominent was her father? If his wealth was widely known an assumption could have been made that his daughter had valuables in her house.

"Are we looking at someone in Naomi Chapman's world then?"

"Might be. I also wonder if the midnight visitor is connected to the robbery. Thinking along those lines, it could have just been staged to look like a home invasion."

"Sounds like you're using your imagination like Felicity did. Everything you just said might as well be fiction, for the lack of fact or evidence."

"Hey, I'm just brainstorming. Spit-balling. You know, to see if anything sticks."

"Nothing is quite yet, anyway."

She wasn't sure if she appreciated Trent's honesty... "Nice."

He held up a hand. "We need more to go on here before we rush to any conclusion."

"I'm not..." She wasn't going to repeat herself again. Rather, she picked up by painting the scenario. "Faye Douglas wouldn't cause neighbors any alarm or make them pay any special attention."

"Even in the middle of the night?"

"Who knows? Chapman and the maid could have been friends. We'll have to see what Douglas tells us." She pointed at the gray-sided townhouse numbered 372.

Trent parked on the road out front, and they walked up the driveway. People were yelling inside, the open windows doing little to conceal the heated argument in progress.

"Get out of here!" a woman screamed.

Stomping footsteps thundered toward the front of the house. The door was flung open, and a man came out. He stopped short at the sight of her and Trent.

"I never want to see your ass again!" A woman filled the

open doorway. She crossed her arms and glared at them. "Who are you?"

"Prince William County PD, ma'am," Trent said. "We need a word, with both of you."

"Just great, Charlie. You had the neighbors call the cops."

"Me? Maybe if you gave your mouth a rest sometimes..."

"Enough. In the house." Amanda nudged her head toward the door, and Charlie trudged toward it as if he were walking to his execution.

The woman stepped back with a snuff of derision but let them all inside. She smacked Charlie's arm though, to which he reacted with a sharp, "Did you see that? She hit me."

Amanda wasn't about to fall into this domestic dispute unless it became absolutely necessary. "Are you Faye Douglas?" she asked the woman.

"What is it to ya?"

"Detective Steele. My partner, Detective Stenson, and we need to ask you some questions."

The woman pointed at the man. "He started this whole thing, I can assure you."

Amanda held up a hand and shook her head. "We're not here because of your arguing, though I do suggest that you refrain from physical assault."

"See?" Charlie smirked. "Keep your hands off me."

Faye shot him daggers, then turned the look on Amanda. "If you're not here because of this rat bastard, why then? And if it doesn't involve him, can he please leave?"

Trent turned to the man. "Who are you?"

"Charlie Doug—"

"He's my no-good cheatin' husband." Faye made a dramatic show of rolling her eyes. "But I'm finished putting up with his crap. I'm getting myself a lawyer." She spoke with her gaze on Charlie but worded things as if she were talking to Amanda and Trent.

"I told you, I never slept with her."

As much as the idea didn't thrill her, Charlie sticking around might be useful. "If we could just speak with both of you... Possibly somewhere we could all sit down, take a few deep breaths."

Faye shot more lasers at Charlie but acquiesced and took them to the living room. To call the place a sty would be unfair to pigs. Guess it was the same for maids as it was for mechanics and handymen: while they tended to other people's issues, their own fell apart.

Once everyone was seated, Amanda started things off. "How long have you been married?" The question was purely motivated by her goal to ascertain whether Charlie had been around at the time of Chapman's murder. She certainly had no desire to play marriage counselor.

"Twenty *long* years," Faye said. "I'd be free on good behavior if I'd just killed him."

"Really, Faye? Again with all that hostility in front of the cops," Charlie mumbled.

"As we made clear, we have questions for you, Faye," Amanda said, "but, Charlie, you might have something to offer." As she verbalized that, she built on her fictional scenario. If Chapman had found out that Faye was a thief and threatened to turn her over to the police, it would have affected the family's livelihood. What's to say Charlie didn't step in to prevent that from happening?

"Whatever it is, ask and leave," Faye said and added, "Please, for the love of God, let's get this over with quickly. I need a break from that man."

"You worked for Naomi Chapman fifteen years ago, correct?" Amanda got to the point.

"I'm sure you know I did, or you wouldn't be here," Faye responded. "Though with that said, I don't know why you're interested in me after this long."

"Her murder was never solved," Trent said. "And you were brought to our attention."

"Well, I had nothing to do with it."

Interesting she'd go right there. "Why would you assume we'd think you did?"

"Isn't that much obvious?" Faye raised her eyebrows, creasing deep furrows in her forehead. "You're here now. But if you did your homework, you'd know the police questioned me and had no suspicions."

Dennis said Douglas had found Chapman, but nothing beyond that. If he ever considered her a suspect, he hadn't been forthcoming on that point. And it wasn't like he was armed with Shirley's testimony to Faye's shady employment history, or her sticky fingers. "Do you know why they looked at you?"

"I found Naomi. That seemed to be enough to question me for hours."

There wasn't currently any sign that Faye was affected by Chapman's murder, but it had been some time ago. "Forgive me for saying this, but you don't seem too broken up about Naomi's death."

"Hey now," Charlie jumped in. "She was upset for a long time. She even saw a shrink for a bit."

"A therapist." Amanda made the politically correct revision, a compulsion that she couldn't ignore. She'd never much cared for the slang term, even when it was acceptable.

"Whatever. Faye saw her for six months after..." Charlie added.

"It would have been quite shocking to find her like that." Amanda flipped her approach. Empathizing often worked to get people to talk.

"It was horrifying." Faye's eyes glazed over, and she licked her lips. "I remember it like yesterday. I'd just let myself in through the garage. I had my earbuds in, listening to some music. All I was thinking about was getting started and getting done. But I rounded the kitchen peninsula and— Boom! She was right there. So much blood." Faye took a deep breath after relaying all this. There wasn't much evidence of emotion as she had rehashed it all in robotic manner. Her time in therapy may have helped her detach from the experience.

"Were you and Naomi close, friends even?" Trent asked.

Faye was quick to shake her head. "She was the boss, I worked for her. She didn't even know I was there unless something wasn't done quite to her liking."

Such as stealing from her, Amanda thought, but refrained from saying as much out loud. "Such as?"

Faye played with the hem of her T-shirt. "She was finicky. If I missed a spot dusting, or, heaven forbid, a hair tumbleweed made itself known after I did the floors, she'd have a bird."

"She was a rich and spoiled daddy's girl," Charlie pushed out.

"Other than that, how was your professional relationship? Were there ever any other types of disagreements between you? Maybe over your pay, or did she ever make false allegations?" Amanda tacked on the last question, hoping to slip it in there somewhat obscured.

Faye's eyes narrowed slightly, but she shook her head.

"She never falsely accused you of, say, stealing from her?" Amanda framed the question in a kind manner, removing any trace of judgment by putting the onus on Chapman.

"I'm going to guess you heard about a situation with a previous employer several months before I started to work for Naomi." She paused there, but neither Amanda nor Trent confirmed. "But whatever, it was a tough time, and I admit that I helped myself to some cash that was lying around a client's house."

"But she paid it all back," Charlie rushed out, coming to his wife's defense. The act barely made a dent in the woman's hardened exterior.

"No charges were ever laid. I'm sure you could see that for yourself." Faye raised an eyebrow. "As Charlie said, I paid it back and just wanted to put the whole sordid mess behind me."

"I can understand that. Can we assume you never took anything from Naomi?" Amanda tried to soften the confrontational question with a precursor.

"Not once. I just did my job and left."

Amanda bobbed her head. "The night she was killed, where were you?"

"I answered all that back then, but I was here with Charlie."

"All night?" The fact she remembered her whereabouts on a single night fifteen years ago wasn't a surprise given the surrounding context of finding Chapman dead the following morning.

"That's right. From the time I left another client's home at five."

Charlie was nodding.

Then Faye Douglas hadn't been Naomi Chapman's midnight visitor. But Amanda was curious if Felicity had visited Faye. "Do you happen to know Felicity Kelley?"

Faye looked at her husband, back to Amanda. "I've heard of her."

The couple's eye contact disclosed there was more to it than that. "Did she come around, possibly asking questions about Naomi after all this time?"

Faye worried her bottom lip.

Amanda considered what might make the woman so coy and landed on a reason. "We don't suspect you in her murder, if that's what's concerning you."

Faye ballooned her cheeks, blew out. "Good. I heard about it on the news. Sad. She seemed like a nice person too. When she showed up at my door a couple of months back, I was starstruck."

Trent passed a brief glance at Amanda. To Faye, he said, "Why was she here?"

"She was interested in talking about Naomi's murder. She didn't think it had anything to do with a break-in."

They might be venturing down the right path, after all, in considering Felicity's poking around got her murdered. "She said that in so many words?"

"Pretty much. She was convinced someone made it look like a robbery to cover the murder."

Convinced was a strong word. The skin tightened on the back of Amanda's neck. "Did she mention any suspects she had in mind?"

"Wait a minute." Faye angled her head left, then right, straightened it again. "Is this why you're really here—the author's murder?"

"We're not at liberty to disclose that." Amanda got up and handed Faye her card, but the woman crumpled it and shoved it into a pocket of her shorts.

"Nothing personal," Faye said. "I just need to move on with my life."

Amanda and Trent thanked the Douglases for their time and left.

Faye Douglas was the second person to point out that the past was best left behind. Amanda disagreed. She had a strong feeling the key to solving Felicity's murder necessitated a trip back in time.

THIRTY-THREE

Amanda settled in a conference room down at Central. A stuffed evidence box from the Chapman investigation was on the table, and doubts crept in. What if they spent hours scouring all of this, and it had nothing to do with what got Felicity Kelley murdered? It would certainly help if they could get their hands on Felicity's research or manuscript notes, but they were still waiting on access to her cloud storage. And that was assuming she kept a backup of all that there.

She and Trent looked in the history of Felicity's phone, but it didn't date back further than a few months ago, so it must have been a new device. To access call logs prior to that, to when Felicity was in possible contact with her mole in the police department, they'd need to wait on the service provider.

It was defeating to consider what they didn't have so she turned her attention to what they had. Amanda's father had told her before the best place to start was at the beginning. Amanda was sure the origin of all this was Chapman's murder.

Trent walked into the room with two coffees and handed one to Amanda.

"Thanks." She took a sip, then popped the top off the box and pulled out a handful of files. "Time to get to work."

Trent reached in and retrieved a manila envelope. He lifted the flap and took out a series of photographs.

"That looks more fun than all this." She set the files on the table and gestured for him to sit next to her.

He'd look at a photo and then pass it to her.

Amanda studied each image closely. There were ones of the back door with its broken window, the shoe prints in the garden, shots of the kitchen. She looked closer at the peninsula: double sink, spotless countertop except for a bottle of bourbon, and a rocks glass with a bit of amber liquid inside. If there had been ice, it had melted by the time of this photograph.

Based on what Bishop told them, Chapman had gone out to celebrate with her colleagues at Taps and Cocktails bar. Then she decided to have a final nightcap at home? Not unheard of, and she'd likely have already imbued a significant amount of alcohol to affect her better judgment. But nightcaps were typically done with company. Her midnight visitor? But if so, where was the second glass?

Amanda continued looking at the photographs. The next several showed Chapman from different angles.

Due to the thorough coverage of the pictures, Amanda could piece together the layout of the home. The door, that was the supposed burglar's point of entry, was to the rear of the dining room. The peninsula served as a boundary marker for where the kitchen began. There was a spot that Chapman could have used for a breakfast counter with two stools. One was tucked in, and the other was tipped back on the floor near Chapman's body. She'd likely been sitting in it when she was shot.

Chapman, fully clothed in dress pants and a blouse, laid supine with her right arm at her side, her left one slightly curled as if she had touched her wounds. Her legs were parted, her right leg slightly bent. There was something about the positioning of the body that felt off though.

"The intruder was said to have come in the back door," she began, and it had Trent looking at her. "That meant they had to round the peninsula, sticking to the inside of the kitchen, and then shoot her. But Chapman would have been alerted to their presence long before then. Why wouldn't she have made a run for it? I mean she obviously didn't or she'd have been shot in the back. Instead, she took three bullets to the chest."

"I was considering the same thing."

"If we both were, had Felicity as well?"

"Only if she had gotten her hands on these pictures somehow."

"Right. Well, the evidence in the Chapman case was last signed out thirteen years ago by Bishop." He might have had loose lips, but Amanda couldn't see him copying photos for a personal collection or giving them to a civilian. Just thinking a cop—former or active—would share confidential case information set her redhead temper ablaze. It was unforgivable if it had factored into Felicity's murder. And while Dennis had made that trespass, she was more concerned that Felicity's contact may still be active with the PWCPD. "Regardless, we need to plug that leak if it's still in the department."

"I wholeheartedly agree."

Amanda was just lost on a next step in that regard. She grabbed one of the photos that showed Chapman and the peninsula. "Why would the intruder even bother to go that way?" She traced a finger through the kitchen. "If Chapman was at her counter having a drink, wouldn't the perp just shoot her from the back door? But that's not what the trajectory shows." She was referring to a diagram that laid all that out.

"They were only about three feet away."

"On her side of the counter. Though it is possible, I

suppose, that the perp got closer and then something made them pull the trigger on Chapman."

"Then she knew the intruder, or was told to stay put at gunpoint."

"Either way or both?" Amanda's shoulders sagged, frustrated. "If only we could find out what Felicity saw in all this—whether it was something in the photos or the case in a broader sense."

"I think we should keep going with this and we might find out."

Amanda sat back in her chair and cradled her coffee cup. She took a few sips, thought it all out. "Well, it's not like we've uncovered anyone who had motive to want Felicity dead within her circle."

"Unless you're forgetting Sheldon Lowe."

"I'm not, but his motive? He loved Felicity."

"You could say he worshipped her."

"But we haven't gotten any concrete evidence against him yet. Means and opportunity seem to be missing. There's no connection between him and Chapman that we've been able to find. That's assuming the cold case has any tie." She massaged her forehead. Her mind was a tangled mess of thoughts. And there was all that awaited her in the files.

"I really think we need to stick to our first instinct with this. The cold case matters. We already know that Felicity spoke to different people connected to Chapman."

"No disputing that, but how did she find them? Through her police contact with the loose lips?"

"Not sure if we'll be able to answer that one or not, but I can scour the call history on her phone again. This time with an eye for anyone she might have called that could be connected in some way to Chapman."

"It wouldn't hurt, and take time to follow up on the warrant to access her storage cloud too, please. I'm going to keep going with this for a while longer with focus on interviews and suspects. You finish up sooner, come join the fun."

Trent stood and pushed in his chair. "A tag-team approach —I like it."

"I imagine you do." After all, he wouldn't be holed up in this room with files upon files to wade through.

He grinned and left, closing the door behind him.

As soon as he was gone, a sense of overwhelm blanketed her shoulders and sat heavy on her chest. But she pushed it aside along with any doubts that mocked her decision to pursue this avenue. She knew in her gut there was something in this, she just had to find out what that was.

THIRTY-FOUR

Amanda was going cross-eyed when Trent knocked on the door and came into the room. She squinted to make out the time on her phone. No wonder her eyes were sore. She'd been poring over the files, analyzing every word, for over two hours. But she didn't want to miss any possible clue or link that Felicity might have followed. Not that she believed Felicity would have had access to all of this. Still, something in the mess of the boxes could have made it to her attention by another route.

"Tell me you have something," Amanda said as Trent dropped into a chair across from her.

"I do."

Finally, good news! "Fantastic. Hit me."

"If we needed any more evidence of how deeply Felicity Kelley investigated the case, we have it. A closer look at her call history confirms she had been in contact with Edmond McCormick, the previous owner of Between the Pages, Chapman's parents, and a woman by the name of Victoria Eaton. Any of these names ring any bells for you?"

"Yep." She put her hand on a piece of paper she had set aside to revisit. "Eaton was Chapman's best friend. She was interviewed and gave Chapman glowing praise, saying that she beat out six other interns for the paid job—who go unnamed in the file."

"Bishop must not have seen collecting their names to be of importance. He was looking at Chapman's murder as a fatal home robbery, not as being personally motivated."

"Except, what's to say it wasn't both? Now, apparently, Eaton was at Chapman's promotion celebration at Taps and Cocktails. She told Dennis that Chapman's fellow interns smiled to her face but badmouthed her behind her back."

"That shouldn't come as a surprise. They all wanted the job she got."

"And it's not just that. They could have been jealous of Chapman already. She had a rich father who gave her advantages in life. The promotion was just a cherry on top."

"Sounds like she had a golden horseshoe up her ass." Trent smiled at his turn of phrase.

"Until she didn't."

"Right. Well, this is a list of numbers and associated names that were on Felicity's call history for the last month." He held up a printout and added, "I figured if anyone Felicity contacted factors in, it would be due to more recent contact."

"Because of her choosing to make a last-minute revision to her plot? Though that was only two weeks ago. What led to that change? I think we should speak with everyone on your list." The page looked rather full. "How many are we talking about?"

"It looks worse than it is. Whittled down, I say we're just looking at the people I mentioned a moment ago."

"Did you pull a general background on all of them?"

"Yep. No criminal record across the board."

"We'll have a chat with them, anyway. I also think we might want to find out who benefited from Chapman's death—not in terms of insurance, but rather who wound up with her promotion. It might have to do with what the best friend said about her fellow interns being two-faced."

"On that note, we should find out the names of all the interns who were working at Between the Pages at that time."

"We'll be talking to the owner from back then, so we'll ask him."

"In agreement."

She smiled at him. "You're always so cooperative."

"I try." He laughed. "All right, so I laid out my gems. Your turn."

"Going back to the best friend's comment, it doesn't look like Dennis interviewed any of Chapman's fellow interns."

"I know I said it was understandable earlier. There was that string of home robberies, but still... Shouldn't Bishop have, at least, considered someone closer to Chapman knew about the jewels and set out to rob her? Seems to me he dropped the ball."

Amanda saw Trent's point, but they also had the advantage of hindsight. "Not sure. I mean, Felicity's murder has us looking back from a different perspective."

"Fair enough, I suppose."

"All right, so I uncovered some more here. Chapman's blood alcohol confirmed she was intoxicated, unfit to drive, but not about to pass out."

"Just drunk enough to think she can keep drinking." Trent smiled. "Could be why she opted for a solo nightcap. Just to keep the party going for a while longer."

"Could be." Not that she was going to argue science with him. Even after a person stopped drinking the body was still processing the consumed alcohol, adding further intoxication. "Chapman left the bar at eleven thirty and accounting for a fifteen-minute drive to her house, she was home by quarter to midnight."

"In time for her midnight visitor."

"As you pointed out before, if there even was one. After

reading the files, none of the neighbors noticed any unknown cars on the street or in her driveway. But Chapman was found wearing what she had on when she went out that night. That makes me think she was expecting someone."

"It could just be as simple as she hadn't changed for bed before she was shot."

"True enough, but you need to see this." Amanda shuffled three photographs over to Trent. "These specific items were stolen and insured by Chapman's parents."

"Wow." The picture of an ornate ruby brooch elicited this response.

"An heirloom passed on from Naomi's great-great-great grandmother. It's priceless but was insured for two hundred thousand. Then the next piece, if you want to go to the second photo?"

Trent shuffled the ruby to the back. "Cufflinks." Obviously unimpressed.

"They might not look like much, but they are made of onyx and platinum. Value is fifty-five thousand."

"And the third photo..." Trent brought it to the front. "Diamond earrings."

"Not just any diamond earrings. Tiffany. Valued at forty grand."

"Holy hell."

"Yep."

"Tell me she kept all this in a safe."

Amanda shook her head. "She should have, but she didn't."

"Wealthy *and* careless."

"But did the intruder know Chapman had items of such high value or strike it lucky? Or were they stolen simply to cover up a murder?"

"We certainly have work ahead of us. It's five to five now. Talk to those people or leave this for the weekend and pick up on Monday?"

She hated taking days off in the middle of an open investigation. As it was, she would be stepping back on Sunday for a gathering at her parents' to celebrate Zoe's birthday with family, since she was in Florida when it actually hit.

But she'd already been on the job for the past three days when she was originally scheduled to be off. While overtime pay was monitored closely and often frowned upon, she was more concerned about displeasing Logan and Zoe.

Thinking about it strictly from the standpoint of Felicity Kelley's case, some separation might do the investigation good and insert objectivity. It might save her and Trent from spinning and using up time that could be better spent in other ways. "I can't believe I'm going to say this, but let's take the weekend. But *first* thing Monday morning, we'll pick it up from here— unless we think up another avenue we'd be better off pursuing."

"All right. I'll help you get these files sorted away and then head out."

And that's what she and Trent did. A half an hour later, she was headed home, the fresh summer breeze blowing over her face as she drove with the windows down. She felt free and unencumbered, even though Felicity Kelley and Naomi Chapman weighed on the back of her mind.

"Mandy!" Zoe ran through the patio door, through the house, to the front door to greet Amanda. The girl wrapped her arms around her and squeezed her tight.

Amanda laughed. "Happy to see you too."

"I thought you were going to work forever." Zoe backed up and looked at Amanda with widened blue eyes.

Logan came out from the side hallway and hugged and kissed Amanda in greeting. "This is a nice surprise."

She'd certainly made the right decision to cut out for the weekend. Zoe's words sliced deep and stung, and she was happy to prove the girl wrong. In this moment, Amanda felt so incredibly blessed. After she lost Kevin and Lindsey, she didn't think she'd ever find happiness, let alone have a family again. But then came Logan and Zoe. Both had wormed their way into her heart. She loved and cherished this gift, but there were times when it also scared her to death. It was never far from her mind how fragile life was. Here one minute, gone the next. A macabre viewpoint she came by honestly.

"I was playing in the garden. Come outside." Zoe tugged Amanda's hand.

"Just let me get changed, and I'll be right there." She could hardly wait to exchange the dress pants for cotton shorts and the collared shirt for a tee.

"Yeah." Zoe clapped her hands and ran off into the backyard.

Amanda turned to Logan. "Playing in the garden?"

"Libby and Penny stopped by around lunch and dropped off Zoe's birthday gift."

Libby Dewinter's relationship with Zoe predated Amanda. Libby had been a family friend of Zoe's parents, adopted aunt and godmother to Zoe. Penny Anderson was Libby's life partner. "That was nice, but they know we're doing a celebration at Mom and Dad's on Sunday. They were invited."

"Guess something came up, and they're off for the weekend. A last-minute getaway."

"Nice for them." It must have been something special to yank Libby away from Zoe. Hopefully not couple problems. "And I take it this gift has something to do with why Zoe is playing in the garden?"

"Yep. Just be happy she didn't plant any seedlings yet."

"What?" Amanda was grinning, just at the thought of Zoe's little fingers digging in the earth. She would probably be a terrific gardener as she had more patience than was to be expected for a girl her age. She was also very understanding and sympathetic—two additional qualities that would come in handy for growing plants to maturity.

Logan was smiling. "They got her a gardening kit for kids. It has a little shovel, trowel, who knows what else. I'll confess, I don't have a green thumb."

Amanda laughed. "Neither do I, so Zoe's on her own. Poor girl, and the dark fate of her plants. Speaking of, flowers or—"

"Vegetables."

"Huh. She'll be putting food on the table for us before long. Or does that smack too close to child labor?" She winked at Logan and slipped out of her shoes.

"By the way..." Logan pulled her in for another hug. "If you didn't figure it out, I'm happy to see you. Does this mean you're home for the weekend?" His voice held a hesitancy as if he didn't quite want to give himself over to believing that.

"That's the plan." She tapped a kiss on his lips, but he extended it. She didn't resist.

After they parted, she walked down the hall with lightened steps and did a quick wardrobe change.

By the time she got to the backyard, Zoe was seated cross-legged in front of the garden bed that traveled the fence line. Her fingers were in the dirt, and she was singing away, some cheery tune with words Amanda didn't recognize. It could have been one she'd learned from her parents, but Amanda wouldn't put it past Zoe to have come up with it on her own. The older Zoe got, the more aspects of her zany personality came to light. She'd randomly burst into song or make strange noises, sometimes in imitation of animals, other times, who knew what. Amanda had to wonder if that was something she had witnessed her mother or father do when she was younger, or if she came by this on her own. The best person to ask would be Libby. But for right now, Amanda was just going to soak in the rest of the day's sun with her family.

THIRTY-FIVE

Last night had been so peaceful and relaxing, it had recharged Amanda's spirit. So often the cases she worked kept her mind awake as she flipped thoughts of them over, examining them from various angles. But time with Logan and Zoe had squeezed out the Felicity Kelley and Naomi Chapman investigations. She had actually let herself *be* in the moment, and it had been glorious.

Even now, as she was stirring awake, she breathed slowly, her mind uncluttered.

The sun was snaking its way around the bedroom curtains and bleeding across the wall and hitting her in the face. The warmth was nice, but she turned away before opening her eyes.

The alarm clock told her it was nine thirty, and she nearly swore. She never slept that late, and even though she didn't have a lot planned for the day, she felt as if she were running behind. She'd felt Logan slip out of bed some time ago.

Just breathe, she coached herself. After all, why should she feel shame in resting when it had been exactly what she needed?

She left bed, with some reluctance, and jumped in the shower. Only after, did she venture into the rest of the house.

And no one was home.

"What the—?" She called out Logan's and Zoe's names and then looked out at the driveway. Logan's Dodge Ram was gone. He and Zoe had gone somewhere. *How strange...*

She padded to the kitchen and found a note on the counter in front of the coffeemaker.

Gone to pick up breakfast and coffee from Hannah's. We love you!

She really had struck it lucky—for a second time in life. That thought only intensified her insecurities. She had been given so much, she couldn't fathom losing it again.

She had barely finished reading the note when she heard Logan's truck in the driveway. At the same time, her cell phone started ringing. It was probably her mother looking to confirm something about the party tomorrow or even one of her siblings. Or Kristen telling them to come over for a swim. Or her best friend, Becky Tulson, looking to spend some time with her.

One look at the caller ID, and her heart sank. It was none of those people. It was Malone, and while he was a family friend, he never made a habit of calling her on the weekend.

Zoe's squeals of laughter could be heard from outside before the front door opened, and she and Logan came in.

"You're up. And you got our note, I see." Logan was smiling as he pointed to it in her hand.

Amanda held up her ringing phone and answered—even though it was the last thing she wanted to do. If only she could stay here in this safe, little bubble with Logan and Zoe, sip her coffee from Hannah's, and enjoy whatever it was they got for breakfast. "Detective Steele," she said, unable to put it off any longer.

"It's not good, Amanda."

Neither is that greeting... "What is it?"

Logan put a hand on the small of Amanda's back, offering support. The longer they were together as a couple, he was becoming more in tune with her emotions, how to read them, how to handle them, how to ease them.

Zoe, just having turned eight, couldn't read Amanda quite as well. But she must have sensed something was wrong as she stood still and looked up at her. Concern or confusion marked her expression.

Amanda had no idea what she would do without Logan and Zoe and refused to give it any serious thought.

"There's another body, Amanda," Malone told her.

His words were like lead, but they were having a hard time sinking in. It suddenly felt as if the investigation was collapsing around her. They'd been so certain they were on the right track, and now this... If she and Trent had been faster about piecing together the clues, could this murder have been prevented?

"You heard me, Amanda?" Malone asked.

"Ah, yeah. Just give me some time." With that, she hung up and drew in a few deep breaths.

"Why don't you set up the patio table for breakfast?" Logan urged Zoe to gather some plastic plates and cutlery and take them outside.

When Zoe cleared the patio door and got to work, Logan returned to Amanda's side.

"You need to get back to work?"

She met his gaze, her heart fracturing. Leaving now was the last thing she wanted to do, but this was the job she'd signed up for. "What did I do to deserve you?" She touched his cheek, peered into his eyes, still processing what Malone had told her. She just wished to shut it out, as if by doing so that would mean it hadn't happened.

Logan took her hand in his and kissed her fingertips and then pressed her palm to his chest. "You can talk to me."

"I need to go. There's been another..." She couldn't get

herself to say *murder* as if it would taint the moment. She felt to blame in a roundabout way. If she hadn't surrendered to believing she could take an entire weekend, then things might be different. This must be the universe inserting a course correction.

"You do what you need to do. Zoe and I understand, Mandy." He made sure to match her gaze as he spoke, and it drove home the sincerity of his words.

"Thank you."

"Can you eat before you go, or...?"

"Is there anything I can take for the road?"

He nodded. "I got some blueberry muffins."

"Thank you. I'll just say goodbye to Zoe." She hugged and kissed Logan, then broke the news to Zoe she had to leave, that the job was calling again. And while Zoe seemed to show the same understanding as Logan, Amanda felt all sorts of guilt and regret. If only she hadn't let herself get involved in the Felicity Kelley case to start with, then Malone would have pushed this new case to Hudson.

Before leaving, she plucked a coffee from the takeout tray and one of those muffins. As she drove to Central, she couldn't help but recall some of her final words to Trent last night. She'd told him that by taking the weekend, they might realize there was another avenue to pursue. When she'd said that, she had no idea it would mean they'd be looking at another murder.

THIRTY-SIX

"Victim is Jane Burr, forty-two, found inside her home," Malone informed Amanda and Trent once they arrived on scene.

Burr's residence was in Woodbridge, and after Malone's call, Amanda reached out to Trent. They met up at Central, grabbed a department car, and came over together.

Malone went on. "She was single, lived alone."

"What did she do for work?" Trent asked.

"She was the office manager for Fine Furniture Limited in town."

As much as Amanda wanted to forget Malone's call had happened, that another life was lost while she and Trent misread the clues in Felicity Kelley's case, the next step couldn't be put off forever. "Where can we find her?"

"She's in the primary bedroom," Malone said. "Up the stairs to the right of the entry, room at the end of the hall, also on the right. Actually, I'll just come up with you."

Amanda put booties over her shoes and entered the home, raising her badge to the officer at the door. If that hadn't been enough to clear her, Malone was right there telling the uniform to step aside.

CSIs were already on location, and she knew from Malone's call that a medical examiner was on the way too. More than likely Hans Rideout, as that was who tended to be sent to their scenes.

There was a buzz in the air that accompanied police presence but also the sedate coolness of a place where there had been a murder. It was an impossible essence to ignore or overlook. For Amanda, as she took each step to the second level, her self-judgment weighed in. She and Trent had dropped the ball, made too many assumptions...

Amanda cleared the doorway for the primary bedroom— spacious floor plan, with a king-size bed, seating for two with a coffee table, and a flatscreen television was mounted to the wall above a gas fireplace. The seating arrangement faced the fireplace, and it was running.

A bottle of champagne and two flutes were on the coffee table.

Amanda laid a hand over her stomach. This was looking eerily familiar to the scene described in Felicity Kelley's *The Romeo Killer*.

"She's lying in front of the fireplace," Malone told her, though this was unnecessary.

The killer had followed the script more closely with this murder.

Standing to the side of one chair was CSI Blair. She was taking photographs. Donnelly was setting down evidence markers next to the champagne bottle and flutes.

Amanda took her steps across the room slowly and deliberately. Her mind was preparing her for what she was about to see. And while there turned out to be no surprises, that didn't make the sight any easier to assimilate.

The woman was dressed in a white robe, the collar opened to expose a black negligee. The handle of a knife stuck out from her chest. Blood had bloomed from the wound, saturated the robe, and pooled onto the floor.

"The Romeo Killer strikes again," Trent said reverently and met Amanda's gaze. She could read that he had regrets too. Had they given up on the theory of a serial killer imitating Felicity Kelley's book too soon? But they had just followed the leads they had—none of which led them to make that conclusion.

"I knew this was going to be hard for you guys to see," said Malone. "I know you were hung up on the differences between *The Romeo Killer* and Kelley's murder. That's why you were interested in Kelley's latest project, why you signed that confidentiality agreement with her publisher. But how does this scene line up in comparison to the bestseller?"

"Pretty much perfectly from what I can tell, and from what I remember," Amanda responded.

"So, either we're looking at a serial killer perfecting the scene, or someone who wants us to think that." Malone put his hands on his hips.

She hated to think that meant Burr was simply collateral damage in the game of a demented killer. But if so, there was a potential lead in that. "If the latter is true, the killer must have been someone we've already spoken to, set on edge. But who?" She wracked her brain and as each man's name surfaced, she released them. No one stood out. She turned to Trent. "I hope we didn't fail this woman by abandoning the theory of a copycat serial killer." She fell silent, thinking about those differences that Malone had alluded to. It was possible they read far too much into them.

"Well, one of those differences was hard to ignore, Amanda," Trent said, indicating he must have been thinking about Malone's words too. "All of Kelley's paperwork was destroyed. That seemed far more personally driven than one would expect from a serial killer."

Malone rubbed his beard. "Don't drive yourself crazy by

second-guessing yourself. Besides, the killer could just be watching you."

"And why doesn't that make me feel better?" Still, she took her first full breath since Malone's call. He'd reminded her of her father's words. What unsettled her stomach was the knife handle looked like the one left in Felicity Kelley. It could have been from the same set. Was it as Malone had suggested—a desperate act from Felicity's killer to complicate the investigation?

"Who found her?" Trent asked Malone.

"Lee Steedman. He says he's Burr's boyfriend. He was here to take her away for the weekend."

There must have been some weekend special out there Amanda wasn't aware of.

"Anything to back up what he said?" Trent asked.

"There's a packed suitcase in the closet, and her toiletries and makeup are on the bathroom counter. Ida does that before we are about to go away so she doesn't forget anything."

Ida was Malone's wife. "Then that part of his story seems legit." Amanda refused to become paranoid and entertain it was done to support his cover story though she'd still see if there was a connection between Steedman and Felicity Kelley. "Anyone pull his background yet?"

"First thing, and no record," Malone said.

"Where is he now?" she asked.

"Out front with Officer Wyatt."

She motioned for Trent to join her outside. They found a gray-haired man leaning against a Mercedes in the driveway, Wyatt standing next to him. Neither of them had been there when they had arrived, but she'd guess he was Lee Steedman.

Wyatt excused himself from the man and helped close the distance.

"What's he telling you?" Amanda asked him.

"He was here to pick up Burr for their getaway. He let

himself in with his copy of the key and found her in the bedroom."

Amanda glanced at the man. He repeatedly pushed his hand through his hair as if unsure how to occupy his hands, and his face was flushed. Finding his lover that way couldn't have been easy and would be an image he wouldn't be forgetting any time soon. While she saw a man in shock, she had to consider his nervous energy might be guilt. "What's your take on him?"

"Do I think he's involved? Nah, I wouldn't say so. He's a bit of a wreck."

Amanda nodded. "All right, well, Trent and I will talk with him now."

"You got it."

Wyatt walked off, and Amanda and Trent joined Lee Steedman. "I'm Detective Steele, and this is Detective Stenson. We understand that Jane Burr was your girlfriend and you found her?"

"That's right." He sniffled and seemed to avoid eye contact.

Again, it was too soon to decide the reason—pain or guilt. "Take us through everything, please." She held up a hand when Steedman opened his mouth to protest. "I realize that you would have been through this already. For that I apologize, but as the lead detectives on your girlfriend's investigation, we could benefit from hearing your statement directly."

"Fine." Lee flailed a hand in reluctant surrender.

"What time did you arrive?" Trent asked.

"It was just after nine o'clock. I knocked, rang the bell, then let myself in. It's what I normally do, but it was so quiet. I called out her name, and there was no... *no* response." He choked on the last word, and his eyes pooled with tears.

"Then what did you do?" Amanda wanted to keep Lee talking, not derailing due to grief.

"I went upstairs, thinking she might have slept in. She loved sleeping." Lee scratched an eyebrow. "That's when I found her."

"And what did you do next?" Amanda asked.

"I called nine-one-one."

"Did you touch anything?" She wasn't going to handle him with kid gloves. Catering to his dips in emotions would demonstrate a weakness, should he be the killer.

"Absolutely not. I backed out of the room immediately."

"You never tried to resuscitate her or check for a pulse?" Amanda needed to be clear on the matter. If he denied such contact and they later found evidence to the contrary, Lee Steedman would have some explaining to do.

"No. I could tell that she was... gone." His shoulders sagged with the admission.

"All right," Amanda said. "I had to ask because it can be a natural reaction to offer help in such a situation. Sometimes it takes a while for acceptance to sink in."

"I'm still waiting for that, but as I said, it was obvious that she was... *that she was...*" Lee clamped his mouth shut, and his chin quivered as another wave of grief crashed over him.

"You backed out of the room, went outside, and then what?" she asked.

"I waited for the police to arrive. That's all, I swear. I know nothing else." His voice was shaking, as was his hand when he put it through his hair again.

"How long have you and Jane been a couple?" Trent asked.

"Just three months."

"But you already had a key to her place?" The progression seemed awfully fast, but then again, some people were quick to let others into their lives.

"I can imagine what you're both thinking." Lee looked from her to Trent and back again. "It was fast, but we were meant for each other. As corny as that might sound. We just hit it off from our first meeting, and the rest of the story wrote itself."

She cringed at his analogy. "When did you get the key?"

"After a month of dating." Lee smiled, though the expression wasn't fully born. "She insisted I take it."

"Did Jane ever mention if anyone was following or watching her?" Amanda was under no illusion her killer was a close friend. She'd ask about those who may have had an issue with Jane, but it wasn't a priority.

Lee shook his head. "Not that she ever mentioned to me."

"Do you know if Jane left the house last night?" Trent asked.

"Why would that matter? She was killed here," Lee pushed out.

He struck Amanda as defensive, though she wasn't sure why. "That's true, but it doesn't mean that her killer didn't latch on to her somewhere—"

Lee sobbed, the sound and sight of it was heartbreaking. Amanda looked away, glanced at Trent, who shook his head. She took that to mean he was of the same mind as her. Lee Steedman wasn't the killer they were after.

After several minutes, and once Lee composed himself, she asked, "What is it, Mr. Steedman?"

"She went out last night." Tears fell and blazed trails down his cheeks. "She had a stressful week and called me around four and said she needed to go out for a drink. She asked me to join her." He gasped a sob, then shook his head, and stood straighter.

"I'm guessing you didn't go?" Trent angled his head.

Lee shook his head. "I couldn't." He made quick work of swiping his damp cheeks, as if he were suddenly embarrassed by them.

"Why was that?" Whatever had kept Lee from joining Jane last night was eating away at him. Had he been with another woman? Made up excuses to avoid the outing?

"To start, you need to know that I'm an investment banker and cater to very wealthy clients. It means I'm often on call.

Last night, one such client demanded a meeting. If I had refused, he would have fired me."

Amanda noted the shiny Mercedes behind him, and it reinforced her belief in Lee Steedman. They could verify his employment, but the car alone confirmed he made good money. "Sometimes those type of things can't be helped. Did Jane go alone or with friends?" She'd circle back to asking for the client's name—assuming Jane Burr had been murdered last night.

"Alone. Which she hates." Lee looked down at the ground and pawed with his polished shoe at the driveway like an anxious horse.

"And where did she go?" Trent asked.

"Tipsy Moose Alehouse."

Amanda was very familiar with the place. It was where she'd met Logan. "What time was this?"

"Right after she finished work at five."

"Do you know when she got home?" Amanda was piecing together a timeline.

"She texted at ten saying she had more than a few drinks and ended up getting dinner too. But she said she'd just gotten in and couldn't wait for tomorrow... today." His eyes blanked over.

What he told them was easy to verify with a look at Jane's phone, but they could also tell from Lee's. "Would you be able to show us that message on your phone?"

"Ah, sure." Lee pulled out the device, swiped to the correct screen, and showed it to Amanda and Trent.

"Did she say why her week was stressful?" Amanda wasn't sure how the answer might affect the investigation.

"A couple of orders came in with the wrong finishes—not Jane's fault but still a headache. It might not sound like a big deal, but she's selling high-end furniture where she works.

We're talking thousands of dollars for a couch, and there are more custom options than Starbucks offers for coffee."

That's saying a lot!

Lee continued. "It takes months for orders to be fulfilled. Customers are required to put down fifty percent upfront and pay the remaining upon delivery. One of those customers canceled their order and demanded a refund. The other was none too happy and said they'd wait but requested a deep discount for their trouble. All this reached Jane's boss. The errors weren't her fault, but she still got in crap for not redeeming both sales."

"Sounds like she had a tough boss," Trent said.

Lee nodded. "The guy's a real asshat."

"This question might strike you as odd, but did you or Jane know Felicity Kelley?" She'd exercised patience getting to this point but couldn't wait any longer.

"Felicity Kelley? Isn't that the author of *The Romeo Killer?* Oh my god." Lee slapped a hand over his mouth.

Amanda suspected he was putting the pieces together—the murders in the book, how he had found his girlfriend.

Lee dropped his arm. "I read the book, and the guy—the killer—murders women by stabbing them in the heart. And I found Jane in the exact same way he left his victims." He met Amanda's gaze, his eyes widened. "Is someone out there copying the murders from the book? Why my Jane?"

"There are many answers we have yet to figure out, Mr. Steedman." She kept her tone even and calm. The last thing they needed was for him to run off to the media in a panic, shouting *serial killer*. "We will need the time of your meeting, along with the client's name and phone number."

Lee gave them that information and added, "We were together from five until midnight. Long meeting, but it's not like I could get away. Please only call him if it's absolutely necessary. But you have my word, I would never do anything to hurt Jane."

Amanda handed her business card to Lee. "We're very sorry for your loss. If you would like counseling or someone to talk to, let me know and Victims Services, a unit with the PWCPD, can come out and talk with you."

"That won't be necessary. I'll get through somehow."

Amanda recognized the tough front from enforcing it herself after Kevin's and Lindsey's deaths.

Lee pocketed Amanda's card. "Does this mean I'm free to leave? Not that I have any idea where I'm going now. Guess I should call the hotel and cancel the booking."

"You are free to leave," Amanda told him, her heart hurting for the man. She and Trent walked toward the house.

Lee pulled out of the driveway just as the ME's van parked in front of the house.

Amanda turned to Trent. "We need to hit the bar and confirm if Burr was there last night. Someone on staff could have seen her leave with a man or noticed one paying her attention."

"Agreed, but I don't think they're open for a couple hours yet. Eleven thirty, I believe."

"That's right. Well, there's lots to keep us busy until then."

She entered the house with Trent; Rideout and Liam weren't far behind.

Malone was still in the bedroom, watching over CSI Blair as she continued to process the room. Donnelly must have been elsewhere in the house. Malone stepped out of the way to let everyone inside.

"How did it go with Steedman?" he asked.

"I don't think the guy did this. He's too broken up," Amanda said. "He has an alibi for last night, which we'll have to confirm. Before we do, we need TOD. He did give us a lead though. According to him, Burr spent the bulk of last night at the Tipsy Moose."

"Sounds like a potentially solid lead to me," Malone said. "She could have picked someone up or been followed home."

"What we were thinking," Amanda said. "We also want to see if we can find a connection between Burr and Kelley."

"What I would like to know," Trent started, "is why Kelley and Burr? What was it about them? Or is it as you essentially suggested, Sarge, that Burr was killed to muddy the investigation?"

"Only upside in that is we hopefully won't be looking at any more victims," Malone said.

"I wouldn't be so sure. If he is willing to kill just to cover his true motive, who knows where this will stop?" Amanda rubbed her forehead, feeling a headache moving in. Why couldn't their murder cases be quick open-and-shut dealies? It seemed like she and Trent were doomed to get the complicated ones. She looked across the room to where Rideout and Liam were getting to work on the body, and it wasn't long before they were pulling a Queen of Hearts playing card—folded into eight squares—from the vic's mouth.

"And there it is," Amanda muttered, shaking her head. That was the last piece that wrapped this crime scene with the neat bow of the Romeo Killer, confirming he'd jumped from the pages of fiction into the real world. To make it worse, *her* world, and that pissed her off beyond measure. Two murdered women within days, and where were she and Trent in terms of catching up with the killer? Behind the eight ball, as the expression goes. Or no further ahead, seeing as that was their starting position. She just had to keep the faith that eventually there would be a breakthrough. It could never happen fast enough.

Malone's face hardened as he fixed his hands on his hips. "We're going to need to get in front of this, not that I should need to say that to either of you."

"You don't," Amanda said.

A few seconds of tense silence passed between them, with Malone breaking it. "Can we afford to make the assumption this isn't a serial killer?"

"We'll keep our minds and our eyes open, but I'm really not convinced." She still felt there was something telling in Felicity's paperwork being burned. Was the killer trying to hide their tracks? Cover up a secret Felicity had discovered? That could fit if Felicity had found out who killed Naomi Chapman. But in the vein of keeping an open mind... "Did we find the vic's phone?" She directed this to Blair.

"Yep, it's bagged," she said.

"Was there any indication items were missing from the home or paperwork destroyed?" Amanda asked, but felt she knew what the answer would be.

"Nothing I've noticed or Donnelly has mentioned."

The answer was the expected one, but it still had the skin tightening on the back of her neck.

"Time of death, Rideout?" Trent asked the ME.

"Preliminarily, I'd say between nine and eleven last night. I'll do more tests at the morgue to narrow it down and confirm."

"We were told she didn't get home until ten o'clock," Trent countered.

"Hey, you're doing my job for me. TOD between ten and eleven then."

"It doesn't get much narrower than that," Malone said.

"It does not. This also means that Burr's killer didn't wait long to act after she returned home." They'd need to call Lee Steedman's client to confirm he was with him during that time. "At least we know who didn't murder Jane Burr."

"Sheldon Lowe," she and Trent said at the same time.

"Yep, and since it's clear we're looking at the same guy for Felicity's murder, he's in the clear there too." How she hoped it was that simple. The thought ran through her mind—what if this is a copycat of a copycat? How much detail hit the news?

"To think if he never led us on a car chase, he wouldn't even be facing charges." Trent raised his eyebrows.

It was crazy what panic would make people do, but it wasn't like Sheldon was entirely innocent. He was a stalker. But her mind was more on what entered her thoughts a moment ago. She and Trent had spoken with a lot of people. Had one of them slipped word to the media, hinting about Felicity's murder being much like her book? "Has there been any mention or rumor out there that someone imitating the Romeo Killer murdered Felicity Kelley?" Just verbalizing the question made her nauseous.

Everyone fell silent. Trent was the first to speak.

"Someone copied a copycat... Then are we looking at someone in Burr's life who saw this as an opportunity to kill her and have blame land elsewhere?"

Amanda hadn't even played out the theory to that possibility. She wished she'd gotten around to asking Lee Steedman about those who didn't like Jane. They'd have to revisit him.

Malone held up a hand. "All right, before we get too carried away, let's see what's circulating online. Heck, I'll see to that in a minute. Rideout, run us through what you're seeing here. Cause of death?"

"What you see is what you get here," Rideout said. "Knife wound to the heart. Death would have been instant."

Amanda butted her head toward the knife. "Same as the one used on Felicity Kelley?"

"Looks like it's from the same set." Rideout pulled it from Burr's chest with a gloved hand and looked at it as Liam rushed over with an evidence bag. Photographs were taken, and Rideout said, "Yes, same set, different type. A chopping knife for Felicity, as you know. This one's a carving knife."

"The killer may be taking knives from his own kitchen," Trent suggested.

"Find me the killer, and I'll let you know," Blair said lightly.

Rideout tucked the knife into the bag, and Liam zipped it up and handled it from there.

Donnelly entered the room and shook her head, but Amanda would need more than that to decipher her message. "What's that for?"

"I searched for signs of forced entry. Found zip."

"Then she let her killer inside." Much as she and Trent had figured for Felicity Kelley and Naomi Chapman. Was it a mere coincidence that aspect spanned all three cases? Had all three known their killer, or had he used the same tactic to gain entry to their homes? Either way, it was one element that added some proof to there being one killer. It also meant they were on the right track, looking at the Chapman case to provide direction. "We'll need uniforms canvassing the neighborhood, see if anyone noticed whether Burr had a visitor last night."

Malone nodded. "They're already out there asking that ahead of TOD, but they are inquiring about the last twenty-four. I figured that ought to have covered it. What's the next step for you two? The bar probably isn't open yet."

Amanda consulted the time on her phone. There was still thirty minutes until opening, but she might be able to talk herself inside. "It will be soon. We'll head over now."

They pivoted to leave the room, and Malone called out, "I'll let you know what's hit online."

She nodded, still somewhat shaky at the thought of a copycat of a copycat.

"I can tell you're freaking out a bit here, concerned all the murders aren't linked, but my gut tells me they are," said Trent. "So does what I'm seeing. Even if rumor hit the news of someone copying the fictional killer, that can't explain how the knives are from the same set."

She didn't respond, wondering if she was being paranoid, but they'd already heard of a leak in the department. Maybe she was just the right amount paranoid. "Have you heard whether we have access to Kelley's cloud storage yet?"

"You'd be the first I'd tell, but no approval when I checked a moment ago."

Was it too much to wish for this cop's name to be in the cloud?

"What about you? Any word from Briggs on the fan emails?"

"Nope. I'll follow up with him. But what next?" Not literally, rather an exasperated cry out to the cosmos.

"It might be best not to serve that question up to the universe."

"You might be right."

They got on the road to the Tipsy Moose Alehouse, and while Trent drove, she texted Briggs on his personal number.

THIRTY-SEVEN

Amanda had a response from Detective Briggs before Trent parked in the lot for the bar. "Briggs said he'd get to it tonight when he goes in. He apologized for the delay but said a lot has come across his desk lately."

"It would help his shift pass faster, but it's a sad reflection on the world."

"Our lives are a sad reflection," she countered. It was unfortunate there was a need for the justice system. But crime and violence would never go away, and if she gave too much thought to human atrocities, it would send her spiraling into the darkness. She preferred not to visit there willingly.

She made two more calls from the parking lot—one to Lee Steedman and the other to his client. She hung up and brought Trent up to speed. "Steedman's alibi is solid, and he can't think of anyone who would have wanted to hurt her."

Trent looked over at her. "That should add more assurance —not a copycat of a copycat."

"You're probably right."

"Oh, I *am* right." He grinned.

She smiled back, again loving his confidence and the way he had of grounding her when it was needed.

They got out of the car and knocked on the door of the bar, even though it wasn't open for another ten minutes.

Alex Hurley, aka Moose, the owner of the bar, responded with a scowl in place. His expression softened at the sight of Amanda.

I might come here too often...

"You're a little early, Amanda, but for you..." He stepped back to let her and Trent inside, though Trent got a look through slit eyes. More bark than bite. To Amanda, Moose said, "You just can't wait a minute longer to sink your teeth into our bacon cheeseburger and onion rings, can ya?"

That sounded delicious and just the mention of it had her taste buds watering and her stomach rumbling. That muffin was long gone. She held up her hands. "You got me." Sometimes it was better to surrender in these situations than resist. If she and Trent relaxed, Moose would too. And if he was at ease, he'd be more cooperative. If they played this right, he might even let them look at the bar's surveillance video without requesting a warrant.

Moose seated them in a booth and asked if they wanted a beer. They both declined. "All right, now I know something's up."

"Yeah, we're both hungry." Amanda tapped the table. "And I will take that bacon cheeseburger with all the toppings and don't go light on the onion."

"I'll have the same." Trent extended the menu to Moose.

He collected the menus but remained at the side of the table for a few beats before walking off. "I'll be back with some ice waters."

"Add lemon to mine, please," Trent called out. Moose shot him a thumbs up over his head but kept walking. Trent leaned across the table to Amanda. "What are we doing?"

"Eating an early lunch."

"I gathered that much, but do we really have time to be—"

"Your waters." Moose set down two glasses, half ice, half water, by the look of it, a lemon slice in Trent's, and gave them each a paper straw on the side. "Shouldn't be too long, and you'll be munching away."

"Fantastic. Thanks, Moose," she said.

"You got it." Again, he flashed a thumbs up before leaving.

"I didn't know that he was"—Trent jabbed his eyes toward the owner's retreating form—"Moose."

"Yep. Alex Hurley is *the* moose the place is named after."

"Well, I pieced together he was the owner, but— Neat. Where did he get the nickname?"

"That is top secret." She settled back into the booth, grinning wickedly.

"You're not going to tell me?"

"Not my story to tell."

"Huh. That's how this is going to work."

"You're a detective. Figure it out." She met his gaze, and his eyes widened.

"No?"

She lifted her shoulders and pressed her lips together, though she was having a hard time holding back from laughing.

"It's some reference to his sexual prowess?"

"Prowess? Is that even a word anymore?" She was smiling now, not to be helped.

"What I mean is he's, ah..." Trent's cheeks flushed. "He's..."

"Well-endowed? That, I wouldn't know."

"Here it is... Fresh off the grill." Moose set down the orders, and the smell alone should be illegal. The sight was heaven—a perfectly toasted bun, strips of bacon poking out, melted cheddar cheese oozing onto the plate, the glimpse of red onion. To the side, a generous heap of golden deep-fried onion rings, a little container of coleslaw, and a wedge of tangy pickle.

"Thank you," she said.

"You bet. Enjoy." Moose walked off again.

No problem there...

She and Trent said little as they ate. When she popped the last bite of onion ring into her mouth, she could hardly believe she'd eaten the entire meal. She was hungrier than she thought, and surprisingly, it wasn't sitting in her gut like a boulder.

Moose checked on them after their first few bites and later to clear their plates. He raised his eyebrows at Amanda and gestured toward her empty dish. "I must have outdone myself today."

"You did that, but I was starving. What can I say?" She smiled at him, not taking offense at his reaction because he knew she rarely devoured the entire thing.

"Just the check then? Two... One?"

"One is fine," Amanda told him.

"Cash, or will you need the machine?"

"The machine, please."

"Charging it to the department?" Trent asked after Moose left to get the check.

"Not this time."

"You don't need to cover mine." Trent went into his pockets and came out empty. "No cash, but I have credit and debit." He held up the two plastic cards, and she shook her head.

"No need."

"I'll owe you then."

"If you wish."

Moose returned with the check and the card machine. Amanda settled up, adding a nice tip. Moose didn't miss this when he was ripping off her copy. His eyes widened, then narrowed. "All right, now I really know you're after something. What is it, Amanda?"

She pulled her phone and brought up a photograph of Jane

Burr. "Do you recognize her as being in here last night between five and ten?"

Moose held eye contact with Amanda, but then relented and took her phone. He held it to within a couple of inches of his nose. "Yep, she was here and sat right there." Moose pointed to a stool at the bar.

Amanda took her phone back. "You wouldn't happen to have video coverage on that section, would you?"

Moose crossed his arms. "I do."

"It would be really nice if you'd let us take a look at that for the time she was here." She tagged on a pleasant smile, hoping Moose couldn't resist it.

"Will this get my bar into trouble?"

She sat up straighter and answered honestly. "I don't see how."

"Very well then. Come with me."

She hopped out of the booth, flashing Trent a cocky smile. Showing interest in people paid off almost every time.

Moose took them to an office positioned off the kitchen. It had two desks, two chairs, and a four-drawer filing cabinet. "Come around here." He motioned for Amanda and Trent to walk behind one of the desks. He gestured toward the monitor. Video feeds showed in four squares, covering the rear of the building, the front lot, the cash register, and the bar with some of the restaurant.

"Which one do you want to start with?" Moose asked.

"The one that covers the bar." She thought the front lot might come in handy later on, but one step at a time.

Moose brought up the file for yesterday and forwarded the footage to 4:59 PM.

"Can you skip ahead a bit?" She sure hoped this endeavor would give them a lead to follow.

Moose did as she had asked.

At ten after five, Jane entered the frame. "Back to regular speed, please?"

Moose complied and, on screen, Jane approached the bar, dropped onto a stool, and flagged down Moose.

"She was a single malt scotch on the rocks," he said. "I've got a memory like a steel trap."

That was impressive given how many drinks he would have served over his lifetime. With recollection like that it was no wonder he didn't need a notepad when he took food orders.

Jane started off alone and the seats next to her were empty, but as the evening wore on, the place filled up. One grace was Jane was seated at the front of the feed, so it was easy to keep their eye on their mark.

Amanda had Moose play the footage at increased speed to cover the time more quickly than watching it pass live. At seven fifty-five, a man in a baseball cap sat down beside Jane, but he kept his head lowered.

"Who is that?" she asked Moose and pointed.

"Heineken Zero."

Smartass. "Does he have a name?"

"I'm sure he does, not that I know it."

She simpered. "Has he ever been in before?"

"I ain't never seen him."

The Tipsy Moose Alehouse wasn't the only bar in Prince William County, but it was one of the more popular watering holes. If Moose didn't know him, the man was likely from out of town.

"Want me to resume the movie?" Moose asked, a slight lift to his lips.

"Please," she said.

As it played at regular speed, Jane and the man got cozier. But while she was knocking back scotch, he was drinking non-alcoholic beer. His motive could have been to get her into bed, but there was something off about his movements. They were somewhat twitchy. He was also good at obscuring his face—either blocking it with his hand, elbow perched on the bar, or letting the bill of the cap do the job.

Amanda had Moose speed up the feed.

At nine thirty, Jane settled her tab and got up. The man in the cap didn't leave with her, but he wasn't far behind. He'd slapped bills on the counter, so any chance of tracking him down by a credit card ended there.

"Can you get a closeup of his face?" Trent asked.

"Let me see. I feel like I'm on one of those cop shows, and it's gonna be me who cracks the case wide open." Moose smiled at Amanda and let it stay for Trent. She'd be fine with it; she wasn't in this for credit, only justice.

Moose reversed and forwarded the feed in search of an ideal angle. No luck.

"What about outside? Can we see his vehicle, possibly his license plate?" she asked, feeling desperate to take whatever she could get.

Moose loaded the footage from the outside camera. The man arrived from the direction of the road, an area the camera didn't cover. As he entered the bar, he walked with his head down. Averting the camera intentionally or coincidentally? When he left, again, he walked toward the road.

"He must have gotten dropped off by a taxi or car service," Trent said. "They usually let their fares out up front."

They were leaving with nothing. Just a faceless man in a baseball cap chatting up their victim at the bar. She still thanked Moose for his help.

"Anytime. By the way, you didn't need to warm me up by buying lunch, but thanks!" Moose grinned.

Amanda stepped outside not feeling like she'd won any prize, but she had a full stomach. "No clear shot of his face, even from sitting at the bar," she said to Trent as they walked to the car.

"Which he did a good job of hiding. Suspicious, if you ask me."

"I completely agree."

"Washington Nationals."

"What?" His statement had her confused.

"His hat had the logo for the Washington Nationals. They're the Major League Baseball team for Washington, DC."

She figured the man must be from out of town, not being someone that Moore recognized. It also removed a niggling thought that a PWCPD officer was somehow involved. "He could live in DC. Though, he could just be a fan."

"Or new to town. *Or* visiting town..."

"I get it. Lots of variables, but I'd put money on him being the killer. You saw the way he engaged Jane. And he goes to a bar and drinks non-alcoholic beer. I know it's becoming more popular to do that, but was he doing so purposely to keep his head clear?"

"Could be. And assuming he's our killer, did he come here to stumble across his next victim? Jane Burr just ticking off that box?"

Random selection was tougher to reconcile than victims who were targeted. The former was all about chance, wrong place, wrong time. "Malone could have been right. Burr was collateral damage, a means to muddy the investigation."

"Speaking of Malone...?"

She shook her head. "No word yet, but I'm confident the same killer took out Kelley and Burr. Quite likely Naomi Chapman."

She got into the passenger seat while he settled behind the wheel.

"My gut is telling me the same, but how did the killer keep tabs on her? How would he have known about her progress? And the flip side, how would Felicity have even been able to identify the killer? It's not like she had the investigation files."

"Well, we do, and we still haven't solved it."

"Thanks for that."

She smirked. "Just keeping it real. But it does seem like Felicity was tenacious about ripping at the case. The fact she spoke with the people surrounding Chapman tells us that much. It might have to do with why her paperwork was destroyed, although... Remember there was paper in the upstairs shredder? I wonder if Blair or Donnelly got anywhere with that. Actually, I'm going to pop a message over to Blair about it right now." Amanda took out her phone.

"I guess it's time to pick up where we left off last night. We go talk to those people Felicity did, starting with the owner of Between the Pages."

She tucked her phone away. "Sounds like a plan to me."

Trent got them on the road, and she thought through the implication of Burr being randomly selected. Her epiphany gave her chills. "Did the killer strike again because he's aware of our interest in the Chapman case?"

Trent looked over at her but didn't say a word. He didn't have to.

The person they were after could very well be someone they spoke to face to face—or someone in the shadows. But what was to stop him from coming after one of them?

THIRTY-EIGHT

It was sad for Amanda to think that it had just been last night when she and Trent had decided to step back from the investigation for the weekend. Yet here they were the following day picking up right where they had left off—with yet another murder to solve. The only thing simplifying this mess was once they solved one, they likely solved all three cases.

The background on Edmond McCormick, the previous owner of Between the Pages, showed no criminal record. He was in his sixties and living in Triangle, only a few blocks over from Felicity Kelley's house.

At his place now, Amanda noted it looked much like Felicity's, a turn-of-the-century brick structure that had been nicely maintained.

Trent rang the bell. A man peeked through the sidelight before he cracked the door open.

"Yes?"

Amanda and Trent had their badges up. Trent confirmed the man was Edmond McCormick, gave the brief introductions, and added, "We'd like to ask you a few questions about Naomi Chapman."

"That poor girl." Edmond opened the door wider and gestured for them to enter. "I heard about her murder on the news."

Amanda glanced sideways at Trent, uncertain where the older man's mind was. "Whose murder, Mr. McCormick?"

"That author's, of course." His tone became snippy, and he shut the door behind them and took them to the living room.

"You're talking about Felicity Kelley?" His mind was bouncing around, and she wanted to keep up.

"Yes." Edmond let out an impatient huff as he dropped down into a chair with plastic wrapped around the arms.

Amanda and Trent sat on a couch, and she considered how she wanted to start the conversation. Their purpose was to uncover exactly what was said between Edmond and Felicity. "Did you know Ms. Kelley?" She'd begin playing it as if they were in the complete dark about their communication.

"Uh-huh. She popped by here for a visit, say about... Well, a few months ago." His shoulders drooped. "Can't remember exactly, but she was a nice girl. Very smart, but very stubborn."

"What was she stubborn about?" Amanda couldn't have asked for a better segue; she had a feeling this would lead the discussion right where she wanted it to go.

Edmond winked at her. "Wouldn't you like to know?"

That's why I asked... Given the way the man's reactions were all over along with his replies, she'd wager Edmond battled with dementia. "If you would be so kind as to share the reason with us..." She smiled, feeling for the man if he was losing control of his mind.

"She wanted to talk about... what was it now?"

Amanda drew inward. *Would he be able to help them?*

"Ah, yes. It was about that Naomi girl."

"Naomi Chapman, sir?" Trent asked, before he passed the slightest side-glance at Amanda.

Edmond pointed a finger at Trent and beamed. "Yes, that's the one."

"Why was she interested in her?" It was probably best to continue playing this as if she and Trent were clueless.

"She said that she was murdered. Some time ago." Edmond rubbed his scruffy jaw.

"She was. You remember that Naomi worked for you at Between the Pages?" Amanda asked, but instantly regretted it due to Edmond's wicked scowl and his stiffened posture.

"I remember just perfectly, thank you."

She held up a hand in surrender. "I apologize. I didn't mean to imply that—"

Edmond waved a hand. "I shouldn't get so worked up. It's no secret my mind isn't what it used to be."

Amanda refused to touch the statement, and she certainly wasn't going to repeat her question unless it was necessary. She'd give Edmond time to pick up with the answer.

A few seconds later, Edmond said, "I remember Naomi. Beautiful girl."

"She must have been smart as well to get that promotion from intern." It was a pet peeve when women—or men—were characterized primarily by their looks.

"Mmm." Edmond teetered his hand as if to imply that Naomi had been lacking in the brains department.

Amanda angled her head. "I don't understand then. Why give her the promotion if the others were more qualified?" She and Trent had batted around the idea that a jealous colleague might be behind Chapman's murder, and if they saw she hadn't earned her place, that might have served as the catalyst.

"Kurt."

Trent lowered the tablet. "Who is Kurt?"

"He was smart, knew what he was doing. He had a promising future ahead of him, but he left and found another job before I could promote him."

Amanda was grateful that these pockets of memories remained for Edmond. The mind was a mysterious thing. "When was this?" She wasn't going to make the same mistake of adding "do you remember" a second time.

"Not long before Naomi's murder."

"Did you tell Felicity about Kurt?" she asked.

"Who?" Edmond kneaded his brow. "Oh, the author. Yes. She took my picture, and I haven't gotten it back yet."

My picture... He made it sound like Felicity snapped one of him, but Amanda suspected he meant she took a photo Edmond had in his possession. "What was the picture of, Mr. McCormick?"

"All the interns that year. They were a good bunch." His eyes glazed over as his mind had taken leave.

Had Felicity suspected, like Amanda and Trent, that Chapman's killer may be among them? "Would you have any other copies of this picture?"

"Nah, sorry. And don't bother to ask me their names. No chance I'll remember any besides Kurt."

"Would you have any of their names on file in storage? We could look it up that way," Trent said.

Edmond shook his head. "Nah. So much time has passed. And it's not like I need backup for audits at this point."

"You held on to the picture though. It must have meant something to you," Amanda said.

"It did. I had it framed, and it hung there." Edmond pointed to a nail on the wall.

There was no framed photo recovered from Felicity Kelley's house showing a bunch of unfamiliar faces. All that adorned her walls were unnoteworthy and impersonal prints picked up from department stores. The only pictures of any meaning were the ones on her mantel of Felicity with her sister. Had the killer taken the one of the interns? If so, it would suggest yet again she and Trent were on the right path—

possibly the same one that had gotten Felicity Kelley murdered. "You mentioned Kurt. Do you have a last name for him?"

Edmond pressed his lips, tapped the top of his head. "Nope."

She and Trent would find this Kurt guy, even though Edmond said he'd left before the promotion was handed out. He might give them the names of the others he'd interned with prior to leaving.

Amanda stood, not feeling they were going to get any more out of Edmond.

"You should know something else." Edmond's voice cut through clearly, more lucid than he'd been this entire time.

She turned to him. "What is that, Mr. McCormick?"

"Naomi didn't deserve that promotion." Shadows crossed the older man's face and aged him. "It's been a regret I've had to live with all these years."

"If she didn't earn it, why give it to her?" Trent asked, still seated and leaning forward.

"Not proud of myself, you see, but I had a problem back then." He paused as if he expected Amanda or Trent to interrupt. When they didn't, he continued. "I was a chronic gambler, in hock up to my eyeballs. I was close to losing everything—my house and my wife. Her dad offered me a way out."

At this point, Amanda didn't need Edmond to say any more as she was quite certain she could see where he was headed. Regardless, she remained silent.

Edmond added, "He paid me a lot of money to promote her, but I was to make a big deal as if she'd earned it. His daughter was never to know what he'd done. But he saved me. All my debts were paid off, and I've never rolled the dice since."

That tidbit could have added more fuel to an already volatile situation. Take a jealous intern, putting in the hard work, then Chapman gets a handout. "Thank you for your honesty and trusting us with this information. Did you happen to mention this to Felicity Kelley as well?"

"Who?" His eyes clouded over. "And what can I do for you two?" His brows angled down like pointed arrows. "Please get out of my home."

"Sorry to have bothered you, Mr. McCormick," she said and made for the front door with Trent.

They loaded into the car, and Trent got the air conditioning running.

He slid his hand around the steering wheel. "That poor man is losing his mind. No one should ever have to go through that."

"I couldn't agree more. But even still, he gave us tremendous leads."

"Uh-huh. Chapman only got the promotion because her father paid for it."

"Did one of the other interns find out and take issue with the bribe? I know I would, but even if they didn't know that part, McCormick just told us Chapman wasn't the best candidate for the job. Her fellow interns would have observed that much."

"We need the names of those interns. Only thing is, McCormick doesn't have the records anymore."

"We just know of a Kurt, no last name. Our best shot might be Ian Moss at Garrison & Marrow. If not him, then Human Resources. They might be able to look up the unpaid interns that came over from Between the Pages."

"Except, there were five years in there between Chapman's time and the acquisition. Those unpaid interns could have gone on to get paid positions."

"Good thinking. Then we're interested in employees that were taken on."

"I think it's worth a try, but it's not likely to go anywhere until Monday."

It was extremely frustrating to feel on the cusp of unraveling everything only to hit a wall. Then again, they could be all wrong about the interns. There might be nothing there at all. "Okay, what about Chapman's best friend, Victoria Eaton? She mentioned the other interns."

Trent bobbed his head. "She might have names for us."

"I say let's get over to her place and have a chat. Hopefully she's home on a Saturday afternoon."

"Let me get her address." Trent tapped into the onboard computer.

"On another note, we know from Kelley's phone records that she contacted Chapman's parents. Did she ask them about the bribe or net something else from them? I think we need to find out. You wouldn't happen to have their number, would you?"

"Yep." Trent paused what he was doing on the computer and pulled out the tablet. He prattled off the digits as she pecked them into her phone.

She listened to the line ring repeatedly and had a feeling where this was going to lead. No sooner had she accepted her fate than she landed in voicemail. She left a message for them to call once they got the message.

"I have an address for Victoria Eaton."

Amanda gestured out the windshield. "No time like the present. Hit the—" She was going to say *gas pedal*, but her ringing phone cut her off. Caller ID told her it was Malone. "What have you got for us?"

"There's one way to answer the phone."

"It's efficient," she said with a smile and put the call on speaker. It felt like an hour before Malone spoke.

"There's nothing online about Felicity Kelley's murder resembling ones from her book."

Amanda let out a breath, even though she'd since put the possibility of someone copying a copycat out of her mind.

"So that's good news. You're looking for one killer. I have something else for you too. One of the canvassing officers came back with this little tidbit. A neighbor across the street from Burr's house saw a cab from Benji's Taxi drive past around ten o'clock last night. Apparently, this eyewitness is a little sketchy on the exact time but was confident in saying *thereabouts*."

Tingles danced over Amanda's neck and down her arms. The man in the ball cap had approached the Tipsy Moose Alehouse, from where taxis and car services drop off their fares... "That's interesting."

"Talk to me," Malone said.

Trent jumped in and informed him about their trip to the Tipsy Moose and the mystery man wearing a Washington Nationals baseball hat.

"And you're sure this guy got into a taxi?"

"He was most likely dropped off by one anyway," Amanda said. "That part isn't covered by the security camera. But Moose didn't recognize the guy, so he's either new to town or visiting."

"Let me get this straight. This guy just saddled up next to Burr and made conversation with her for hours. You sure he was a stranger to her? If so, why would she let him into her house?"

Amanda pinched her eyes shut for a moment. It was far too easy to go down rabbit holes during investigations. "We don't have all the answers, but he could have established some trust.

"Chatting with someone at the bar is one thing, but for that person to show up on your doorstep shortly after is quite another," Malone pointed out.

"Now, you said the taxi was seen out front around ten. That was when Burr texted her boyfriend that she got in. So that man could have followed her from the bar. But there's nothing saying he didn't threaten her at knifepoint or gunpoint," Amanda suggested.

"Or maybe Burr was going to hook up with this guy. Consider that?" Malone asked.

"I got the feeling from talking with the boyfriend their relationship was in a good spot. While taken on its own, the scene might speak to a romantic rendezvous, we can't ignore the stark resemblance to the murder in *The Romeo Killer*. And the knife being from the same set as the one used on Felicity. We need a warrant for the security footage from inside the cab. It might give us a look at the fare's face."

"Might be tough, but I'll see what I can make happen. Anything else before I go?"

"Just that Trent and I feel our strongest lead rests with the Chapman case. We were just about to head over and talk with her best friend."

"Always trust your instincts, Steele. I do. Keep me posted." With that, Malone hung up.

"Huh. He trusts *your* instincts," Trent said.

"He meant ours." She shook her head, and he smirked as he put the car into gear.

THIRTY-NINE

A woman in her late thirties answered the door, and Amanda held up her badge. "Are you Victoria Eaton?"

"I am. Come in." She let Amanda and Trent inside, and they took seats at the table in the dining room. A fan swirled overhead, the light off, as the room was bright enough with the late afternoon sun streaming in through the window.

Amanda managed to tamp down her curiosity until they all got situated. It normally took more effort to get themselves invited into a person's home. Victoria must have been expecting police to show up at her door. "Thank you for being so willing to talk with us."

"Well, she's dead... that crime author, Felicity Kelley. The article came up as a suggestion on Google for me. I figured you would have seen that she called me and been curious. I mean you guys do that, right? Look at call histories?"

"We do," Amanda confirmed.

"She wanted to talk about Naomi, but I didn't want to. That time was painful for me. Hardest time in my life to date, truth be told."

Amanda nodded, understanding Victoria's viewpoint. She

also appreciated that she was being so open with them. Before she could open her mouth to speak, Victoria continued.

"Ever since I saw that Felicity was dead, I've been beating myself up about not hearing her out."

They'd been trying to figure out how Felicity had assembled the pieces in the Chapman case, and it would seem she hadn't received much help from Victoria. Hopefully that would change for her and Trent. "Would you be willing to answer some questions for us?"

Victoria licked her lips. "About Naomi?"

"Yes."

Victoria took a breath, straightened her posture, and said on a breath, "All right."

"During a police interview after the murder, you brought up Naomi's fellow interns. Why was that?"

"The police were interested in who might have known about her jewelry. Naomi wasn't exactly quiet about flaunting what she had. I was her best friend, but I knew about the heirloom brooch she inherited. It was worth *a lot* of money. I assume whoever killed her took that, and these pricey cufflinks she had, and her Tiffany studs..." Victoria looked at her and Trent as if seeking confirmation, but the stolen items weren't to be public knowledge.

Amanda didn't recall reading mention in Victoria's statement that Naomi Chapman flaunted her wealth. Such a tidbit might have not only aided the investigation but steered it in a completely different direction. "Did you mention this much to the detectives at the time?"

Victoria seemed to hesitate, then shook her head. "I didn't want to make Naomi look bad, you know. I didn't want them thinking she was a spoiled brat, which she was, and I'm only now comfortable saying that out loud."

If she had been bold enough, Chapman's killer might have been caught years ago and Felicity Kelley and Jane Burr could still be alive. "Did her fellow interns know about the items you just mentioned?"

"I'd be more shocked if they didn't."

"Do you know the names of the other interns? I saw from the file that you celebrated with everyone at the bar the night she died," Amanda said.

"After all this time? All of them? No way. That feels like another lifetime. But I do know who got Naomi's promotion in her place. He was a worm and not worthy of it."

"Do you have a name?" Trent asked, the question rushing from his lips.

"Wendell Barrett."

Trent pecked on the tablet.

When Amanda and Trent had first turned their thoughts to the Chapman case, they'd considered the person who might benefit with her out of the way. They finally had a name. "Do you remember a Kurt by chance?" Edmond McCormick mentioned he was gone before the promotion, but Amanda still thought she'd ask about him. He could have felt pushed out by Naomi. Then the news of her promotion could have found him and prompted him to murder.

Victoria shook her head. "Never heard of him. But I have something for you." She walked to a curio cabinet, in a corner of the room, and returned with a manila envelope, which she gave to Amanda.

She moved it over in her hands. "What is this?"

"You might have noticed my car in the driveway on your way to the door? The logo on the door for my photography studio?"

"I did," Amanda said.

"My passion for photography dates back to my teenage years. That night at Taps and Cocktails, I took a lot of candid shots. Every one I took is in there." She nudged her head toward the envelope.

Amanda withdrew a stack of prints. "How many are there?"

"Forty-three."

"This is terrific, Naomi." Amanda shuffled through the top few photos, letting Trent see them too. Unfortunately, many were shadowed, dark, and out of focus.

"If you'd forgive me, but I didn't know all that much about flash and angles—even in my early twenties. I hope they'll still prove useful."

"It all helps. Thank you." Amanda put the pictures back into the envelope.

"Please just find out who did this to her. Naomi may have been a lot of things, but she didn't deserve to be murdered. Same for that author. I wished I had spoken to— Oh. I'm just putting this all together. I'm not sure how I didn't before now. I just thought Naomi's case was reopened, but there's more to it, isn't there? Felicity Kelley was asking about Naomi. Now she's been murdered. Then you two are at my door..." Victoria's glassy eyes met Amanda's gaze. "Do you suspect the person who killed Naomi also killed that author?"

Again, Amanda thought it was interesting how the mind worked and processed information—not everything clicked together at once. "That's what we're trying to figure out."

"Please let me know if you do. I'd love some closure."

Amanda dipped her head, and she and Trent saw themselves out. This had certainly been a worthwhile stop. They had the name Wendell Barrett and a potential goldmine in the photographs. While many weren't in focus, a close examination might yield a familiar face. And just that spark of possibility filled Amanda with the fuel she needed to keep going.

FORTY

The home of Wendell Barrett was Amanda and Trent's next stop. This was now territory that Felicity Kelley hadn't traveled. At least, she hadn't found out about him from Victoria Eaton and Felicity's phone records didn't connect her to him. It was going on four forty-five by the time they were pulling down his street. She had called Logan to touch base but couldn't provide an ETA on when she'd be home. It felt like they were on the verge of solving all three murders.

"I understand," Logan said. "You're on a case."

Three, technically. "You sure you understand?" She wouldn't normally push the matter. It must have been guilt over leaving him with Zoe so much. Though he knew he was signing on to be a father figure before he had moved in. They'd had a serious talk where she'd laid it all out—how she worked unpredictable hours and she'd expect him to watch Zoe if he could. He'd gladly accepted those terms.

"All right, saying that I understand is pushing it a bit," he said, his smile traveling in his voice across the line. "But it is what it is. You're putting bad guys away, and Zoe and I couldn't be any prouder of you."

"Thanks. I love you."

"And *we* love you."

After ending the call, she put her phone away as Trent was parking in the driveway of number 238, Wendell's house.

They knocked several times and were about to leave when the door opened.

"Yeah?" A man in his late thirties squinted in the afternoon sunlight. His eyes were puffy, and the tip of his nose was red.

"Wendell Barrett?" Trent asked him.

"That's me."

Trent flashed his badge. "We're Detectives Stenson and Steele, and we have some questions about Naomi Chapman."

"What about her?"

The fact they didn't need to jog his memory after fifteen years was noteworthy. Then again, even if he was innocent, how many people could say they knew someone who had been murdered? "It might be best if we came inside for this conversation." She could already feel the eyes of nosy neighbors on them.

"You don't want to do—" He sneezed and held up a finger while he fished a tissue from the pocket of his jogging pants.

"Bless you," Trent said.

Wendell blew his nose. "Summer cold. Nasty as hell, and I wouldn't wish it on my worst enemy. We can just talk here." He stepped out of the house and sat on the porch swing, the only available spot to sit.

As much as Amanda didn't like towering above people, it couldn't be helped.

"Why do you—" A nasty cough ripped from his lungs. It had his eyes bulging and tears forming.

Amanda and Trent moved back.

Wendell cleared his throat. "Why do you want to talk about Naomi? Didn't she die in a home robbery?"

It was rather convenient he had gone right there. Possibly a way of trying to nip this conversation before it got started. "Let's just say, we're revisiting the case. You may know that her killer was never caught."

"Really? She was murdered ages ago."

"Fifteen years ago, to be precise," Amanda said.

Wendell shrugged and mumbled, "Ages ago."

"What was your relationship like with Naomi Chapman?" Trent intercepted.

"Relationship? That's pushing it. She loathed me. Heck, she looked down her nose at everyone. Truthfully, she was a horrible human being." He coughed some more.

Amanda found him horrible for passing such a judgment when Naomi Chapman couldn't defend herself. Once he got his coughing under control, she said, "We heard she wasn't shy about letting others know about her wealth."

"She rubbed it in any chance she got. You'd think it was something she'd accomplished. Meanwhile, it was her Daddy Dearest with the money. It wouldn't surprise me if he paid Mr. McCormick to promote her. She wasn't the smartest tool in the shed."

Technically, it was sharpest *tool...* But her focus was more on what made Wendell say what he had. "Why did you make that suggestion... that her promotion was bought?"

"Oh, just that she had her father wrapped around her little finger. She got everything she ever wanted in life. All she had to do was ask for it and—*poof!*—it would appear."

Whether Wendell was guilty or not, he probably wasn't alone in suspecting Chapman's promotion had been bought. "Well, you ended up benefiting from her death, Mr. Barrett. You got that promotion in the end." If Wendell picked up on her implication—not well veiled—he never indicated in any way.

"I would have rather beat her out fair and square. Getting promoted after everything that happened with Naomi was rotten. The interns had no respect for me and questioned my right to advance. But my life turned out all right. I'm a literary agent and have a firm of my own. Now if only I can shake this blasted cold."

On that note, Amanda took another step back, as a further precaution.

"Were you transferred to Garrison & Marrow when they acquired Between the Pages?" Trent asked.

He nodded. "For a few months, but I didn't enjoy being a number in a big house. That's why I branched out on my own."

"You mentioned Naomi rubbed the fact she was wealthy in your faces. Did she ever mention anything specific that she had of value?"

Wendell's face blanked. "Where to start? Her BMW, her designer clothes and handbags, her diamond earrings from Tiffany's... Probably more that I've forgotten by this point."

There was a detectable bitter undercurrent, but was it strong enough to propel him to murder three women? He knew about the forty-thousand-dollar earrings and that meant the other interns may have too. "What about a ruby brooch or onyx cufflinks?" She wasn't saying these were among the stolen items, so she felt okay about asking this.

"Never heard of those. Doesn't mean she didn't brag about them when I wasn't around."

That it didn't... "Where were you the night of the robbery?"

"That was fifteen years ago. How do you expect me to remember that?" Wendell laughed, but his expression turned serious just seconds before he set off in another coughing fit. After it settled this time, he popped a lozenge in his mouth. "Are you seriously suspecting me of killing her?"

"Did you?" she countered.

"If you think one of us interns did this to her, I'd start with Kurt Archer." He was talking around the hard candy, and it clicked against his teeth.

What were the chances there was more than one Kurt? Edmond McCormick told them he was the one worthy of the promotion, but he was gone. "We've heard of Kurt, but we were told he moved on before Naomi got the promotion."

"Because Naomi got him fired. He was lucky to get other employment so quickly."

Edmond McCormick had failed to mention any of this. He made it sound like Kurt left of his own will, and if Kurt found fast employment, financial motive would be less likely. "How did she get him fired?"

"She messed up proofing a galley before a substantial print run and made it look like Kurt's fault."

"What is a galley?" Trent asked.

"Right. I guess you'd have no reason to know. Galleys are the last chance to catch and correct any errors before a book goes to print. If errors are significant enough, the run needs to be recalled and a new one done. That was the case there. If I remember right, it was an earlier version of the book and had some sections a lawyer had suggested be removed. Made public, the author and Between the Pages would have been vulnerable to legal action."

And yet, Edmond thought Kurt deserved the promotion. Given his dealings with Naomi's father, he may have suspected Naomi had framed Kurt. Yet he still fired him... Though it seemed he liked to remember Kurt leaving of his own initiative. Maybe that was Edmond's dementia at work.

"When did this happen exactly?" Trent asked.

"The week before Naomi's promotion."

Amanda gave her closing spiel, handed over her card, and she and Trent left. Neither spoke until they were in the car.

She clicked her seat belt into place. "If Wendell suspected Naomi's promotion was rigged, it's entirely possible other interns did too."

"Yep. And this Archer guy has strong motive. Setting him

up to get fired? That's heartless. It's feasible he was in touch with the remaining interns and hearing about Naomi's promotion from them set him off—new job or not."

"Very possible. And Naomi may have set Kurt up because she viewed him as competition. She must not have realized her father was going to secure her promotion."

"You know if her father never stepped in, we might not even be in this spot. Three women may still be alive." He glanced over at her.

"I'm trying not to think about that."

Trent took his phone out and was checking something on it. The clock on the dash told her it was now after five. Their visit with Wendell Barrett had been brief but informative.

"Do you need to cut out for the day?" she asked.

"Not that. Just checking to see if I have any messages. Thought I heard my phone chime. Turns out no texts, but I do have an email. We have access to Felicity Kelley's cloud storage."

"Take us to Central. Let's log in and have a look."

FORTY-ONE

Amanda and Trent were in his cubicle, and he was logging into Felicity Kelley's cloud drive. She was sure she held her breath as she waited for the password to be accepted. It turned out she need not have bothered. There was nothing there.

"Son of a..." Trent said. "But it would have been too easy, right? We need a challenge."

She shook her head. "For once, I'd take easy. We've hit a wall with her cloud storage, but we also talked about Felicity keeping backups on separate hard drives. The killer might have taken any drives, but it's possible she might store a backup drive or sensitive material somewhere secure...?"

"A safe deposit box maybe?"

"Good thinking. We'll check with Blair and Donnelly on Monday to see if there were any keys that might belong to one, or evidence of any receipts for its rental. There's no time to sit around sulking about this. We have a lead we can still follow today. That's if you're up for it?"

"I'm assuming you're talking about Kurt Archer. I mean, why not? It's not like I have someone waiting on me. But what about Logan and Zoe? I'm sure they're missing you."

"They are and I them, but they understand I put away bad guys. So, let's put on our capes and go catch one." That netted the trace of a smile.

Trent looked Kurt up in the system and scribbled his address on a piece of paper, which he tore off and took with him.

According to his file, Kurt Archer was single and living in Dumfries. They found him in his backyard after knocking on the front door and getting nowhere. Music started up, and they followed the direction of the noise, which took them through a side gate.

"Prince William County PD," Amanda called out ahead of them, to announce their presence and give them validity for being there.

Three men, all late thirties, topless and deeply tanned, sat around a small patio table. They must have been pounding back beers, given the number of empty bottles kicking around.

"Whoa, look." One of them, who was tilting back, balancing precariously on the rear legs of his chair, pointed at Amanda and Trent as they stepped onto the patio.

Another one tossed back the rest of his beer. The third stood, turned off the music, and came over.

She and Trent were holding up their badges. "Are you Kurt Archer?"

"That's me." He winked at her, and she felt slimy and pissed off at the same time.

"Detective Steele, and I suggest you keep your distance." She held up a hand and stepped back.

"She's not into you, man."

"You've been told."

Just great, the peanut gallery is weighing in! "Is there somewhere that Detective Stenson and I can talk with you?"

"Something wrong with right here?"

Kurt's buddies were leering so badly, she would have thought they'd just gotten released from a long prison stay. For all she knew, they could have. "Actually, yes, there is." She motioned for him to follow her around the side of the house.

"I'll be right back," Kurt told his friends.

"Good for you," one of them replied and let out a cat whistle.

Amanda took a deep breath. Alcohol really did turn some people into idiots. She pivoted and Kurt was right there, mere inches away. She moved back, because why waste her breath and ask him to give her space?

"Here, put this on." Trent thrust a T-shirt toward Kurt. He must have swung by the table for it before joining them at the side of the house.

"If I must." Again, he winked at Amanda, and she was grateful she had some patience and tolerance or she might have hauled off and hit the guy.

After Kurt put his shirt on, she said, "We have questions about Naomi Chapman."

"Who? Oh, right, *her*." That couldn't have come out with more disgust or disdain.

"You're not a fan?" Trent asked.

"Nope, never was, and especially wasn't after she got me fired. But I do all right."

There was a point in his favor that he'd been forthcoming about what Naomi had done to him. Whether he was currently doing all right was debatable. "What do you do, Mr. Archer?"

"Oh, Mister? I like that. So formal." His grin faded, likely in direct correlation to the grimace on her face.

"May I remind you that I'm an officer of the law and here on a serious matter," she pushed out.

He held up his hands. "Sorry. But, uh, yeah, I work for a

landscape and snow removal company these days. Me and the guys just got off for the day."

It surprised her he'd kept the conversational thread and answered her question. "Naomi Chapman. What was the relationship between you two?"

"Enemies. I'm sure she felt threatened by me. But she won in the end. Got me fired."

This was the second time he made this admission. She acted as if this was news. "How was that?"

He told them the same story they'd heard from Wendell Barrett.

"That would have sucked. How did that make you feel?" Trent asked.

"It pissed me off, torpedoed my publishing career before it started. But I got my revenge."

The back of Amanda's neck tightened, as her entire body stiffened. Could he be the man in the Washington Nationals hat? But given his love for alcohol, it was likely Moose would have recognized him. She also couldn't imagine Kurt chatting up a woman at a bar while drinking non-alcoholic beer all night.

Kurt held up a hand. "I just keyed her precious Beemer. I didn't... kill her. Wish I could have stuck around to see her reaction to her ruined paint job though."

The act of vandalism was news. Naomi must not have been too affected by it or her friend would have likely mentioned the incident when she was interviewed.

"Where were you the night of the robbery?" Trent asked.

Kurt looked at him. "You really mean did I murder her?"

Trent hitched his shoulders. "Just answer my question."

"You really think I killed her?"

Drunk or not, he had *some* brain cells left. He was just a little slow arriving. "It has crossed our minds. Did you?"

"Ah, no. She messed up my life enough, thank you. I certainly wasn't going to prison for her ass."

Huh. Valid point. Still, she said, "If you could answer the other question though... where you were that night."

"It really was forever ago."

"Try to remember. For me." Softening her voice was as far as she was willing to go to play her feminine wiles. The thought of tagging on a smile made her want to gag.

"I'm quite sure I was with my girlfriend. Don't ask me how you'd reach her now. We've long since fallen out of touch."

That answer had hardly been worth her effort. "We have ways of finding people. Her name?"

"Mia. Something or other."

"Charming," she mumbled. "Then from what I'm hearing, you don't have an alibi?"

"I do, I do, I swear."

She'd let the matter go—for now—and focus on another purpose for being here. "Do you remember the names of the other interns who worked with you at the time?"

"Nope. I put all of it out of my mind. Just remember Naomi because of what she did to me and then finding out she was murdered."

Amanda pulled her card and handed it to Kurt. "Only call me if you remember Mia's last name." She wanted to make it clear she wasn't interested in hearing from him for any personal agenda he might have.

He laid a hand over his chest. "You're breaking my heart."

"I'm sure you'll be just fine." Amanda spun to leave, and back at the car, she shared her earlier thought with Trent, "What is it with booze and its power to transform people into idiots?"

Trent just laughed.

"On a more serious note, we can't exactly verify Archer's alibi, but I don't think he did it." She laid out her thinking about the guy on the video chatting with Jane Burr.

"Me neither. Booze is also a kind of truth serum. His reaction to Naomi said it all for me. He hated her; he wasn't going to risk going to prison because of her."

"Yet he risked jail time by keying her car."

"Carries a lighter sentence than murder."

"Just a tad." She smirked at him as her phone rang. She held up the screen for Trent to see *M. Chapman*—Naomi's father, Michael—the caller's ID. "Detective Steele," she answered. "Thank you for returning my call." She proceeded to ask about his conversation with Felicity Kelley, leaving out all mention of his bribe to Edmond McCormick. After about five minutes, she hung up.

"So, what did he say?"

"He provided Felicity with photos of the brooch, cuff-links, and earrings. I asked if he suspected anyone, and his response—*to a cop*—was if he had any, he'd have dealt with them."

"Can't say Mr. Chapman takes things sitting down."

"Nope. And while we might not have any names to go after, we know that Kelley had her hands on photos of the insured pieces of jewelry."

"She really was a little sleuth, reaching out to all these people and digging up what she did. It's quite impressive."

"She had a knack for it, that's for sure. I think our theory about her getting close to the killer is gaining more credit by the minute. We speculated Felicity's killer was someone close to her, feasibly a person with whom she had face-to-face dealings. Just throwing this out there, but did she spot this person with one of those stolen items?"

"She could have, then tipped her hand. Even if not intentionally."

Amanda's mind bounced around the possibilities and landed on one undeniable. "She definitely knew her killer. I think we should step back, take the rest of the weekend, and come back to this on Monday."

"You're brave enough to give that another try?" He smiled at her.

"If you are." She laughed, but a part of her feared that taking time off might bite them in the ass again.

FORTY-TWO

Amanda enjoyed Sunday, the day of rest as her father liked to call it, without any word from Malone or the PWCPD. At least she and Trent were afforded some reprieve. The gathering at her parents' for Zoe's birthday had gone beautifully, and the girl wound up with more toys than she needed. But on that point, the girl deserved the moon and stars. She had certainly rescued Amanda. And now her light was shining brightly for Amanda's entire family and Logan.

But her buying time out for family hadn't come without some willpower. As it was, she'd succumbed to compulsion and checked her email Sunday morning. All that was there was a message from Briggs with names and addresses for each of the fans who sent email. With the current leanings in the investigation steering them to the Chapman case, she found it easy enough to set it aside.

But now that Monday was here, it was full throttle again. Zoe would be off to spend the day with her on-again, off-again friend Maria and a few other girls at Maria's house. Logan was scheduled back to work at the construction site his employer had been contracted for.

Amanda was behind her desk at Central at seven that morning. She'd started the day by pulling backgrounds for those select Felicity Kelley's fans—for due diligence—and nothing sparked. No criminal records anyway.

She next turned her attention to the photographs Victoria Eaton had given them. Flipping through them, she examined each image closely. Victoria certainly hadn't been a gifted photographer when she was younger, with so many of the shots being out of focus. Amanda wasn't even sure what she expected to see but still held a glimmer of hope she'd recognize someone. That was long gone after going through them a few times.

"For you." Trent entered her cubicle and set an extra-large coffee from Hannah's on her desk.

She leaned back in her chair and let her body relax. "You are the best."

"We take care of each other... Ah, keep each other in coffee anyway." He lifted his cup to hers in a toast gesture.

And that wasn't awkward...

"Any luck there?" Trent flicked a finger toward the photos, and she shook her head.

"Nope." She told him Briggs came through with the sender names and addresses for the fan mail and that they turned up nada in the system.

"Well, we are looking at things from another perspective now. Do you still want me to contact Human Resources at Garrison & Marrow to see if we can get the list of employees that came over from Between the Pages?"

"Yep. I say go for it. Go right to Ian Moss, run it past him. It seems everyone around there needs his approval."

Trent retreated to his cubicle while she stubbornly returned to the photos. After learning what they had about Naomi Chapman and the dynamics with her fellow interns, she was more confident than ever that one of them had killed her. The robbery was beside the point. As Dennis told them, there weren't any other fatalities with the string of home invasions at the time. But had the murder been premeditated?

Gah.

Her phone rang, breaking her concentration. It was CSI Blair, and Amanda answered before the third ring.

After greetings were exchanged, Blair said, "Donnelly and I were able to assemble some of that shredded paperwork. We were in yesterday for a few hours to do it."

"You two must be mind readers. I was going to follow up on that today. Tell me it paid off."

"That remains to be seen. But we made out one thing that might help. We pieced together the letterhead for Locked Up Tight. Looks like Kelley rented a safe deposit box there."

Amanda's heart kicked up speed. "Did you find a key in Kelley's possessions that could have belonged to one?"

"There was indeed."

"Where would that be now?" If Blair had it in Manassas, that presented a delay of another hour—the drive there and back.

"I have it here, but I can meet you halfway if that makes it easier for you?"

"That it does." They arranged a meeting spot, and Amanda could hardly wait for Trent to get off the phone.

Passing through the doors for Locked Up Tight brought back the past for Amanda. She'd been here during a previous investigation. The memory stirred bittersweet feelings as it had to do with the murder of Logan's estranged wife in June of last year.

One relief for Amanda was the person at the counter wasn't someone she recognized or knew from before. She told the woman they were with the PWCPD and showed Felicity's key.

"This is for a box belonging to Felicity Kelley. We need to see its contents."

"I'm going to need to see a warrant."

They'd got that ball rolling before they left to meet up with Blair. Amanda gestured to Trent, who brought it up on his screen.

The clerk glanced at it. "All right. What number is it?"

"That we don't know," Trent told them.

"Let me look it up in the system." The clerk typed and, a moment later, said, "Box 2392."

"Just to confirm, when was the box last opened?"

The clerk consulted the screen. "Last Tuesday at three thirty in the afternoon."

Amanda hadn't expected that. Felicity would have come here pretty much upon her return from Washington. Also, the same day she was murdered. Did Felicity see something while at her publisher's that had her on edge? Possibly the killer himself? It was starting to feel like the world was closing in on itself. But if Felicity came right here, did that mean this box might hold the key to the killer's identity?

She thanked the clerk, and the three of them walked to the box. After unlocking it, the clerk set the insert on a table in a small space with a curtain for privacy.

"Give a shout if you need me," she said, walking away.

"Will do," Trent said as Amanda lifted the lid on the box. This time her anticipation was high, but she braced for disappointment.

It turned out there was no need for that. There was a backup drive inside.

Trent was grinning. "Love it when we're right about something."

"You and me both."

"It's just the drive in there?"

Amanda took another look and nodded. "But it may be all we need."

They locked up the box again and left with the backup drive in hand. With every mile closer to Central, she swore her heart ticked up speed.

Please, point us right to the killer!

FORTY-THREE

Back at Central, Amanda stood behind Trent as he connected the drive to his computer.

"I think Felicity had a feeling the killer was on to her and that's why she put this in the box," she said.

"Let's see what's on it first."

It was the rare occasion he talked her down. "Right. Yeah, of course. I just have a feeling something good is on it. The timing alone... right after returning from Washington."

"We're about to find out." Trent gestured to the screen, where the file directory was now showing. There were only two folders: *Current book* and *Research*.

She told Trent to click on the latter, and there was a list of several documents and images. Trent opened one labeled *Chapman Crime Scene*.

It was a sketch of the crime scene, likely drawn by Felicity Kelley's own hand. It showed Chapman as a stick figure with the tipped-over stool and a question mark over her head. There were arrows drawing a path from the back door, through the kitchen and around the peninsula.

"This looks like the real deal," she said.

"She found out exactly what it looked like."

"Her contact within the department." With everything going on it had been a while since she'd thought of this, but he or she needed to be found out and reported.

"That or the maid. I wouldn't put it past her to share the details of how she found Chapman."

"A possibility. She didn't tell us she'd shared as much with Felicity, but that doesn't mean she didn't."

"I'd say Kelley was hung up on the intruder's supposed route too." Trent pointed toward the screen.

Just as they had been... "Let's see what else there is."

Trent opened more image files. They found ones of the brooch and onyx cufflinks that she would have obtained from Chapman's parents. There was also a picture of a framed photograph.

"The interns. Probably the picture she got from McCormick. Print that in color, Trent."

He sent it through to the printer, and it started whirring as it warmed up. In the meantime, she had him enlarge it, and they studied the image. One man's face was circled.

"He look familiar to you?" she asked.

"Nope."

"Me neither." She snatched the photo off the printer, stared at the man again, feeling disappointed she couldn't place him. Though there was this tiny fluttering inside her. A recognition on some level? "What about the documents? Anything that says so-and-so is the killer?"

Trent smirked and shook his head. "We can only hope."

"Well, Felicity locked up the drive for some reason. And there's that circle..." Was it too much to hope for something more definitive? Though she knew the answer to that question without dwelling on it for long. It was point-less to expect life would be that easy. She recalled her thinking about the timing—Felicity's trip to Washington and opening the box. "Have you heard back from Ian Moss yet?"

"Only to say he'd have HR get it over."

She nodded, and they kept working. They found news articles and opinion pieces within the research folder. Amanda eventually wheeled in her chair because she couldn't continue to stand.

Much of what they found covered the Chapman case, and there was a lot on how beauty and good looks affected promotion, as well as how popular opinion influenced unfairly. One article was entitled "How Attractive You Are Equals More Success." The rest were similarly headlined.

Trent flumped back in his chair. "What does any of this have to do with the Chapman case?"

"All I can think is Chapman was a beautiful woman, and she got everything handed to her in life…" Honestly, she was at a loss too, but they must be missing some small thread that stitched all this together.

"Daddy's money had a lot to do with that."

"But was it the only reason? She was stunning."

"I don't think that swayed McCormick."

"Except his pick would have been Kurt, if he hadn't essentially been forced to fire him. And Kurt was the best-looking of the bunch."

Trent rubbed his forehead. "How does any of this get us to the killer?"

"That I don't know."

An email notice popped up in the bottom of Trent's monitor. It was from Ian Moss, and he wasted no time opening it.

"What happened to HR?" she asked.

"Don't know." There was an attachment, but a scan of the message told them Ian Moss had decided to handle the matter himself. Ian added that the spreadsheet included everyone—in paid positions and interns—who had been transferred from

Between the Pages at the time of acquisition. He had marked those who were still currently employed by Garrison & Marrow with an asterisk.

"He gave us more than we needed. Wonderful. But all we need to focus on to start are those who are still current employees."

"You know something I don't?"

She took a few beats before sharing her thinking.

Trent was swiveling in his chair by the time she'd finished. "Someone Felicity saw the day of her murder..."

"What I suspect anyway. Hard to ignore she went into her safe deposit box upon her return from the champagne lunch."

"So, it could have been anyone she saw in the building—I get it now. Active employees. And we'd also speculated she saw someone wearing the jewelry."

"Yep." Talking it through out loud had her more confident this theory was right. "You get those backgrounds?"

"Consider it done."

"Just before you do, please pop out the drive. I'm going to look at it some more on my computer."

"Just a thought on that..." He handed over the drive. "You might want to read what she had written so far in her book. She might have named the killer."

"In that case, I'll skip right to the end." Although she highly doubted Felicity Kelley would have given the real killer's name to her fictional one.

"I'll be busy for a bit here. There are fifteen names."

"Well, hop to it." She rolled her chair out and went to her cubicle. Once there, she skimmed more articles about beauty affecting wealth. Study after study concluded it determined a person's bottom financial line. Such a sad reflection on the world.

An hour passed, two, maybe more. Her stomach was rumbling. Trent had finished pulling the backgrounds. None of them showed a criminal record. He was now working to see if he could link any of them to Felicity Kelley beyond working for her publisher. After all, it had to be someone who had reason to cross paths with her.

Amanda started on Felicity's book and, according to the word count, it was sitting around eighty-five thousand. That sounded like a lot, and she figured it was complete. She skipped to the end and scanned it, looking to see if she could decipher the killer's identity. She found the name. "Hey, Trent, anyone on that list named Isaiah Miller?"

"Nope."

"There goes your idea. That's the name of the killer in Felicity's latest book. Assuming by the file date of earlier last week, it was the latest version. But all right, back to the drawing board." She opened a Word document entitled "Author Letter" and proceeded to read.

Felicity was thanking and acknowledging everyone who helped with the book. Amanda stopped when she came across the following:

> *I can't express my gratitude enough to those in law enforcement who answered my questions about procedure. Though you requested to go unnamed, your personal investment in this project meant the world to me and helped me see things from a different perspective.*

No names or initials, but there was one word that had Amanda tingling with an epiphany. *Personal.* "Trent." After he looked over the divider, she said, "I stumbled on something here. I think whoever this cop is who helped Felicity knew her personally." She took out her phone and selected Celeste Sweeney's contact. "It never occurred to us to check with Felicity's best friend for the identity of her contact within— Well, you know." She didn't want to say the PWCPD for prying ears. The line stopped ringing, and she was sent to Celeste's voicemail. She begrudgingly left a message and ended the call.

"I'm going to need a little more information to go on here," Trent told her, and she directed him to read the text on her screen. He came around to read it. "Personal."

"That's the word that stuck out to me."

"Hence, the best friend. Let's hope she knows and can tell us who this person is." He returned to his cubicle, and her mind drifted. Her gaze did too, but it landed on the printed photo with the circled face.

Who are you?

She lifted it closer and narrowed her eyes, concentrated. There was a hint of familiarity, just a vague one. She shuffled through the photos she got from Victoria Eaton and searched for the man among them. Two had him in the frame. In the group shot, he was smiling but appeared self-conscious. He was quite overweight, his teeth were crooked and slightly yellow, and he had a problem with acne.

But as she studied the one photo, his right hand was wrapped around a beer glass. There was a gold band on his pinkie.

With that, everything slipped into place. Why he looked vaguely familiar, why Felicity Kelley had been interested in the effects of beauty on advancement, even why she'd named her killer Isaiah Miller. "Trent, I know who our killer is."

FORTY-FOUR

Amanda didn't get a chance to lay it all out for Trent before Malone came scurrying over with a printout in his hand.

"I just got the video from Benji's Taxi," Malone said. "The owner there is a great guy, Terrence Phillips."

"Yeah, I spoke with him in the past," Trent said.

Amanda just wanted Malone to get to his point. She was on the verge of exploding with what she'd just uncovered.

"He sent this picture over right away. It's from the taxi that was seen outside Jane Burr's house the night of her murder. Timestamp says it's nine fifty-five. You'll see that he's wearing a Washington Nationals baseball cap. Here..." Malone gave it to Amanda, but Trent was already to his feet and standing with them. "Tell me you recognize him."

"Ian Moss," they said at the same time.

"I reached that conclusion, Sarge," Amanda rushed out, almost breathless. "Just before you got here, I was about to share my findings with Trent. To start, Moss didn't always look like he does now." She grabbed the photos of him from her desk and pointed him out to Malone and Trent.

"He was right there. I didn't recognize him at all. He looks so incredibly different now," Trent said.

"Don't give yourself a hard time of it. I didn't recognize him at first either. The guy, as you can tell from the taxi photo, Sarge, is trim and good-looking. From talking with him in person, he has bright-white flawless teeth. He's shed at least a hundred and twenty pounds. His skin has cleared up." She realized she was talking fast, rattling all this off, but it felt like their efforts were about to pay off. "Trent, you saw all that research that Kelley did." She elaborated for Malone's benefit. "She had gathered a bunch of studies that showed attractive people are more likely to be successful, get promotions, and make more money than those who aren't so genetically blessed."

"Somehow that doesn't surprise me," Malone said.

"Moss was overlooked because of how he looked fifteen years ago—or at least that's how he might have felt. He probably hated Naomi Chapman for being everything he wasn't, having what he didn't have. And from what Trent and I have found out, Chapman pushed her money and success in people's faces. It's not a stretch to imagine that she picked on Moss. That's if she paid him any attention at all. But look at this..." She took the photo back from Malone, showing the younger Moss holding a beer glass. She tapped a finger to the image. "See the pinkie ring, Trent? Do you remember that?"

He met her gaze. "Yep. I saw it when I shook his hand."

"That was what pulled it together for me. And then Felicity named the killer in the book she'd been working on Isaiah Miller. That was probably on purpose too. Otherwise, why pick a name with the same initials as Ian Moss?"

"Word games aside, we have enough to move on this," Malone said.

"We're going to need to notify the Metro PD in Washington that the PWCPD is coming to town," she replied.

"You let me handle that." Malone gave the stack of photos back to Amanda and walked toward his office.

Trent was standing there, shaking his head. "We said the killer needed to be keeping tabs on Felicity. Moss fits."

"Felicity must have come across something that had it all clicking together. One of the jewelry items, as we'd thought before?"

"And in his case, that would most likely be the cuffs. At the champagne lunch? Why be so bold? Especially if he knew what she was working on, which he must have."

"Remember, though, the cufflinks weren't public knowledge."

"Here's another thing, he had to see the similarities between Felicity's book proposal and Naomi Chapman. Why didn't he reject it from the start?"

She had the answer to that one. "Turning it down could have looked bad for him. He probably didn't want to risk drawing any unnecessary attention."

"So, we can assume he approved the book and kept a close eye on Felicity. He would have known all about her sleuthing. He felt threatened and did what he felt necessary to keep his secret."

"It all fits, every last bit of it. Meanwhile, he's top dog at a large publishing house, smiling, shaking our hands. The whole time he was probably freaking out inside while outwardly over-compensating. Then he takes it upon himself to send the list of employees, making it seem like he was doing us a favor."

"Yeah, when really, it was all so he could leave his name off the list," Trent inserted.

"He's a real piece of work, who was doing a good job of covering his ass until Felicity Kelley turned up to ruin his life. And now it's time to finish what she started." She could hardly wait for the arrest and search warrants to hit her hand.

FORTY-FIVE

For the past few hours as Amanda and Trent waited on the warrants to come through and for everything to be arranged with the Metro PD, they did a deep dive into Ian Moss. It didn't reveal a criminal record, but it shone a light on his upbringing and background. Presently thirty-eight, Ian had grown up below the poverty line. His mother had died during childbirth, and his father was an alcoholic and couldn't hold down a job. The family home was a rundown shanty in a rural part of Prince William County. The fact that Ian had been able to pull himself out of that wreckage, excel in school, and get himself a paid ride through college was nothing short of impressive. It was just everything that came after that tarnished his crown. Now, Amanda looked forward to ripping it from his head and seeing that smug look of his disappear when she read him his rights and slapped on the cuffs.

The time eventually arrived. Warrants were in hand. While they were bringing him in, officers would be searching his residence and car. The latter turned out to be a BMW of the same model that Chapman had—a fact Amanda didn't view as a coincidence.

She and Trent entered Garrison & Marrow, accompanied by two uniformed officers with the Metro PD. They announced themselves to Cara at the front desk and said they were there to speak to Ian Moss, but she was not to notify him they were heading up.

Cara said they should be able to find him in his office. After which, she gave them directions. "Should I let his assistant know to expect you?"

Amanda shook her head. It was best that they have the element of surprise on their side. If they were right, Ian Moss had killed an innocent woman just to muddle the investigation. He clearly saw life as disposable when it served his purpose.

The four of them loaded into the elevator and made their way up to the twenty-fifth floor.

Amanda approached the assistant's desk holding up her badge. "Detective Steele, and I'm here with my partner, Detective Stenson, and officers from the Metro PD."

The young woman's face flicked over Amanda's shoulders, and she swallowed roughly, her eyes bulging.

"We're here for Ian Moss, but you're not to alert him we're coming."

The assistant nodded and held Amanda's gaze. It felt like there was something she wanted to say, but she remained silent.

In that stillness, Amanda heard voices from Ian's office. She turned to the assistant. "Is someone in there with him?"

"Uh-huh. Melody Schmitt."

Amanda's shoulders sagged as she faced Trent and the officers. "We can't risk going in hot. Let me—" She held up a hand and stopped talking.

Ian was looking through the window in his door—directly at her and everyone else. He shuffled out of sight and returned with Melody, his hands gripped around her arm.

"Never mind. Let's move."

They all forged ahead and entered the room. The office was

a massive space that included a living room and bar area, a meeting table and chairs.

"Mr. Moss, you need to let go of Ms. Schmitt and come with us," Amanda said calmly. No one had their guns out yet, but all it would take was the slightest provocation.

"I'm not doing that!" he roared.

Trent and the officers raised their guns. Amanda resisted, deciding to play Good Cop, hoping to deescalate the situation.

"Let me go!" Melody tried to pull away, but Ian yanked her closer to him and practically dragged her across the room toward his desk.

"You need to stop moving right now," Amanda told him, a hand up, palm toward him. "We just need to talk. That's all."

"*Pft.* You must think I'm pretty stupid." He tugged on Melody and used her as a shield, proving his intelligence.

Amanda approached slowly, holding up both hands now. "Let her go, Ian. She doesn't need to be caught up in this."

Melody was sobbing, and her shoulders were heaving.

"Melody," Amanda said softly, earning her gaze. "It's going to be all right, okay? Just breathe. Take slow, deep breaths." As she spoke to her, she was hypervigilant about what Moss was doing. He hadn't stopped moving and continued to creep with Melody ever closer to his desk.

Amanda drew her weapon. "You need to stand still, Mr. Moss. Immediately."

He didn't comply, but in a fluid movement, Ian opened the top drawer of his desk and pulled out a gun.

Melody screamed and started shaking violently.

"Come on, Ian, let her go," Amanda petitioned again. "No one else needs to get hurt."

"She should have left it alone. Let *me* alone," he snarled. It was clear he was referring to Felicity Kelley.

"Please, Ian. It's over."

"It's over when I say it's over!" Ian lifted his gun to the ceiling and pulled the trigger.

Overhead, something groaned and hissed. Sparks rained down. His bullet must have hit electrical wiring.

Melody tugged, trying again to get away, but he fastened his hold on her and held the gun to her cheek. She screamed—the muzzle would be burning her flesh. Amanda cringed for her.

"We have to go, Ian. Now."

"I'm not going anywhere! You just leave!"

How long could they stand there, face to face, angling off against each other? She wasn't trained in hostage negotiation, but this was the position she found herself in.

Smoke was curling from the ceiling tiles into the room.

Think! People who took hostages always wanted something. For Ian it would be his freedom and not a request she could grant. She thought if she could distract him somehow, she might open a window of opportunity. She ran through the scenario of throwing an object his way. Instinct would have him wanting to catch it before it hit him. Failing that, he'd freak out and fire a hail of bullets. Not acceptable. But causing a distraction was the only way she could conjure a positive outcome. Just how to do it.

"Get out of here!" Ian roared.

"You know what? Ian, they're going to go now." Amanda cautiously glanced over her shoulder and received questioning looks from Trent and the Metro PD cops. But they backed out of the room.

"No!" Melody cried out.

"I want you to leave too," Ian barked at Amanda.

The distinct clicking of the door shutting confirmed the others were gone. *Now, follow your own advice and breathe,* Amanda told herself. "I can't do that. But it's just me now. Naomi must have hurt you badly, I can see that now."

"I don't want to talk about her."

"She thought she was better than you, didn't she?"

"She thought she was better than *everyone*." He adjusted his hold on Melody.

If only there was some way for the editor to get the jump on him, but even if Amanda could find a means of communicating a method to her, it was too great a risk. She didn't want the woman's life on her shoulders.

The hole that Ian had made was extending as flame ate tile, widening it, and smoke was billowing from the aperture. Surely sprinklers had to come on soon. It might provide enough distraction to do something, but she had to keep him talking until then.

"You were the one who deserved that promotion years ago. I mean, look where you are." It took all her effort to project enthusiasm for his accomplishments. His path was paved with blood. She hadn't doubted they had been right about him, and his actions now weren't giving her any reason to reconsider.

The room was becoming hazy, and Melody coughed. Still not enough to distract Ian. Rather, it looked like he was pressing the muzzle harder to her cheek. Between hacking, she was crying.

As Amanda stood there, feet away, she felt so helpless. Even armed with a gun.

Watching the smoke descend, she flashed to the past when a killer had trapped her in a fire. She'd come close to dying that day... "We can't stay here any longer, Ian. Let Melody go, come with me, and—"

The overhead sprinklers came to life, and the click of them turning on had Ian flinching. In just a mere fraction of a second, he faltered. He used the back of his gun hand to wipe his face.

Amanda wasted no time signaling to Melody for her to duck down, and took aim.

Direct hit.

FORTY-SIX

Another long day meant Amanda would be home late, but she did catch the bad guy. Well, she and Trent, with a little help from the Metro PD—if she was being generous in throwing credit around.

They had searched Ian Moss's house and turned up the ruby brooch, onyx cufflinks, and the Tiffany diamond earrings. He'd kept them all this time. Maybe because he was afraid to pawn them. They also found the knife set in his kitchen that matched the ones used on Felicity Kelley and Jane Burr. They pulled two decks of discarded playing cards from his trash and their style was the same as the Queen of Hearts cards left in Kelley's and Burr's throats. A pair of his running shoes, size ten, matched the impressions left in Felicity's home. An area rug was rolled up and stuffed into a garbage bag in the garage, and the blood on it was likely to come back a match to Felicity. Her laptop was also found in Ian's place. But another takeaway was the framed photo of the interns that Edmond McCormick had treasured. Whether the owner of Between the Pages would still treasure it once he discovered one of them had turned into a killer remained to be seen. Regardless, they'd make sure it was returned to him.

Amanda was with Trent back at Central, and she was exhausted. There were a few moments she hadn't been sure if she was going to get Melody and herself out of there alive. Thankfully, the editor was quick to respond to Amanda's gesture for her to crouch down. Paramedics treated her on scene and released her. The emotional and mental recovery would take longer to heal than the burns to her cheek.

Ian Moss was another story. Amanda's bullet pierced his chest, but he was still alive when he was raced off to the hospital. Only time would tell his fate.

"All this to protect his secret," Trent said, shaking his head. "Two more women killed, all because he was trying to cover up his first murder."

"It's truly heartbreaking. Even more so when you consider that Jane Burr was simply in the wrong place at the wrong time."

"I agree. Moss must have sensed we were getting closer to him and panicked. Did what he knew how to do."

"It just all makes so much sense, looking back."

"It usually does."

She nudged him in the shoulder for his smartass attitude. "Felicity's handwritten note 'could it be' makes more sense now. She was probably struggling with where her research was leading her. I bet she suspected Moss before the champagne lunch."

"That wouldn't surprise me. I'm just impressed by how much she dug into the Chapman case."

"And while her efforts ended up bringing justice, if she'd left it alone, she'd still be alive and so would Burr."

"I think we do need to focus on the good. We stopped a killer and now three women's families will have justice and closure."

"Suppose you're right." She couldn't help but dredge up the question that if a cop within the PWCPD hadn't opened their mouth and directed Felicity to Bishop, could at least two murders have been avoided? Then again, things might have turned out the same way. Felicity was determined to get answers. Either way, Amanda wanted to know who that cop had been. She hadn't heard from Celeste Sweeney yet, but she'd follow up with her. They had good news to share anyhow.

"One thing that still remains—what was the final tip-off for Felicity? Had she seen Ian with one of the stolen items of jewelry? The cufflinks we thought before?"

"We may never know." Amanda's phone rang, and Celeste Sweeney's name came up on the screen. She answered immediately. "Thank you for returning my call. We need to talk. Could my partner and I come over now?"

FORTY-SEVEN

FELICITY KELLEY

Day of the Champagne Lunch

Another dream was coming true. Today Felicity was headed to her publisher's—in the back of a limo!—to sign a huge international rights deal for *The Romeo Killer*. All because it had met with so much success and secured a movie deal. She still had to pinch herself when she thought *box-office hit!* The media described it as overnight, but that was a laugh. She'd worked hard for years to get to this point.

Word play, as her friend Celeste called it, and Felicity couldn't deny that's exactly what it was—and so much fun! There was something magical about how the words spilled onto the page, as if she were a conduit for some omniscient being who was feeding her their story.

The limo came to a stop outside Garrison & Marrow, and the driver came around to get her door. He tipped his hat and smiled at her. "I will be ready when you are, ma'am."

So proper, so formal... She loved it, and how far a cry it was from her regular, everyday life when she preferred to sit on the couch, legs curled underneath her, laptop under her fingers, cranberry juice in a wineglass on the table beside her. She never mixed alcohol with writing; she took the craft far too seriously.

"Thank you," she told the man as she got out and smoothed the front of her pants.

She was dressed like a penguin today—as her sister would say—business suit in a deep plum that had a long jacket that reached mid-thigh. The style might be dated, but even at twenty-eight, she had observed that fashion trends circled around. Regardless, the dressy heeled boots and her Gucci handbag—a gift from Justine, who wouldn't accept Felicity's pleas that it was just too much—had her walking on air.

As Felicity entered through the lobby doors, any nerves settled. For just a second.

Eve... She felt her sister's presence, even if she couldn't see her. She had been a warrior, not afraid of anything. Fierce and beautiful and... Felicity's eyes welled up. *She missed her so much.*

Cara smiled at her. "Ms. Kelley, how nice to see you. Mr. Moss, Ms. Livingston, and Ms. Schmitt are already waiting for you in the Tower."

Felicity cleared her throat, said, "Thank you," and headed up in the elevator.

The 'Tower' was the top floor where Ian Moss, Publisher, had his office. Felicity suspected only A-list authors ever saw the space or made the trip to the twenty-fifth, though it was talked about as a revered sanctuary among authors in the know at conferences.

And while the signing could have been done over the internet, Justine had wanted a chance to parade Felicity around like a pony, remind the staff at Garrison & Marrow who she was and how important her work was to the publishing house. The other part was that Justine reveled in celebrations.

Felicity hugged her purse to her on the ride up, her mind mulling over her latest project. No title had been decided on yet, but the working one was *The Murdered Intern*. No one knew where Felicity had taken her inspiration for the project, or how close it came to the publishing house in which she found herself now. Or even closer still to one of the people she was about to see.

The elevator dinged, and its doors opened.

She took a deep, steadying breath.

Ian's assistant, Emily, got up from her desk, which was posted just outside the sanctuary, and parted the double doors. Emily walked in ahead of Felicity with poise and confidence. "Ms. Felicity Kelley is here," she announced.

There was a round of applause from the three people inside —Ian Moss, Justine Livingston, and Felicity's editor, Melody Schmitt.

"Bravo." Ian grinned and got up from a leather chair, running a hand over his jacket and doing up its buttons in a swift, practiced movement.

"Hello, darling." Justine was smiling and touched Felicity's elbow as she sat next to her on the couch. "So very proud of you," her agent added.

In her fifties, almost skeletal thin, sporting a stylish bob, her hair a blend of silver and white, Justine always looked and smelled amazing. *Like money*, Felicity's sister would have said.

"Thank you."

The "sanctuary" had warm, honey-colored wood floors and was larger than a studio apartment. To add to the impressive furnishings and footprint, floor-to-ceiling windows afforded a bird's-eye view of Washington.

Next to Ian was a champagne bottle on ice. The coffee table that stretched the length of the couch had two silver trays—one with four flutes and the other with a small stack of paperwork.

The *contract*, Felicity realized.

Melody hadn't said a word yet but was smiling warmly.

"Hello, Melody," Felicity said to her.

"Hello to you. I'd ask how you are but..." Melody laughed. She had a glorious one that usually made Felicity feel lighter every time she heard it. But at this moment, her nerves were edging in again. She'd come here with suspicions, hoping they were baseless.

Her heart was beating wildly, and she flinched when Justine tapped her knee.

"You're ready for this." Justine, her champion and cheerleader, smiled at her.

"I am."

"Let's not delay this any longer then." Ian grinned and shuffled forward on the cushion of his chair. He retrieved the paperwork from the tray. As he did so, the cuff of his shirt poked out from the sleeve of his jacket.

Felicity's breath froze, her eyes fixed on the black onyx stone. Her world collapsed in on itself. Her suspicion wasn't wrong, after all.

Ian was watching her, his eyes piercing hers. His were dark, his face shadowed.

He knows I know...

She had to get out of there as soon as she could.

EPILOGUE

Present Day

It was two days after Amanda put a bullet into a man, and she still felt no remorse. She'd had time to live with it, jump through the bureaucratic hoops, file the necessary reports, hand in her gun, and get a loaner. Even Chief Buchanan had stopped by her and Trent's desks and congratulated them on a job well done. Then he and Malone walked off to his office. Amanda had the feeling when they'd interrupted them last week, there was tension there. Likely to do with Malone taking the Kelley case from Hudson and handing it to Amanda. Whatever it had been, the matter now seemed resolved.

Celeste Sweeney had cried joyful tears when they told her they had caught Felicity's killer. "At least she will rest now."

But the best friend wasn't the only one who received closure. Celeste informed her and Trent that Felicity used to date an officer with the PWCPD, and the timeline fit. Amanda tried reaching out to him but was unsuccessful getting through. From what she could tell, he was no longer in law enforcement. At least his lack of judgment didn't risk him leaking more confidential information to civilians. That didn't help repair the likely damage that had been done though. It left her with a sickening feeling of the matter being unresolved, but life didn't always serve up endings wrapped in a neat bow.

But the time was here to get some answers—hopefully. Ian Moss could finally have company. He came through surgery, after his survival had been touch and go.

They walked into his room in a Washington hospital, and he groaned at the sight of her. He even seemed to shrink back. But the man had a right to be afraid of her. She had put a bullet in him.

"We have some questions for you," she started.

"What do you want now? Haven't you done enough?"

"I'm just getting started." She walked to the side of his bed. Numerous lines were going into his veins. One was likely for pain medication. "Let's start with Chapman. Tell us what happened there."

Ian flushed and let out a deep sigh. "Naomi was a witch. I deserved that promotion far more than she did, but because she was beautiful and had a powerful and rich daddy, she got the job."

"She made you feel insignificant," Amanda empathized.

"Like a piece of crap. But she made me realize one thing, that I'd never get anywhere as long as I looked like I did. So, I took control and made myself over." He paused there as if he wanted a compliment, but where it counted, the man was ugly as sin.

"Tell us about that night fifteen years ago. You went to Taps and Cocktails to celebrate her promotion," she said, starting him off.

"Why, I don't know. It just made me miserable."

The pictures of him attested to that. "Did you go to Naomi's house planning to kill her?"

"I was prepared for that outcome."

So blasé and unapologetic. "Go on, tell us." She encouraged him as if she and Trent were relishing his every word, pretending to be awed by his genius. Whatever it took to keep him talking.

"I knocked on her front door."

The reason for the front light coming on...

"She let me in with a dramatic sigh and roll of her eyes. Witch. But I played things up like I was there to celebrate her achievement more. She took out Scotch and poured us a few shots."

The nightcap, but there was one inconsistency... "There was only one glass."

"Because I took mine with me after I killed her."

"What did she do or say to trigger you?" Amanda tiptoed toward that question. If she asked the wrong way, wrong words, wrong tone, she feared he'd clam up and stop talking.

"She laughed in my face and said that someone as ugly as me would never get ahead in this world. Can you believe it?" His face turned red, and his jaw clenched. "I just snapped, pulled out the gun I had brought with me, and shot her three times. *Pop, pop, pop.*" As he retold this part of the story, his eyes darkened.

"But then you had the brainwave to make it look like a home invasion," Trent interjected. "The shoeprints in the back garden, the broken window in the door. Obviously, the theft of the jewelry. But none of that was your original plan."

He smiled at Trent and shook his head. "But it all worked perfectly until Felicity started snooping around."

"How did you know she was? Well, aside from the fact you were probably aware of her book proposal—a murdered intern at a publishing house," Amanda said.

He rubbed his wrists along his bed rail, and Amanda wasn't sure why. She didn't think it had to do with the fact the handcuffs were bothering him. "I have been keeping an eye on her since the project's approval. In recent months, I started following her."

"*Stalking* her." Amanda wasn't in the mood to pussyfoot.

"Sure, whatever you want to call it. But she was nosing around too much, talking to people she had no business talking to, asking questions. She was an author for God's sake, not a cop. But she wouldn't let it alone. The day of the champagne lunch, I just knew that she knew..."

"How's that?" Trent asked.

"It was in her eyes, her energy. But I messed up. I wore the onyx cufflinks I'd stolen from Chapman. But how was I to know Felicity had found out about them?"

Amanda shrugged. "She was serious about her research."

"Don't I know it."

"Is that why you destroyed all her paperwork, out of fear your name was there somewhere?" Trent said.

"Yeah."

"Well, your name wasn't, but your face was. She made a backup of her research and put it somewhere you could never get to it, including this..." She motioned for Trent to show him the intern group photo on the tablet he had with him.

He barely looked at it and shook his head. "Where did you get that?"

"Doesn't matter. We found Felicity's area rug in your garage, but what did you do with the coffee table that she hit her head on?" she asked.

"I burned it."

As they'd figured, but it was one more question answered. "Where did you get the gun you used to kill Naomi? There's no record of you having a permit for one."

"Off the street. It's easy enough if you're determined."

"Tell me this, will the rounds pulled from Chapman be a match to the gun you just held on poor Melody Schmitt?" Ballistics would confirm, but she wanted to hear it from him.

He angled his head. "What do you think?"

"I think they will."

"Ding, ding, ding."

She really disliked this man!

"Why did you kill Jane Burr?" Trent asked.

"That woman from the bar?" He laughed, short and insincere. "I only killed her hoping it would throw you off my track. After you asked for access to Felicity's latest project, I got a bad feeling. I figured if you thought a serial killer was out there, you'd forget about Naomi."

"You were right about one thing. There was a serial killer. *You.* And because of Felicity Kelley, you'll be going to prison for a very long time. And the Tipsy Moose Alehouse... why there?"

"Why not?"

Amanda turned to leave the room, and she and Trent said goodbye to the officer posted at the door on the way out.

She let out a deep breath and faced Trent. "Well, we did it. Time to go home."

"Don't have to tell me twice."

They had the rest of the day and week off to compensate for all the overtime they'd put in during the past weekend. Also, to account for Amanda's vacation being cut short. They were expected back first thing Monday morning though.

But that was then. Right now, she couldn't get home fast enough.

Amanda walked in the front door and found Logan curled up on the couch, reading *The Romeo Killer*. "No, no, no."

Logan looked up and smiled at her. "It's actually really good."

"If you were me, you might have a different opinion. I'd prefer never to lay eyes on it or hear about it again."

"Good luck there. It's going to be a blockbuster hit." He was on his feet now, finger stuck between the pages. He moved in for a kiss, and she held up a hand.

"Not until that thing's away." She pointed at the book.

"Fine. I'll closet read." He tossed it to the table by the front door and greeted her properly with a tight hug and a passionate kiss.

After, she pulled back and said, "Where is—?"

Zoe came running through the patio door barefoot and covered in dirt. Amanda didn't get a chance to run before the girl caught her and wrapped her dirty hands around her pant legs.

She looked up at the ceiling. *Can't beat 'em, join 'em.* "Let's go garden."

Zoe squealed, and Amanda took Logan's hand as they stepped outside. She planned to salvage as much time with these two as possible before Monday came around.

Life was about laughter and love, and she was blessed with both.

A LETTER FROM CAROLYN

Dear reader,

I want to say a huge thank you for choosing to read *Her Last Words*. If you enjoyed it and would like to hear about new releases in the Amanda Steele series, just sign up at the following link. Your email address will never be shared, and you can unsubscribe at any time.

www.bookouture.com/carolyn-arnold

If you loved *Her Last Words*, I would be incredibly grateful if you would write a brief, honest review. Also, if you'd like to continue investigating murder, you'll be happy to know there will be more Detective Amanda Steele books. I also offer several other international bestselling series for you to savor—everything from crime fiction, to cozy mysteries, to thrillers and action adventures. One of these series features Detective Madison Knight, another kick-ass female detective, who will risk her life, her badge—whatever it takes—to find justice for murder victims.

Also, if you enjoyed being in the Prince William County, Virginia, area, you might want to return in my Brandon Fisher FBI series. Brandon is Becky Tulson's boyfriend, who was mentioned in this book, but you'll be able to be there when they meet in *Silent Graves* (book two in my FBI series). These books are perfect for readers who love heart-pounding thrillers and are fascinated with the psychology of serial killers. Each install-ment is a new case with a fresh bloody trail to follow. Hunt with the FBI's Behavioral Analysis Unit and profile some of the most devious and darkest minds on the planet.

And if you're familiar with the Prince William County, Virginia, area, or have done some internet sleuthing, you'll realize differences between reality and my book. That's me taking creative liberties.

Last, but certainly not least, I love hearing from my readers! You can get in touch on my Facebook page, through Twitter, Goodreads, or via my website. This is also a good way to stay notified of my new releases. You can also reach out to me via email at Carolyn@CarolynArnold.net.

Wishing you a thrill a word!

Carolyn Arnold

www.carolynarnold.net

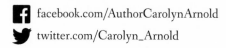

facebook.com/AuthorCarolynArnold

twitter.com/Carolyn_Arnold

Made in the USA
Middletown, DE
01 March 2024

50599545R00191